Whale Heart

Greenland Crime Series book #5

by Christoffer Petersen

Whale Heart

Published by Aarluuk Press

Copyright © Christoffer Petersen 2020
First Published 2020

ISBN: 978-87-93957-80-0

www.christoffer-petersen.com

Note to the Reader

Whale Heart is the fifth book in the Greenland Crime series of novels featuring retired police constable David Maratse. More thriller than mystery, it is not a stand-alone novel. Therefore, readers will benefit from reading the other books in the series starting with *Seven Graves, One Winter*.

Many threads and character arcs are pulled together in this novel from the other novels in the series, closing some storylines, while opening others. This is not the last Maratse novel, but some open threads had to be closed to make sense of the ongoing saga, and to give the characters time to breathe.

However, from an author's point of view, I enjoyed writing *the* novel where Maratse and Petra finally get to spend some quality time together, as much as you can, between murders.

Whale Heart is a fictional story written in British English. The *Xue Long* does exist, but has been used fictionally, although readers will discover it did visit Tuktoyaktuk in 1999, which is where this story begins.

Having doomed spies, doing certain things openly for purposes of deception, and allowing our spies to know of them and report them to the enemy.

Sun Tzu, The Art of War

Northwest Passage
Tuktoyaktuk, Canada, 1999

Prologue

With a tilt of the head and a narrowing of the eyes, the twin cranes stretching over the bow deck of the MV *Xue Long* looked like pincers. The deep red hull of the Chinese icebreaker contrasted sharply with the white superstructure towering above it, and the black windows streaked with tears of rust. The centre of the ship was dominated by two more cranes, larger than the combined size of the bow cranes, each with two great arms and hooks adding to the *Xue Long*'s impressive lifting capacity. The open deck between the cranes was equally impressive, revealing the original intent of the *Xue Long*'s designers to create a cargo and supply ship suited to the Arctic. A single globular eye the size of an industrial gazebo, bolted to the top of the structure to the rear of the ship, completed the fanciful suggestion that the ship shared some similarities with giant crustaceans. The eye was constructed of a multitude of hexagons, lending it a more insect-like appearance appropriate to its purpose – invading public, private, and sovereign spaces, leaving no trace, and shifting its gaze back to the horizon at the twist of a dial. But the *Xue Long* was not content with looking from afar, as the captain steered a course towards the tiny village of Tuktoyaktuk in the Canadian Arctic.

A tall, thin Chinese man lingered at one of the square windows on the bridge. "How long?" he said, as he scanned the grey skies above Tuktoyaktuk.

Wén Hai, the captain of the *Xue Long*, an older man enjoying the privileges of seniority and good political standing, narrowed his eyes as he regarded the younger man standing next to him on the bridge of China's first and only icebreaker. The dark stranger who, apparently, enjoyed even more privileges than his rank – classified – had irritated Wén Hai since his arrival and subsequent commandeering of the *Xue Long*, something Wén Hai had been promised would never happen, and certainly not as they plotted a course through the Northwest Passage, under the very noses of the Canadians.

"Until we reach Tuktoyaktuk?" Wén Hai said.

"Until the helicopter returns," said the younger man.

The man turned from the window, giving Wén Hai but a moment's eye contact, and causing one more surge of pressure in the captain's blood, as he struggled with the blatant disdain with which the man treated him.

"Hong Wei," the captain said. "I don't appreciate you sending *my* men in *my* helicopter, on a hunting expedition."

"They are not *your* men," Hong Wei said, tugging at the wispy beard he had been cultivating for over a month. "Not your helicopter. You sail at the privilege of the People's Republic of China. We serve at the people's pleasure. Need I remind you of that?"

Wén Hai gripped the side of his chair as he bit back his preferred comment, choosing a more appropriate tone within an inch of what he knew was expected of his position. "You can remind me of *your* mission," he said, pitching his voice with sufficient grit to reassert his authority.

"*My* mission?" Hong Wei crossed the deck to the window on the port side of the ship, tapping strong fingers against the salt-licked glass. "*Our* mission, Captain, is to send a message to the world that China is a power to be reckoned with – a superpower that the world has overlooked while they were sleeping. We caught them napping while their eyes were fixed elsewhere during the Cold War, and now, when they wake up, when they see this ugly leviathan off their shores…"

"Ugly? You're talking about my ship."

"Yes, ugly. And, no, the *Xue Long* is not and never will be *your* ship. My presence confirms it." Hong Wei gestured at the captain, pointing at his insignia, the subtle decorations denoting his service. "You are confusing service with seniority. While you have amassed an impressive forty years of naval experience, does it not gall you that at just thirty-eight years old, with no naval record whatsoever, *I* can take command of *your* ugly ship?"

"You," Wén Hai said, spittle flecking his lips like sea foam, "have no record."

"You looked?" Hong Wei chuckled.

"As soon as I was told to expect your arrival."

"Good. I would have done the same."

"Your man…"

"Pān Tāo?"

"Yes." Wén Hai glanced away at the sound of the helicopter returning. "Also – no record," he said, turning back to Hong Wei. "So, to repeat my question…"

"Why are we here?" Hong Wei paused to zip his jacket and remove a thin hat from the pocket. "A good question. But first, Captain, how do I look?" Hong Wei held his arms casually at his sides, encouraging the captain to comment on his dirty jeans, the old army surplus jacket – American, and the shit-stained boots one size bigger than his slender figure needed.

"Like one of the natives."

"*Natives*?" Hong Wei laughed. "The Inuvialuit, the *real* people of this part of the Arctic can teach us much, if we are prepared to listen. However, as to your question, I require something from the village. Pān Tāo and I will take that fibreglass hunting boat you picked up in Arkhangelsk, together with the reindeer your men have just brought back from their hunting excursion." Hong Wei pointed at the helicopter hovering over the rear of the ship in anticipation of landing. "That's why you are here, Captain. And that's all you need to know."

Hong Wei left the bridge before the captain could respond. He slid down the stairs, lifting his feet high, his palms hidden inside the voluminous cuffs of the army jacket he pressed onto the railings. Hong Wei's oversized boots thumped on the grille between ladders until he reached the open deck and strode towards the helicopter pad. Pān Tāo looked up from where he quartered the reindeer to one side of the helicopter, ringed by a small crowd of curious crewmen. Blood stained the younger man's face, drawing a smile from Hong Wei as he climbed up and onto the pad.

"More makeup, Pān Tāo?"

"Just blending in," Pān Tāo said. "As instructed."

Hong Wei caught Pān Tāo's eye, then nodded for him to continue, watching the flash of Pān Tāo's blade with appreciation as he deftly pared the reindeer's skin, before crunching the blade through the bone to cut the pieces they would carry into the village. The stink of blood was hot and rich in Hong Wei's nose. There was more blood and reindeer hair on Pān Tāo's jacket, crusting within the light black hairs on his bare forearms as he worked the knife. Hong Wei gave a nod of appreciation as Pān Tāo instructed the crewmen to carry the reindeer to the boat. He stood, wiping the blade of the knife on a bloody rag, before grinning at Hong Wei.

"Hot work," he said, wiping the sweat from his brow. Pān Tāo left a swathe of blood on his forehead, to which the fringe of his thick black hair clung in sticky clumps. He scratched at his thin beard next, adding more blood to his disguise.

"Enough blood," Hong Wei said, laughing.

"Too much?"

"There's a fine line between authentic and horrific."

"And I look horrific?"

"Let's just say Xiá should not see her daddy now."

Pān Tāo grinned again, and said, "She can cope with anything."

"I don't doubt it, but…" Hong Wei gestured at Pān Tāo's face. "There are some things a two-year-old does not need to see."

"How about them?" Pān Tāo said, nodding at the village just visible on the horizon. "The two-year-olds in the village will be used to the sight of blood."

"Used to a lot of things," Hong Wei said. "But, let's let Xiá grow a little older before we expose her to the world, eh?"

"Oh, I intend to teach her everything, as soon as she's old enough, probably before," Pān Tāo said. He curled a bloody hand around Hong Wei's shoulder, steering him away from the helicopter and off the landing pad as they walked towards the *Xue Long*'s midsection.

"I don't doubt it," Hong Wei said.

They paused to watch the patched and beaten fibreglass hunting boat spin in the air below the crane, as the crew lifted it over the side of the ship before lowering it into the sea below. Hong Wei nodded at the two crewmen waiting with American-style frame backpacks, and an old Remington hunting rifle. He waved them forward, taking the rifle as Pān Tāo shrugged the backpack onto his back, slinging the other over his shoulder.

"Lieutenant." Hong Wei loaded the rifle as a junior grade officer trotted across the deck towards them. "Pistols," he said, as the man stopped next to him.

The lieutenant nodded for one of the crew to bring a satchel, out of which he took two Browning Hi-Power 9mm pistols. Pān Tāo took one of them, stuffing it into the waistband of his dirty jeans. Hong Wei took the other, plus the three extra magazines, handing two of them to Pān Tāo before pocketing one for himself. Hong Wei slipped the pistol into a shoulder holster hidden inside his jacket. He cupped his hand and waved the lieutenant closer so that he could give him his final instructions.

"As soon as we're gone, you will wait twelve hours before sailing into Tuktoyaktuk. The captain knows this, as does your commander. But now I'm telling you…"

"Zhāng Min," the lieutenant said, filling the expectant pause.

"Because, Zhāng Min, I'm ordering you to make sure the captain does exactly what I say." Hong Wei tapped the pistol holstered on the lieutenant's belt. "Whatever it takes, the *Xue Long* must not arrive earlier than planned. No matter what you hear, or who gives the orders. Am I making myself clear, Lieutenant?"

Zhāng Min looked at Hong Wei, swallowed loudly, and then nodded. "Yes."

"Good," Hong Wei said. "Then we can begin.

You may resume your duties."

Pān Tāo waited until the lieutenant had walked away before letting out a long, low whistle. "You've done it now."

"Done what?"

"Spooked another innocent young man."

"Nobody's innocent," Hong Wei said.

"Not even me?"

Hong Wei snorted. "You were born guilty, Pān Tāo."

"I suppose I was. But Xiá…"

"Is innocent."

Hong Wei turned to walk away but stopped when Pān Tāo caught his arm. He frowned as he caught the look on his partner's face.

"Pān Tāo? What is it?"

"Xiá," he said. "If anything happens…"

"Nothing will happen."

"Right," Pān Tāo said, lowering his voice. "We're about to enter a country illegally…"

"*Covertly*," Hong Wei said. "There's a difference."

"Not much if we get caught." Pān Tāo raised his eyebrows. "Two foreign operatives, disguised as local Inuit, sneaking into the north, stealing a man's identity, his car…"

Hong Wei laughed. "I'm sure he will let us borrow his car, once we've stolen his identity."

Pān Tāo looked Hong Wei in the eyes, held his gaze for a moment, then continued. "Either way, we plan to infiltrate a country, a mining organisation, and…"

"Pān Tāo?"

"What?"

"Relax."

"I *am* relaxed. It's just if anything happens… Xiá… My parents will look after her, but since her mother died… if I was to die…"

"Xiá will be taken care of. I'll see to it." Hong Wei slapped Pān Tāo on the back, shoving him gently towards the ladder the crew hung over the side of the ship. "It's time," he said, checking his watch. "We need to go."

Pān Tāo nodded, then climbed over the side of the ship and down the ladder. Hong Wei looked for the lieutenant, tapping the face of his watch as he caught the young man's eye. He followed Pān Tāo down the ladder to the boat thumping the side of the ship in the water below. Hong Wei wondered at Pān Tāo's uncharacteristic concerns, deciding that being a father was obviously still new to him, but something he would have to address if he was to continue to be an effective operative for the Political and Economic Intelligence Division of *Guoanbu*, the Chinese Ministry of State Security. Of course, having met Pān Tāo's charming daughter Xiá, Hong Wei understood his partner's concerns, but the interests of his country always came first, and, unfortunately for Pān Tāo, Hong Wei's loyalties were not conflicted.

Not in the least.

But I'll do what I can to protect him, he thought, as he lowered himself into the boat. *And if I can't protect Pān Tāo, then I'll do whatever it takes to protect his daughter, just as soon as the mission is over.*

Hong Wei took a breath of rich salty air laced with the blood of the reindeer at his feet, before nodding that he was ready.

Uummannaq Fjord
Inussuk, Greenland, Present Day

Chapter 1

Towards the middle of January the sun returned to Uummannaq fjord, slipping over the glacier between the snow-clad mountain peaks. The sun shone for less than ten minutes, but its presence was revealed, it could no longer hide, the twilight hours had been extended, now pierced with a ray of the most brilliant light. The return of the sun heralded new times, renewal, and rebirth. The energy that had been sapped by the long winter dark returned as eyes shone brightly, dismissing all wisdom to stare at the sun, if only for a second, then blinded, with big white rings in their vision as the people of Uummannaq and the surrounding settlements looked forward into the year. Not back. Never back. Only onward to new horizons, dreams, and beginnings.

Tucked between the granite knees of the ragged mountain range on the eastern slopes of the Uummannaq peninsula, curving around the fjord to the sea, the people of Inussuk saw the sun reflected on the jagged flanks of the icebergs pinched in the sea ice, locked in the fjord. They stared at the brilliant white slabs of ice, drawing a second-hand glimpse of the sun, knowing it was mirrored, but enjoying it all the same, minus the flares of white rings caused by direct contact. It would not be long before they too were bathed in the first rays of the sun, as it rose above the horizon, circling steadily higher and higher, until it adopted a regular orbit of eternal summer sunshine. Until then, the residents of Inussuk, including one retired police constable, and one recovering police sergeant, their friends, hunters' families, and resident artists now returned for one more season, would have to wait just a little longer – a few more days, before they too could see the sun.

For Sergeant Petra Jensen, anticipating the arrival of the sun was like waiting to open presents on Christmas Eve – as per Greenlandic tradition – *interminable*.

She had waited long enough.

Petra needed the sun to return, to mark the arrival of the new year, and not just with the ticking off of a day on a paper calendar. It was not enough to know that they had passed the first day of January, she needed to *feel* it. To *see* it. To know that there were things to look forward to, and other – darker things – to put behind her, sinking them beneath the surface ice, weighting them down with mental boulders of black granite to descend into the black depths of the deep fjord, never to be recovered.

She knew that some things returned from those dark depths, such as the body of Tinka Winther that retired police constable David Maratse dragged from the deep on a longline, when fishing with Karl in Karl's boat. But unlike Tinka's body, the physical embodiment of the horrors associated with Petra's past would never return. Maratse had seen to that. Only the scars remained – those scratched into her mind, those piercing her soul, and the physical scars poked between the joins on the inside of her fingers with iron gall ink.

The snow covering the deck outside the tiny wooden house squealed beneath the soles of her boots as she took a breath of crisp winter air. Petra made fists, hiding the iron gall scars within the tight grip of her fingers. *These scars,* she thought, *can be hidden.* She looked out to the sea ice, felt the wind tickle her long black hair across the back of her neck, breaking soft sleeves of rime ice from the tips of her hair to crumble onto her collar. She felt the pinch of cold on her cheeks, resisted the urge to press her palms to her face to warm her skin, embracing instead the cold that snapped the air around her, condensing her breath into clouds of thin crystals. The cold was necessary, part of what she called her *cleansing*, which she chose to do every dark morning before breakfast, taking another stab at the dark thoughts gripping her mind, prising the tiny claws free until, piece by piece, she could cleanse those memories, casting them out into the fjord, pressing them beneath the ice. The shards piercing her soul were deeper, and only love could pull them free, something she knew Maratse could help her with – *was* helping her. He had done so every day since his return from Denmark, after his brief incarceration, following the desperate hours in the hospital before Buuti, their neighbour, put an end to one more evil figure, just as Maratse had done several months before.

"Buuti is strong," Petra whispered, with a glance at the house in which Buuti and Karl lived, not a stone's throw from the tired wooden deck upon which she stood. Petra knew that Karl worried about Buuti's silence, but the silence was part of the deal, following the sanitisation of the crime scene, the purging of the truth. While the truth was what Petra lived for, what she worked to seek out and uphold, some things she now knew to be so evil, that the only option was to bury them, and the truth along with them.

I can live with that, she thought. *I* am *living with that.*

With each cleansing, and each day closer to the return of the sun, Petra measured her progress. She joked about having a ratings system, rating each day on a survival scale sliding further and further from suicide, depending upon how tightly the dark thoughts gripped her, how deep they dug those stiletto claws.

"Today," she would say, "I am three days from suicide, stepping into a fourth."

Petra would hold Maratse's hand as she said it, as she placed herself on the scale, clenching his fingers in what she believed was a reassuring grip. But she knew, when she was most honest with herself, that Maratse focused on the words, twisting them in his mind in the negative direction, thinking she was planning for her own death, and that he only had so many days remaining before he lost her.

Forever.

His silence made her talk, repeating the words, as if saying them for a second time would reassure him.

"Four days from suicide."

"Don't," he would say.

"But that's progress."

"*Piitalaat…*"

Petra knew she was punishing him, hurting the one she loved most, cutting him deeply, just as she had been cut. In some twisted way it made sense to make him bleed, to see the sheen of tears, not quite dry, on his cheeks, the welling of more in his eyes, before he turned away, gasping energy in gulps of empty air, before turning to face her again, to take her hands again, to *begin* again.

His tears were love.

She knew it then, now – forever. But she needed to see them, more each day, if only to be reassured that she was loved, that *he* loved her, that he would never leave her again.

It was Petra's idea to start the cleansing, to begin her day with twenty minutes of fresh air, to let the cold pierce the thin weave of her pyjamas, to feel the pinch of winter pressing the rubber sides of Maratse's boots against the skin of her feet. Twenty minutes, in which the fine hairs on her skin prickled, the air inside her nostrils froze, the skin on her cheeks drew tight, contracted, nipples hardened beneath her thin top, eyes grew heavy with round breathy diamonds condensing on her lashes. Twenty minutes to cleanse, to purge the words if not the thoughts, to heal, to allow them both to heal.

And each morning Maratse waited.

As soon as Petra slipped out from beneath the covers of their winter-warm bed, he would open his eyes, and wait. He waited for her to tramp down the steep staircase, waited for the soft squeal as she slipped her feet inside his boots, the shudder of the door and Petra's curse as she broke the layer of ice freezing the door to the deck. Maratse slipped out of bed the second she closed the door behind her. He tugged jeans over his underpants, padding barefoot and bare-chested out of the bedroom, down the same steep stairs and into the kitchen, careful not to look out of the living room window at Petra on the deck, careful not to ruin the spell. He made coffee. He made pancakes when they had milk and flour. He made toast when they had bread. He littered the kitchen table – its legs half in the sitting room, half in the kitchen – with everything they had in the cupboards that might possibly be added to toast, pancakes, even cereal. He emptied the fridge of milk – the long-life kind available in the settlements, the northern villages, and towns. It was *his* ritual, something *they* could laugh about when Petra came back inside the house.

"You emptied the cupboards again," she would say.

"*Iiji.*"

"Peanut butter? On pancakes?" she would ask, holding up an almost empty jar, just a spoonful left, something they had been saving and savouring, until the spring supply boat broke through the ice sometime in May.

"It's good," he would say.

"You always say that."

He always did, for at least as long as their tradition was old, ever since his return from the Danish prison, ever since Buuti killed the head of the *Makakajuit*, Greenland's organised crime ring. Teasing each other about the last spoonful of peanut butter, no matter how old and hard it was, no matter how much it clung to the inside of the glass, was preferable to talking about the past, or measuring Petra's return to health on a sliding suicide scale.

Maratse timed the coffee to perfection, placing two mugs on the table as Petra kicked the snow off Maratse's boots before stepping into the house.

The first warning.

She shivered, loudly.

The second.

Then Petra padded into the living room, face flushed with musty warmth, eyes shining with beads of ice, melting, licking her cheeks in tiny rivulets of thawing breath.

Maratse waited, his hand on the back of his chair, anticipating the moment when they would sit, just after the gentle teasing. He frowned that morning as Petra said nothing. He watched, lips parted, as she reached for the jar of peanut butter, her eyes locked on his, twinkling as she unscrewed the lid.

"*Piitalaat…*" he whispered.

Petra's deep brown eyes blazed into his as she reached for a teaspoon. He held his breath as she worked the tip of the spoon around the inside of the jar, scraping the very last of the peanut butter into a sticky heap on the spoon.

"Wait," he said, as she opened her mouth and slipped the spoon between her lips.

Petra took her time to lick the peanut butter from her teeth, to work it from her lips with the tip of her tongue, her eyes locked on Maratse's, eyes twinkling in the last of the tiny diamonds of ice trickling onto her cheeks. She set the jar down on the tabletop, tossed the spoon beside it, and walked around the edge of the table, reaching for Maratse, plucking at the black hairs wisped in clumps across his chest between the scars.

"The peanut butter jar," she whispered, pressing her lips to his ear, her nutty breath warm against his skin, "is empty. We need more."

"*Iiji,*" Maratse said, swallowing, turning his face slowly as Petra pressed her lips to his.

"We need more," she said, spacing each word with warm, sweet breaths.

"Hmm…"

Petra's breath tickled the light oriental beard that Maratse preferred in the winter, parting the hairs with more waves – peanut sweet – as she pressed her teeth to his bottom lip.

"I have decided," she said, twisting her fingers into the hairs on Maratse's chest, "that we should buy some more."

Maratse swallowed again, then pressed his

hands slowly to her sides, feeling her ribs through the soft layer of her top, his mind racing as he wondered what she wanted him to do next.

"Peanut butter," he said, with another swallow.

"Yes. But we will have to go far to get it. We have to get away."

"Far?"

"Very far," she said, taking his hand and pressing it up under the wrinkled hem of her pyjama top, guiding him to her breast.

Petra had glimpsed the sun on the back of an iceberg, and she was determined to look ahead, always ahead, to live above the dark depths of the sea, and she was going to take Maratse with her.

It was her last cleansing.

They would fly the very next day.

Just as soon as they were finished with breakfast.

Chapter 2

Petra's playful mood continued into the midmorning twilight, just as the sun teased its way over the mountains, striking the icebergs with another shaft of brilliant light. Maratse rolled onto his back, pulling the duvet with him, exposing Petra's legs, her bottom, forcing her to wriggle back under the covers, seeking the warmth of his skin.

"You've gone all quiet," she said, resting her chin on his chest. "You've gone all *Maratse.*"

"Hmm?"

"Exactly." Petra opened her mouth wide, clacking her teeth with exaggerated movements as she pressed her chin up and down into Maratse's chest, waiting for him to respond, slipping a cold hand beneath him and into the small of his back when he didn't.

"Speak, oh moody one," she said.

Maratse turned onto his side, curling a scarred finger through the twist of jet-black hair framing Petra's face. He looked into her eyes, saw his own reflection, looked deeper, searching for something – a sign that this was real, that he wasn't about to wake up, that she was getting better, *healing.*

"How do you feel?" he asked, the words

clumsy but sincere.

"Right now?"

"*Iiji.*"

"Safe," she said. "Warm. A little high."

"High?"

"Yes." Petra giggled. "Drunk, maybe."

Maratse moved his hand to stroke the back of her head as she snuggled closer into his chest. Petra's voice was muffled when she spoke, but her words were sharp, difficult to digest as she started to talk.

"It's taken time to enjoy that," she said. "What we just did. I struggle with the thoughts – dark thoughts, wondering if he's still there, if he can still hurt me."

"He can't."

"I know." Petra lifted her head to look at Maratse. "I know because you made it so. You made sure he could never hurt me. That Jaqqa Neqi could never touch me, or any woman, *anyone*, ever again."

"*Iiji.*"

"And I punished you for it."

"I don't think about it."

"But I do." Petra shifted in the bed until she could see Maratse's face, hold his hand as she opened up, releasing the darkness, into the light. "I punished you because I thought I needed *him* to feel wanted, to feel needed."

"I need you."

"I know," she said. "Which is why you have to hear this. That place he had me – the mental place – it was real, David. More real than you can imagine." Petra gripped Maratse's fingers as she talked. "He conditioned me to think that his touch, however rough, however misguided…"

"Evil."

"Yes." Petra took a breath. "Evil. He was evil, but he was all I had. I thought I would die in that cabin. Every time he left, it was as if he took life – *my life*, with him. I was weak. I hardly ate, hardly drank. I didn't know what day it was. I couldn't measure time, only things – the things he did to me. That was my reality, and when you killed him, I thought you had taken it away, and I didn't know how to get it back, if I would ever come back to reality. Does that make any sense?"

Maratse nodded.

"No, David. You need to say it. I need to hear the words."

"It makes sense," he said.

"Good." Petra closed her eyes, sighing softly, her breath still sweet with peanuts and butter. "That's how I felt. And then, when I clawed my way back to reality – with your help, with Buuti's and Karl's – I punished you again, because right when I needed you the most, you were going away."

"I know."

"But that was the price. I just didn't know it then. Only now, when he invades my dreams, and I push him away, telling him he can't hurt me, that he's dead – now I understand the price." Petra opened her eyes. She looked at Maratse, then pressed her fingers into his skin, running them along his side until she found the stab wound – raised, healing. "The price we both paid. The price Buuti is paying now."

"She'll be all right," Maratse said, taking Petra's hand. "Karl will look after her."

"I feel like I should too."

"When we get back," he said.

Petra flicked her head up, lifting her chin, frowning at Maratse. "Really?" she asked, her eyes softening as her pupils dilated. "You want to go away?"

"Hmm."

"*Hmm*?" Petra rolled closer to Maratse, raising her eyebrows as she waited for a response. She blew a strand of hair from her lips, tickling Maratse's moustache. "What do you mean?"

"You said we needed peanut butter."

"I was fooling around."

"Well," Maratse said, catching his breath as Petra wormed her way onto his body.

"Constable," she said, pressing her lips to his mouth. "What are you trying to say?"

"I'm trying…"

"Yes?"

"*Piitalaat…*" Maratse gasped as Petra pressed a cold hand between his thighs.

"Talk," she said. "Speak…"

"I have money," he said.

Petra frowned, taking hold of him. "What money?"

"From the Berndt Foundation." Maratse took a deep breath. "I still have it."

"Tucked away?"

"Yes," he said, squirming as Petra shifted her

grip. "We could use it, to go away."

"South?"

"*Iiji.*"

"Somewhere hot?"

"Wherever you want."

"Hmm," Petra said, sliding onto Maratse's body. "Spain."

"Spain?"

"The coast. Hot, but not *too* hot in January. You might even enjoy it."

Maratse smiled as Petra pressed her forehead to his. He breathed her breath into his lungs, tasted her sweat on his tongue, felt her body press against his, her skin, her hair tickling his cheeks as he paused, not for the first time, surely not the last, to wonder what he ever did to deserve Sergeant Petra Jensen, and, how on earth he was going to cope as she sealed the bond between them.

"*Piitalaat...*" he breathed, as their bodies became one.

"You're going where?" Karl choked on a lungful of smoke as he turned on the deck to face Maratse. "Spain?"

"*Iiji.*"

"But it's hot in Spain."

"Piitalaat said it would be okay in January."

"She did?" Karl finished his cigarette. He looked up at a howl from Tinka, followed by more from the sledge dogs tethered to the ice around her. "See, even Tinka is sceptical."

"About going away?"

"About Spain, David. You in a hot country…"

"It's what Piitalaat wants. So, I want it." Maratse shrugged. "I'll read books inside with a fan if it's too hot."

"A fan?"

Maratse nodded. "A big one." He waited until the dogs were finished howling, before turning to Karl. "How is Buuti?"

Karl stiffened. "You're not supposed to ask."

"I was there, Karl. I can ask."

"She…" Karl paused, turning on the deck to look through the living room window. The candles Buuti had lit when Petra arrived flickered on the table between the two women. He turned back to Maratse. "She's quiet. I know she's thinking about it. But she's rational."

"Rational?"

"She knows what she did was wrong – killing that man – but she also knows she did the right thing." Karl sighed. "It's hard to describe."

"I understand," Maratse said.

"*Aap*. I thought you would. If anyone can…"

It was Maratse's turn to sigh. After a pause, he pointed at the dogs. "You'll look after them for me?"

"Of course."

"And the house?"

Karl nodded.

"Hmm."

"What?"

"After all the trouble I've caused."

"Trouble?" Karl laughed. "You mean murder,

kidnapping…"

"Hmm," Maratse said. "That too."

Karl clapped Maratse on the shoulder. "After all you've been through. After all *we've* been through. I think Inussuk, Uummannaq, maybe even Greenland, could do with a break. You should definitely go to Spain. Stay there until the money runs out."

"The money?"

"Petra said you had money from the German."

"Berndt," Maratse said, with a nod. "*Iiji.* Plenty."

"And your pension?"

"Karl," Maratse said, turning to look at his friend. "Do you need some money?"

"No, David, I don't need any money. But seeing as you don't use your money, I think it's a good time to go away, have some fun, treat Petra to nice things – she deserves nice things."

Maratse glanced through the window, waving as Petra caught his eye. He leaned closer to Karl, and said, "Any ideas? The nice things. Only, I…"

"Don't know what to buy her?" Karl laughed again. "I wouldn't worry about that. Petra will set you right."

"She already has," Maratse said.

They both turned at the sound of a snowmobile grating across the sea ice towards Inussuk. The dogs stirred, dragging their chains through the snow as the driver bumped the front skis of the snowmobile up and over the ice foot. Maratse watched as the snowmobile approached.

Karl lit another cigarette. The two men waited as the driver clicked the snowmobile out of gear, turned off the engine and dismounted, fiddling with the helmet until he pulled it off.

"Your phones are out," Constable Danielsen said, boots squealing in the snow as he tramped up the stairs and onto Karl's deck. "All of them. I tried every landline in Inussuk."

"I didn't notice," Maratse said, as he shook Danielsen's hand. The constable from Uummannaq wore the lines of the helmet's foam pressed into his chubby cheeks.

"Well, they are. Mobiles too. The whole network."

"And you came all this way?" Karl asked. He gestured at the ice, commenting on the open leads as Danielsen described the route he had taken.

"I skirted around most of them. Jumped the last one," he said, with a grin. "Don't tell Simonsen."

"Not a word," Karl said.

"Anyway," Danielsen said. "The Chief sent me with a message for Maratse." Danielsen smiled, raising his hands as Maratse tensed. "Easy, *Constable*, you've done your time, but now you have to pay for it."

"How?"

"You're wanted in court. That's the message. It's all arranged, including a return flight to Copenhagen."

"David is going to Spain," Karl said.

"Spain?"

"*Aap.*" Karl puffed a cloud of smoke above

their heads. "Where it's hot."

Danielsen frowned at Maratse. "You'll melt."

"He's going to get a fan," Karl said.

"Hmm," Maratse said. He shot Karl a look, drawing more laughter and smoke from the hunter, before turning to Danielsen. "When?"

"Tomorrow. It's short notice, but there are seats tomorrow."

"How many?"

"What?"

"Are there two seats?"

"I didn't look."

"I'll need two seats. Piitalaat is coming with me."

"Sergeant Jensen?"

"*Iiji*." Maratse nodded at the door as Petra stepped out of the house and onto the deck.

"Petra," Danielsen said.

"What's going on?" Petra's face paled in the afternoon moonlight.

"I came with a message for Maratse. They want him in Copenhagen."

"To testify," Maratse said. "Not to stay."

Petra reached for Maratse's hand, gripping it as she stood next to him. "I thought…"

"I know."

"Well," Danielsen said. "That's the message. I'll make sure they know to book two seats. Maybe Karl can give you a lift to Qaarsut in the morning?"

"I'll get them to the airport," Karl said, with a nod.

Danielsen shook everybody's hand before

leaving, gunning the engine of the snowmobile as he navigated the ice foot, and drawing Buuti to the door.

"Come inside," she said, waving them in. "I've made more coffee. And there's cake. Narwhal stew, too, if you're staying for dinner?"

"They are," Karl said, as he ushered Maratse and Petra into the house. "They leave tomorrow."

"Leave?"

"They're going away," he said. "But they won't need much. Some clothes, some books, and a fan."

"Hmm," Maratse said.

"A fan?" Buuti frowned at Karl. "Why?"

"Never mind," he said. "Let's just enjoy this night with our neighbours."

"Friends," Petra said.

Karl smiled. "That's what I meant."

Karl closed the door behind them, trapping the cold air between the door and the layer of ice clinging to the wooden frame. The heat of the living room thawed their cheeks and melted the last of the ice beads in the men's hair and beards. Steam from Buuti's coffee melted the stubborn ice clinging to their eyelashes as they sat around the kitchen table, teasing Maratse about his fan, his money, and all the ideas Petra had how to spend it. Outside, the dogs stirred at the ends of their chains, howling in the wake of the snowmobile, as Danielsen raced across the ice, all the way to Uummannaq.

Chapter 3

The late January streets of Copenhagen reflected the red lights of the commercial-carpeted Mercedes taxis with a sheen of rain, threatening ice if the temperature dropped just another few degrees. Qitu Kalia splashed along the pavement, hugging his leather briefcase to his chest. He thought of Tertu back at the hotel, how she had shaken her head when he chose the briefcase instead of the more practical – and waterproof – backpack. But, as Qitu believed, image was everything, and he would rather arrive drenched with the appropriate accessories, than looking like someone who had just stepped off the mountain path. At least, that was what he thought two kilometres earlier, when he still held out hope for a taxi, or, when he started walking, a brief reprieve in the rain.

Copenhagen rain was like the rain in Nuuk, and when it rained in Greenland's capital city, it was just as cold, just as persistent. Qitu arrived at the agreed location in the same manner as if he had walked two kilometres of Greenland's streets. He shivered as he pressed the buzzer, holding his hand on the unit in the hopes of feeling the connecting buzz through trembling fingers, to offset his poor hearing. The unit buzzed, the door clicked, and Qitu let himself into a nondescript office building, barely a kilometre from Tivoli Gardens.

The instructions he had received in a text told him to take the elevator to the basement. Qitu used the half minute inside the elevator to shake the rain from his briefcase, and dry his glasses – the result of more tests and more failing senses – before stepping out into a long grey basement, dimly lit, carpeted with tired linoleum. He walked left, as instructed, found the second to last door on the right, knocked and waited.

"Qitu!"

Wrapped inside a swirl of cinnamon and black cotton tucked into elastic denims, Kaama Pihl pulled Qitu inside the room. She closed the door and then threw her arms around his neck, burying Qitu's face in her thick, wiry black hair.

"It's been so long," she said. "I was so pleased when you said you'd come. How long has it been?"

Qitu dropped his briefcase and pulled back to read Kaama's lips, frowning a little as he caught up with her rapid Danish.

"University," he said, removing his glasses to wipe the last of the rain from the lenses. "Graduation night, just before I returned to Nuuk."

"And started working at *Sermitsiaq*, right?"

Qitu nodded. "That's right."

Kaama, he noted, had a healthy glow to her ebony skin. She smoothed her hand over her belly, nodding when Qitu asked if she was expecting.

"Due in February," she said, smiling again before she turned to introduce Qitu to a thin blonde woman wearing a tight-knit sweater and jeans, shifting her balance from one foot to other in the middle of the windowless office. "Svea is my better half."

"Svea Pettersson," the blonde woman said, greeting Qitu with a slim hand and a firm grip.

"Swedish?"

"Yes."

Qitu twirled his finger beside his ear. "I just need to focus," he said. "On your lips."

"Sure," Svea said, dipping her head. Qitu dipped his head with her, following her lips until she laughed. "Sorry," she said, lifting her chin.

"It's okay. It's only awkward for a moment."

"Well, Qitu," Kaama said, as she stood next to Svea. "Look at you. Head of Nuuk Media Group."

"It's only a small newspaper," Qitu said, resisting further praise. "We work on a few things. Just the important stories, one or two on the go, no more than that."

"But well-funded?"

"Yes. Privately. Out of Berlin." Qitu shrugged. "It's a long story."

"Maybe later then," Kaama said. She pointed to a small table pushed against the wall. It overflowed with jars of instant coffee, small boxes of assorted teas, and a generous jam jar filled with sugar. "Drinks there," she said. "And over here…"

Qitu took a step forward to look at the wall at the far end of the small office. The space in front of it was clear, save for empty packets of drawing pins on the floor, together with pads of post-it notes curling in the damp office air.

"This is everything?" Qitu said, as he took a closer look.

The wall was plastered with grainy images of people – mostly men, printed in the centre of A4 pieces of paper, around which were scrawled dates, locations, connections and sometimes sums of money in different currencies. The notes were written in black ink, corrected in places with red, highlighted in yellows and blues from the marker pens stuck to the wall with blobs of putty. Newspaper clippings were tacked beneath the photos, all shapes and sizes, from single columns to double-spread features, blog articles printed, company magazines copied, all linked with thick black arrows drawn in shaky arcs straight onto the wall and onto the corners of the papers.

"We have to paint once the lease is up," Kaama said.

"*Aap*," Qitu said.

"What do you think?" Svea asked, her voice laced with subtle traces of doubt that Qitu read in the pinch of her forehead.

What do I think?

Qitu removed his wet jacket and hung it over the back of a chair. He returned to the wall, tracing his fingers along one connecting line after another, pausing to tap the face of one man, then lingering over the article next to it. He followed sums of money – American dollars, euros, Danish kroner, Chinese yuan – from one man to the next, circling around a blank page in the middle, like the eye of a storm. Qitu took a step back, shifting his gaze with broad strokes until he found another blank page, smaller than the rest – A5, perhaps. He pointed at it, then moved on, back to the wall, tracing the lines from banks to businesses, frowning at the headlines of articles announcing company mergers, tacked next to printouts of rare minerals and their relative worth in the markets on certain days – the same days as the corresponding articles.

"These are just the bullet points," Kaama said, stepping to one side of Qitu, turning so that he could see her face. "Everything is backed up and explored in detail on our hard drives. This is just the working desktop – a shared screen if you will."

"I like it," Qitu said, nodding. He pressed his finger onto the blank A4 page tacked to the centre of the media mosaic around it. "This is him. Isn't it?"

"Yes."

Kaama shook her head when Qitu looked at her. She lifted her finger and Qitu turned in the direction she was pointing to look at Svea, following her lips as she continued.

"We know he's Chinese," Svea said. "We've got his associates – the legitimate ones. We have times of meetings that he should have been to, but nothing to confirm he was ever there. We found minutes from meetings but no mention of this man, while all the others were accounted for."

"And no photos?"

"None," she said. "Either the security cameras are turned off when he meets at the banks and offices, or the files are deleted afterwards. I don't believe he walks around the camera's field of vision. He can't. He wouldn't be able to go through any doors."

"This is Copenhagen," Qitu said, pointing at another photo. "That's the hotel I'm staying at."

"You're staying at Copenhagen Towers?"

"*Aap.*"

"You're smiling."

Qitu shrugged. "It's a little posh compared to what we're used to – Tertu and me. The hotel staff are struggling with her pink hair and her tusks."

"Tusks?" Kaama frowned.

"Piercings," Qitu said, tapping his skin between his chin and his bottom lip. "You get used to them, although you need time."

"When do we meet her?"

"Oh, when she's ready," Qitu said. He pressed his lips closed, as if he had already said more than he intended to. "And this," he said, pointing to the smaller blank piece of paper. "Who is this?"

"We're hoping you can tell us," Svea said. She paused to grab a tablet from the table in front of the wall, checking her notes before continuing. "We found something that links a Chinese businessman, visiting Greenland, with a police officer. A constable…"

"Maratse," Qitu said.

"Yes." Kaama put her hand on Qitu's arm. "Do you know him?"

"*Aap*. Quite well."

"Then you can help us. You can fill in the blanks." Kaama's eyes lit up as she reached for the tablet in Svea's hands. "We're pretty sure he's the key. If he can place this person *here*," Kaama said, pointing at the small blank page. "Then we can get a name for this man *here*." She drew her finger along the arc connecting the two pieces of paper. "It could blow the whole investigation open. We might even convince our paper to go to print."

"And get us out of this damned basement," Svea said.

"Before our little nugget is born."

"I don't think so," Qitu said.

"What?" Kaama said. "You don't think he'll talk to us?"

Svea stepped closer to the wall, closer to Qitu. "But he'll talk to you. Right?"

"Constable Maratse is retired. This," Qitu said, tapping the blank pieces of paper in turn, "is the reason he retired, the reason he was invalided off the police force. He has recovered, but he won't talk about it. No one will. His files are sealed."

"Sealed?" Kaama looked at Svea, nodding as she started to speak.

"So this does have something to do with national security." Svea pressed her hand to her mouth, catching Kaama's eye, bobbing her head, just a little, but enough to reveal her enthusiasm. "It's big," she breathed.

"Bigger than we thought," Kaama said.

Qitu said nothing. He turned away from the wall as the two women continued to discuss the possibilities of linking the missing pieces of the puzzle, perhaps even turning them over, revealing the faces lost in a sea of dead ends and spirals of misinformation. Qitu opened his briefcase, pulled out a thin paper folder, and walked back to the wall. He took two tacks from one of the boxes on the carpet, removed a small photo from the folder, and pinned it in the middle of the blank page reserved for the missing piece.

"He's not Chinese," Kaama said.

"No," Qitu said. "He's Greenlandic."

"This is the missing piece?" Svea frowned as she pointed at the photo.

"It's another piece," Qitu said. "This man is Malik Uutaaq. He's a minister in the Greenland government. He's not your missing piece, but I think he's another piece of the puzzle." Qitu gestured at the entire wall. "Only I don't know where he fits in. Not yet. But he's staying at the same hotel as me."

"Why?"

"He's attending a trial related to the *Makakajuit*, a Greenland crime ring. The case is important to Greenland's First Minister, and, for a brief moment, Malik took a leading role in the investigation. He has been summoned to testify to his actions that may have jeopardised an undercover informant. At least, that's what I've heard. I think the First Minister has sent him here to atone for that indiscretion. It has no real bearing on the case. But it does put him in Copenhagen, and I'm not sure that was wise."

"Who was the informant?" Kaama asked. "A Greenlander?"

"*Aap*," Qitu said. He smiled and added the name, "Constable Maratse, retired."

"The same *Maratse*?"

"Yes."

"And the trial is in Copenhagen?"

Qitu nodded.

"And Maratse is coming here?"

"He arrives tomorrow. He's also staying at Copenhagen Towers."

"That's perfect," Kaama said. "You can introduce us."

"He won't talk about his past."

"You just said he was here to testify."

"About something else," Qitu said. He nodded at the wall. "Not this."

"Then we make it about this," Svea said. "We arrange an interview to talk about the trial... whatever that's about."

"Corruption in the Danish Prison Service."

"Okay," Svea said. "That's a whole other article right there."

"Not our department, honey," Kaama said. "But it does give us a way in, a legitimate reason to talk to Constable Maratse." She paused, pressing her hand on Qitu's arm. "Qitu?"

"*Aap*?"

"What do you think about interviewing

Maratse? That's why you brought the photo of Malik…"

"Uutaaq," Qitu said. "It's one reason. But I think it's better if you talk to *him* – Malik." Qitu looked at Svea, and said, "And you need to be the one to do it."

Chapter 4

Malik Uutaaq tugged the hem of his t-shirt to his face, wiping the sweat from his eyes as the pace of treadmill increased, together with the curses his campaign manager swore were supposed to be encouragement.

"Come on, Uutaaq. Forget your eyes, burn that fat. Push it. *Push it!*"

Malik let go of his t-shirt to grab the handrails, cursing as the woman he hired to improve his profile slapped at his knuckles with a rubber exercise belt.

"It's a treadmill, Uutaaq, not a walker."

"Tipaaqu," Malik wheezed.

"What?"

"You're fired."

"Again? That's three times this week." Tipaaqu Jeremiassen walked to the front of Malik's treadmill, dialling down the speed until he was jogging, then walking, before turning it off completely.

"*Qujanaq,*" Malik said, as he stepped off the treadmill. He slumped on the nearest bench, pressed a towel to his face, and leaned his head against the wall.

"You won't win like this," Tipaaqu said.

"Maybe I don't want to anymore."

"No? Then you don't need me."

"Hey," Malik said, reaching out to take Tipaaqu's hand. "Of course, I need you. It's just this thing, tomorrow. Nivi Winther sent me here to punish me. She's making sure I fail, and that I fail in public."

"I'll keep the press off you." Tipaaqu stepped onto the treadmill, dialling it into motion and jogging as she talked. "No one gets an interview unless they come through me."

Malik nodded. He let the towel fall to his lap, then watched as Tipaaqu pounded the treadmill. He could feel the vibrations of her feet stomping through the running machine, echoing around the hotel gym, and pulsing through the wall into his head.

She's in my head, he thought, opening his eyes to study her trim figure, the sweat plastering her hair to her skin – European blended with Greenlandic genes, just like he preferred. *In my head, and my bed.* Malik laughed, reached for the towel, and wiped another blister of sweat from his forehead.

"Tell me about the meeting."

"Tonight's meeting?"

"*Aap.*" Malik reached for a bottle of water. "Why do I need to take it?"

"Because Levi Aaqqii is an old friend of yours."

"He's gotten older," Malik said. "That's for sure."

The elastic holding Tipaaqu's ponytail slipped as she increased speed. She reached up to fix it, raising her voice as the pounding of her feet grew louder.

"He's a businessman. He's been successful, if you ignore the bankruptcies. And, more importantly, lately he's learned how to be discreet. Something you need to learn."

Malik frowned. "Tell me again why I hired you?"

"To be straight. To be honest. To call you out on your shit."

"Yeah, that's what you do. But did I hire you to do that?"

"You hired me to raise your profile, to improve your ratings, and to challenge the First Minister in the next election." Tipaaqu slowed the treadmill. She stepped off and pointed at Malik's towel, grabbing it as he threw it to her. "The fact that I get to insult you is just a bonus. A perk of the job."

Malik thought of the other perks, and wondered, not for the first time, if he should put a stop to the more intimate approach to improving his profile, only to realise he didn't care, that some things mattered more to him – the things that satisfied his other non-political needs. *And that,* he thought, *is probably why I'll never actually* be *Greenland's First Minister.*

"Levi has a proposition for you."

"What kind?"

Tipaaqu plucked the water bottle from Malik's hand and took a long gulp, wiping her mouth with the back of her hand before tossing the empty bottle into Malik's lap.

"A business venture. He needs support from someone in government to encourage and approve foreign investment in certain projects." Tipaaqu took a moment to look around the gym, lowering her voice, sticking to Greenlandic. "Nothing illegal. In return for your support, he – more likely his investor – will make a few generous contributions to your campaign." Tipaaqu raised her eyebrows as Malik looked up. "Serious money can be used to sway opinion. You take this meeting," she said, "and your next job will be First Minister for Greenland."

"It's that simple?"

"It's a lot of money. You can hire ten of me." Tipaaqu laughed. "If you think you can cope."

"This foreign investor…"

"*Aap*?"

Malik chewed the question over in his mind. He knew the answer already. He understood the implications, and why Levi, an old friend, might need a friendly advocate in the government.

"He's Chinese. Isn't he?"

"What makes you think it's a *he*?"

"Don't play around, Tipaaqu," Malik said, swearing under his breath. "Chinese?"

"*Aap*. I think so."

Malik sighed and stood up. The stiffness in his muscles was nothing compared to the streak of concern creasing his forehead and souring any thoughts he might have had about enjoying Tipaaqu's campaign strategy in his bed that night.

"Denmark has already quashed the Chinese plans to build a new airport in Nuuk."

"I know."

"And the Americans…"

"Hey." Tipaaqu slapped the corner of the towel into Malik's chest. "Grow a pair already. You sound like Nivi Winther, always bowing down to Danish concerns, bending to their priorities, at the whim of *their* masters…"

"The Americans."

"Yes, the bloody Americans. It's time someone stood up for Greenland. It's time to accept investment, to start injecting cash into the infrastructure, into housing, to build more roads, to make air travel affordable, to improve our schools and implement a Greenlandic curriculum, for *Greenlanders*." Tipaaqu stabbed her finger at Malik. "With the right promises, backed up by visible cash, I could get you the First Minister job running a campaign that focused purely on schools. Add a few roads into the mix, and I'll secure that seat for life. Nivi is weak. She's lost the support of the people. And this petty war she's waging with you… For what? Punishing you for sleeping with her daughter – her *adult* daughter."

"She was murdered, Tipaaqu."

"So? Not by you." Tipaaqu tossed the towel onto the bench. "Nivi Winther is trying to keep you chained to her past. She's not ready to move on. We can see that. The minute the Greenlandic people see that too, you've won." Tipaaqu lowered her voice as two guests entered the gym. "Levi's money gives us the chance to do that." She sighed. "Take a shower and take the meeting.

You've got half an hour."

The Copenhagen Towers Hotel, squeezed into the centre of the city, boasted fine food and fine wines, superior to that which Malik enjoyed on occasion in Nuuk, but at Danish prices, which meant he could enjoy more for about the same price. When Levi said he was paying, Malik decided he was ready to at least hear what his old friend had to say, and even more so after the first bottle of wine.

"Tipaaqu said you were interested," Levi said, as the waiter topped up their wine glasses.

Levi waited until the waiter was gone before discreetly popping the button of his trousers, folding his shirt over his waistband to conceal it. Malik smiled at the older and portlier man sitting opposite him, tipping his glass to salute the confident manner in which Levi relaxed into his chair. Levi's stomach was more generous than Malik remembered, and there was more grey in his hair. But he still *had* hair, and a trim beard styled in a goatee that gave Malik a curious feeling that he was looking into the mirror, seeing a vision of himself perhaps twenty years into a comfortable future.

"I have some concerns," Malik said, pausing as Levi glanced around him to a table tucked into a dark alcove behind them. Malik turned his head, frowning as he tried to see the faces of the two people seated at the table. It was the third time Levi had looked at them.

"Of course," Levi said. "We understand."

"*We?*"

Levi nodded, then waved to the table behind Malik. "But you've heard enough from me. And now…" Levi gestured at the glass in Malik's hand. "Now we've reached the more comfortable end of the evening, perhaps you'd like to hear it from my associate?"

Levi smiled as a slim Chinese man approached the table. Malik turned to look at him, noting the fine cut of the man's suit, the smooth and dry palm he pressed into Malik's hand in greeting, and the fact that he was taller than Malik had expected.

"Hong Wei," the man said as he drew up another chair to the table and sat down. "That's my name."

"And your lovely companion?" Levi asked, continuing in English, following another glance at Hong Wei's table. "Won't she be joining us?"

"No."

A simple answer, Malik thought, *together with a steel look that leaves no room for interpretation.*

"A pity," Levi said, albeit in a lower voice than the one he used when Hong Wei first approached the table.

"I trust Mr. Aaqqii has explained my situation," Hong Wei said, fixing his attention on Malik, leaving Levi to his thoughts and another glass of wine. Hong Wei placed his hand over the spare glass on the table when the waiter approached, saying nothing until they were alone again. "Mr. Uutaaq?"

~ 52 ~

"You need a friendly face in my government."

"That's correct."

"Someone to speak on your behalf."

"Also correct, although…" Hong Wei paused. "I hope you will understand that, from time to time, it might be important to advise you on the exact wording when you *speak on our behalf*, as you put it."

"You mean you'll tell me what to say?"

"Yes."

Hong Wei tilted his head to one side as he waited for Malik to respond. The new angle allowed the light to fall on the Chinese man's head, highlighting the grey that Malik had missed when he first approached, together with a glint in Hong Wei's eyes that urged caution, more caution than three glasses of fine red wine allowed. Although the alcohol seemed to help Malik's English vocabulary.

"I like to speak my mind," Malik said, shrugging as he took another sip of wine.

"Ah," Hong Wei said. "A pity."

"Wait," Levi said, as Hong Wei pushed back his chair. "You're leaving."

"I don't wish to. But I was under the impression Mr. Uutaaq would be more amenable."

"He is," Levi said. "We had reached an understanding. That's why I called you over."

"Too soon, apparently," Hong Wei said.

He stood, bowing ever so slightly, before returning to his dark table. Malik watched him walk away, saw the candle flicker as he sat down, catching a glimpse of Hong Wei's companion. She was, as Levi had suggested, lovely.

"Perfect," Levi said, switching back to Greenlandic. "That's the end of that then."

"What? Just like that?"

"Hong Wei doesn't give second chances. You blew it."

"You mean…" Malik turned in his seat to stare at the Chinese man's table. He turned back after he failed to catch Hong Wei's eye. "That was it. One chance?"

"*Aap.*" Levi reached for his glass, draining the last drop, then waving the waiter away. He fiddled with his trouser button, cursing until it closed. "I'll get the bill on my way out."

Malik slid the base of his wine glass onto the table. "Levi?"

"Done for the night," Levi said, as he stood. "I'll just have to find another friendly ear in the government. Shouldn't be too hard. You're all equally corrupt. The only question is if you're equally cheap."

"What do you mean by that?"

"Remember the offer I made at the beginning of dinner?"

"One-hundred-thousand US dollars a year, as a retainer." Malik remembered choking when Levi added that there would be more for the campaign itself. "I remember."

"That was his opening offer," Levi said.

Malik caught the nod that Levi cast towards Hong Wei's table. He wondered if he had been played, or if he should ask for more. Either way, Malik realised that he was never particularly good at impromptu speeches, that he often came across better when he spoke from a prepared script.

What difference does it make if the script is Chinese?

Levi stepped to one side as Hong Wei returned to the table, just as his companion slipped out of her chair and walked towards the door to the lobby.

"Mr. Uutaaq," he said, as he sat down in Levi's chair. "I believe you are ready to negotiate."

"Yes," Malik said, as he raised his glass at the waiter. "I believe I am."

Chapter 5

The ambient sounds of pots crashing in the kitchen, the curses that followed, and the last scents of crisp chicken skin and herbs drifted around the kitchen door, as Hong Wei's companion left the restaurant and walked into the lobby. She noted the late-night arrivals and heard their complaints of persistent rain, as they shivered their way to the check-in desk. On her way to the elevator, she heard the snap of the newspaper the man in the comfortable black leather sofa was reading, and the clack of his wife's nails scrolling through her social media feed on her smartphone. The woman's nostrils twitched at the smell of tobacco from the elderly woman shuffling back inside the hotel from the designated smoking area, seeking shelter out of the rain. She caught the faint smell of sweat and aftershave from the stairs leading to the gym on the floor below, as she pressed the button to call the elevator. Each interaction was noted, threat assessed, and subsequently ignored. Hong Wei's companion took a last look around the hotel lobby as the elevator doors opened, and then stepped inside.

"Wait."

The elderly woman, still exuding smoke from

her lungs, spurred her legs from a shuffle to a slow jog as she headed for the elevator. Hong Wei's companion pressed the button to open the doors, giving the woman a flat smile as she stumbled inside.

"Bless you," the woman said. "I thought I was going to miss it." She waited for the young Chinese woman to reply, frowned briefly when she didn't, then carried on regardless, switching from Danish to English. "It's so wet," she said, pausing again in the hope of a response, receiving a second flat smile for her efforts. "Of course, a young thing like you wouldn't feel it, would you?"

Another smile, thinner than the last.

"You don't speak English?" The woman shrugged. "Never mind," she said, as the elevator stopped at her floor. She took a last look back at her elevator companion, before stepping out into the corridor. The young Chinese woman pressed the button to close the door as soon as she was gone.

The elevator stopped again on the seventh floor and the woman stepped out, using the shiny surface of the metal information plaque opposite the elevator to check the corridor to her left, before walking purposefully to the right. She kept her head dipped low, just enough for her long fringe to cover her eyes. An earlier reconnaissance of the corridor had revealed the position of the hotel security cameras, as well as the door to room 717, on the right, approximately thirty metres from the elevator. She walked past it, before slowing to stop at room 719. She tugged a card key from the pocket of her long-sleeved cardigan, pressing one end into the door, while hiding the flexible flat cable linking the card interface to the electronic lock-picking device with her sleeve. The door clicked open just a few seconds later, not much longer than if she had swiped the card too quickly, and again, as so many guests often did when trying to open their room for the first time. The cameras, and the important time stamp on the feed, she surmised, would register little more delay than was normal. Nothing out of the ordinary, and certainly not a Chinese intelligence operative forcing her way into a hotel room on the seventh floor.

The woman closed the door softly behind her and paused, her back to the door, as she listened for sounds that might reveal the room was occupied. She had passed the occupants of room 719 in the restaurant, choosing to leave just as they started their dessert.

The room was empty.

The door to the balcony was closed. The woman walked straight towards it, pocketing her lock-picker. She pulled two elastic hair bands from the hem pocket of her faux leather black stretch pants. She flattened the ends of her sleeves and secured them with the elastics, one around each wrist. The woman took one more elastic from her pocket and smoothed her bobbed hair into a tuft on the top of her head, freeing her fringe and removing all hair from her vision. She closed the buttons of her cardigan, bunched the tails around her waist, and tied them with the sash, before opening the balcony door.

The wind thrust the January rain into her face. She ignored it, pausing only to lick the drops from her lips as she contemplated the short leap between the balconies, from 719 to 717. The soft rubber soles of her flat shoes squealed on the wet railing as she climbed onto it, then again as she leaped across the gap. Her cardigan tails flapped loose in the wind on landing. She readjusted them, retied the sash, and then approached the balcony door, pressing her face to the glass – cool and wet on her forehead – as she surveyed the room. Hong Wei's companion took a moment longer, ignoring the rain, just to be certain the room was empty before she tried the door handle.

If luck was on her side, then Malik Uutaaq would have looked out of the balcony on entering his room for the first time. More luck in her favour would have convinced Malik that he needn't lock the glass door, just pulling it to would suffice. She thought of the short, flat metal file pressed between her thigh and her stretch pants, her backup tool to force the lock if necessary, and then opened the door.

Luck *was* on her side, which was a good thing, as Hong Wei had taught her not to believe in luck.

"You are not lucky," he had said, many times during her training. "Either something is to be, or not. Things – circumstances – will be in your favour, or against you. You must prepare for both. You must never trust to luck."

The woman allowed herself a small smile as she remembered the exchange. There had been many such exchanges during her training, and always a lesson to be learned at the end of each. Hong Wei had tested her with scenarios that eradicated luck, so much so she had given up hope of ever catching a break.

"What about hope?"

"Hope is like luck…" He had said.

"It can't be trusted?"

"Never."

And yet, she had often *hoped* for different outcomes. And when hoping didn't work, she had been forced to adapt, react, and prevail, which, she realised, was what he wanted all along.

However, her smile lingered as she told herself she had *hoped* the door would be open, allowing for a smoother, quieter entry, and it was.

She stepped into the room, closing the door behind her. The rain lashed the glass in a gust of wind like a serpent's tongue darting at her heels. She ignored it, listening again for signs that someone else might be in the room, hidden in the shadows, under a duvet, or showering. She knew Malik's assistant had a key to the room, and that she used it during the early hours, entering his room quietly, when a knock in the corridor might wake a neighbour. The room had the smell of sex and sweat about it, but, as far as she could tell, the bed and the shower were empty.

The *sleep* indicator light on Malik's laptop waxed and waned, prolonging the smile on the woman's face as she tugged a thumb drive from another hem pocket; she had stitched two of these concealed pockets into the waistband of her stretch pants, something she did with all of her clothes. She approached the desk, stepping over one of Malik's belts strewn on the floor before lifting the laptop lid. She pushed the thumb drive into the USB port on the right-hand side. The screen flickered for a moment as the software from the drive wormed its way into the laptop, bypassing Malik's password, and granting her access to the contents. She cloned the computer before digging for anything of interest, sifting through the apps that were already open, saving the others for a more thorough search later.

Malik's calendar was the most promising, allowing her to check the last days of January and the first week of February. Malik had made additional notes, including the arrival time of a flight from Greenland, together with a name: *Maratse*.

Maratse.

She knew the name, remembered Hong Wei talking about an earlier mission at a mining camp north of the Greenland capital, Nuuk. The mission had been frustrated by a woman working for *Politiets Efterretningstjeneste*, Danish police intelligence. The woman had burned the camp to the ground and followed Hong Wei to the *Xue Long*.

"Fenna Brongaard," she whispered, as she closed the lid of the laptop.

She bit her lip as she removed the thumb

drive, slipping it back into her hem pocket. Rumour had it that Brongaard had switched loyalties, that she had been recruited by the Canadians, and was now leading an investigation that, if successful, threatened Hong Wei's current mission to seduce Greenland's government into receiving Chinese assistance, and influence. Hong Wei had taught her not to believe in luck, but was it not luck that brought this man – Maratse – to Copenhagen? Brongaard, she knew, had risked her own life to save the Greenlander. He was important to her, and if, as they believed, she was close to finding Hong Wei and compromising the mission, then perhaps this Maratse could be used to stall her investigation, perhaps even end it.

Luck, she mused, *could be a powerful ally.*

The woman flicked her head to one side, staring at the hotel door as the lock clicked and the door started to open.

She shoved all further thoughts of luck to one side, as she fell back on her training, the countless drills where she had been forced into situations that required a cool head, quick thinking, and, on occasion, drastic measures to complete the mission. She stepped back as the light from the corridor wedged around the door, spilling onto the wall as a hand – a woman's hand – pressed the card key into the slot that would restore power to the room.

The lights snapped on a second later, together with the dull clunk of the restored electricity. The woman at the door stepped into the room, just as Hong Wei's companion dropped to one knee, curling slim fingers around Malik's belt buckle. She recognised Malik's assistant, Tipaaqu Jeremiassen, as she stepped into the light, and closed the door behind her. Her photo was on file, attached to a slim profile suggesting that Tipaaqu possessed a fierce intelligence fuelled by ambition. Despite encouraging Malik to accept Hong Wei's offer of support, Tipaaqu's profile highlighted potential concerns should she decide to make the move from managing Malik's campaign to running her own.

She was, according to the report, too smart to match the interests of *Guoanbu*, but Hong Wei's companion remembered an alternative use for her, something that could provide even greater leverage than money. She and Hong Wei had discussed it, and at that moment, with her hand wrapped around Malik's belt buckle, it was time to act – to react to the situation, and to force the best possible outcome.

Tipaaqu barely registered the movement as Hong Wei's companion – his very *capable* companion – closed the gap between them, clasping her hand over Tipaaqu's mouth as she punched her in the gut. The two women slid to the floor. Tipaaqu reached for her throat as the Chinese woman looped Malik's belt over Tipaaqu's head, pulling it snug around her neck, then tighter as she slapped Tipaaqu's hands out of the way. Tipaaqu's last breath spilled out of her lungs as her assailant pushed her all the way to the floor and knelt on her chest. Her luck had run out, but as Tipaaqu's eyes bulged, flecked with bursting vessels of blood, luck was all Hong Wei's companion could think about. She would keep such *lucky* thoughts to herself, presenting instead a range of possible scenarios to Hong Wei. Scenarios that might just include a hapless retired police constable called David Maratse.

Chapter 6

The delays started in Qaarsut. While the helicopters from Uummannaq island continued to ferry passengers through the snow to the tiny airport on the mainland peninsula, reports filtered in that the snow was heavier further south, preventing the De Havilland Dash 7 from taking off in Ilulissat. Karl suggested he should wait, after dropping Maratse and Petra at the airport building. He parked the snowmobile close to the main entrance, hinting that Buuti would be pleased if he brought them back within the hour.

"Although she'll never admit it," he said, lighting a cigarette. "She wants you to go on holiday."

"We'll take our chances," Maratse said, brushing the snow from the front of his old police jacket. He shook hands with Karl, then stepped back as Petra wrapped her arms around their neighbour in a farewell hug.

"You'll be back," Karl whispered, as Petra clung to him.

"Count on it," she said. "It's only a holiday."

Maratse remembered snatches of previous conversations concerning what would happen when they did come back. As Petra healed – her body and, more importantly, her mind – the question of *when* not *if* she would return to work had been raised. Returning to work meant returning to Nuuk, something neither of them were keen to talk about, and, as such, the conversation remained unfinished, snatched at here and there when one of them felt brave enough to broach the topic.

It can wait, was Maratse's stock response. To which Petra would invariably reply, *but not forever.*

Forever was somewhere between a long dark winter, and old age, concepts that were equally unfathomable in the tumult of their lives, and even more so in the lulls.

Maratse jolted himself into action, putting off the thought and the conversation one more time, as he grabbed their bags from the small sledge Karl had towed behind the snowmobile. His own suitcase had seen better times, while Petra's backpack reflected a more modern and younger approach to travel.

"You're taking that?" she had asked when Maratse pulled his suitcase out from under the bed.

"*Iiji.*"

"It's ancient."

Maratse had shrugged. "It's that or a sledge bag."

The thought of a filthy cotton envelope bag splashed with shit and seal fat convinced Petra that a battered suitcase would suffice.

"Until we buy you something new in Copenhagen."

Karl was right, Maratse thought as he packed earlier that morning. Petra had no problem spending his money, or her own. But as he brushed the snow from their luggage, picking a stubborn clump out of the broken corner of his suitcase, he decided that it wasn't a bad thing, and after so many years of travelling around Greenland, from one temporary posting to another, it was probably time for a new suitcase, maybe even a new outlook as they headed into the future.

Thoughts of a possible future, together with the emotions wrapped around their recent intimacy still bewildered him, as he struggled to think further than the moment. Spontaneity was the way of the hunter, launching the boat at the first cry of whale, harnessing the dogs and heading out onto the ice at the first sighting of a polar bear, feasting in times of plenty, and tightening the belts when hunting was poor. Maratse had adapted the hunting way of life to his police career, always on the move when the opportunity presented itself, travelling with the barest of essentials – a few books, several packets of cigarettes, a toothbrush, and a limited change of clothing. Everything fitted inside his battered suitcase with room to spare. But since moving to Inussuk, his material possessions had increased, even in such a short time, to include a string of dogs, a modest metre of books, and a growing selection of dry foods, herbs, and spices in his kitchen cupboard. The cigarettes had been replaced with more coffee, something Karl teased him about, with a nod to Petra and comments along the lines of Maratse changing his ways. To which Maratse would invariably reply, "Hmm," ending the conversation, until the next time.

"We have to go," Petra said, giving Karl one last hug. "We have to check-in."

Karl looked up at the thick grey clouds quilting the black winter sky. "It's a lot of hurry up and wait. You'll be sitting here for at least a couple of hours."

"*Iiji*," Maratse said, with a glance at the check-in desk just a few metres away on the other side of the thick glass door.

Karl reached for the door to open it as Maratse carried their bags inside. Petra lingered outside, oblivious to the snow clumping in her long black hair

"You'll look after Buuti?" she asked, knowing it was less of a question, more a swirl of complex and conflicting thoughts that were otherwise difficult to articulate.

"*Aap*," Karl said. He took Petra's hand, squeezed it, and said, "What she did…" He paused as a family arrived at the door, kicking the snow from their boots before they entered the airport. "She would do it again, in a heartbeat."

"She shouldn't have to – no one should…"

"Petra." Karl's eyes shone as the words triggered his emotions. "It happened. It's done. We will all move on, put the past behind us. Whether right or wrong, it's easier when the past can't return, when it's gone forever." He let go of Petra's hand to brush a tear from her cheek.

"Besides, it was self-defence, and we're not supposed to talk about it."

"But you do, with Buuti, when she needs to?"

"When she's ready I will," Karl said. "But knowing Buuti it will take a while. Maybe three weeks." Karl winked. "Just about the time you come back."

"Piitalaat," Maratse said, calling from inside the airport.

Petra gave Karl one last hug. "For Buuti," she said, before peeling away and walking into the airport.

Karl clamped his cigarette between his lips, waved once, then climbed onto the snowmobile. If it hadn't been snowing, even a casual observer would have seen a soft stream of tears spilling onto the hunter's cheeks.

Interested passengers could glean new information from the check-in desk every twenty minutes, following a prompt on the single television screen hanging in the corner of the waiting room. The *interested passengers* included a couple of Danish nurses anxious about their connecting flight to Kangerlussuaq and the onward flight to Copenhagen. The remaining passengers took their cues from the clouds, placating small children with hugs and the occasional vacuum-wrapped cookie from the vending machine, while swapping looks and raised eyebrows with their neighbours. Two hours after the Dash 7 should have arrived, Maratse caught the eye of an older Greenlandic woman as she pointed at the grey sky. The late-morning twilight had arrived, pressing soft light through thinning clouds. The Greenlanders stirred, while the Danes waited for *new information*, casting curious frowns at one another, then pricking their ears as the waiting room wriggled into life at the sound of four throaty propellers roaring above them. Petra lowered her smartphone and took Maratse's hand.

"We're going on holiday," she said.

Once in the air, the subdued drama of Arctic travel played out to a chorus of resigned sighs from the passengers, when they learned that the pilot was flying directly to Kangerlussuaq.

"The snow is too thick in Aasiaat and Ilulissat," the captain said, her voice crackling through the speakers in the cabin. "We're flying directly to Kangerlussuaq."

Petra didn't need the Danish translation to understand the change in plans; it was clear from the sighs around her and Maratse that something had changed, and the most likely change would be in their favour. With only a limited number of flights each week, getting passengers to the Denmark flight was often a priority in bad weather.

Petra took Maratse's hand, smoothing her thumb over his rough fingers as the pilot lined up for the final approach to the old American air base in Kangerlussuaq. The light shone in her eyes as the wheels thumped onto the runway, jostling the passengers for a moment before the stewardess welcomed them to Kangerlussuaq, thanked them for their patience, and reminded them that the temperature outside was minus forty-two degrees Celsius, not untypical for Kangerlussuaq, as the cold air sank onto the airport, shop, school and houses of the settlement.

The cold yanked the passengers' breath from their lungs as they exited the aircraft, passing the airport personnel, their faces hidden deep inside frosted parkas. Maratse's bushy black eyebrows frosted with his first breath, and the tips of Petra's long hair were capped with icy sleeves before they reached the terminal building. They thawed inside as they walked through security to join the passengers waiting to board the flight to Denmark.

A middle-aged American man with pale skin and tired eyes caught Petra's attention as he slumped at the information desk, fatigue tugging at his head as he forced his chin up to ask the question, "How long?"

"When the flight from Nuuk gets here, they will start boarding," was the answer.

"And how long will that be?"

The *Air Greenland* assistant consulted a screen set into her desk, before leaning to one side to look around the American. She stared out of the window for a few seconds, before responding.

"Maybe an hour," she said. "We'll know more in…"

"Twenty minutes," the man said, as he pushed off the counter. "I get it."

Petra watched him adjust the satchel he wore

across his chest, as she and Maratse followed him towards the restaurant. She paused as the man slumped into one of four upholstered chairs – the comfiest in the airport – pushed against the glass separating the cafeteria from a small waiting area. Petra squeezed Maratse's hand and stopped walking.

"Don't sit there," she said, to the American.

"What?"

"The door." Petra pointed to a small door just three large chairs from the one the man was sitting in. "It's where people go out to smoke. If you sit there, you'll freeze."

The American glanced at the door, just as a young couple returned from outside, drawing a deep draught of freezing air into the waiting area.

"I wondered why it was empty," the American said, as he pushed himself to his feet. "Thanks."

"You're welcome," Petra said. She smiled as she walked with Maratse into the restaurant.

Maratse pointed at a table with three free seats in the middle row. The floor below it was slick with melted snow from passengers' boots, and the chairs squealed as they pulled them out from beneath the table.

"Ah, if you don't mind," the American said, following close behind them and gesturing at the seats. "I'd like to join you."

"*Iiji*," Maratse said.

"That means *yes*," Petra said, nodding at the chairs.

"*Yes* he minds, or…"

"I don't mind," Maratse said, drawing a smile from Petra as his tongue tripped over the English words.

"That's great, thank you." The American reached out to shake their hands before sitting, introducing himself as, "Connor Williams."

"Petra and David," Petra said, pointing at Maratse. She saw Connor's gaze flick from their faces to the palms of her hands, and quickly hid them.

"Are they, *er*, tribal?" Connor said, as the three of them sat down. "Your tattoos."

"Not so much," Petra said, hiding her hands in her lap.

"I'm sorry," Connor said. He brushed stubby fingers through his thick brown hair. "I'm so tired, my polite switch has been turned off."

"Polite switch?" Maratse said.

"Yeah, erm…" Connor placed his palms on the table. "You know what, I *am* tired."

"It's okay," Petra said. She flashed Maratse a quick smile, then suggested coffee.

"Allow me," Connor said, tugging a handful of Danish kroner from his pocket.

"It's okay," Maratse said. "I'll get the coffee."

Connor nodded his thanks as Maratse pushed back his chair, stuffing the kroner back into his pocket as Maratse walked to the counter.

"This is a real quick turnaround for me," Connor said, dumping his satchel on the floor. "I try to keep up to date with the latest in Greenland and the Arctic, found some article about a resurgence in Inuit tattoos." He dipped his head in a brief nod towards Maratse. "I guess *tribal* wasn't the best word."

"Oh, that won't bother David," Petra said.

"He *looked* bothered."

"David?" Petra laughed. "That's his default look. All mysterious." Petra's cheeks flushed as she said it, adding a little more warmth to the chilly cafeteria.

"And what do you do?" Connor asked, thanking Maratse for a second time as he returned with three coffees and a selection of pastries.

"We're police officers," Petra said.

"Retired," Maratse said.

"Okay." Connor warmed his hands around the coffee mug. "I should have guessed from your jacket," he said, pointing at Maratse. "Only, it looks like you peeled the letters off."

"Peeled them off?" Petra bit back another laugh. "They didn't peel off; they ran away in protest."

Connor frowned. "I don't understand."

"David uses that jacket all the time," Petra said. "Even when he's hunting." She pressed her hand to Maratse's cheek, curling her fingers through his hair. "It's a health risk, really. It needs a wash."

"Okay," Connor said. "I get it. But..." He paused to look at Maratse. "You're a hunter?"

"I hunt," Maratse said.

"He's being modest," Petra said. "He *is* a hunter."

"But you *were* a policeman?"

"I was a constable."

"And a hunter," Petra said. "It's in his blood."

"I see." Connor paused to take sip of coffee. "It's funny, you both speak English. Any other languages?"

"Petra speaks Danish and German, too," Maratse said.

"Greenlandic?"

"I never got the hang of it," Petra said.

"But you do?" Connor looked at Maratse, nodding when Maratse raised his eyebrows in confirmation. "Interesting."

"What is?" Petra asked.

Connor reached into his pocket and pulled out a couple of business cards. He tapped them on the table as he spoke. "I work for a company called *Polar Travel Solutions*. Basically, I scout out locations for adventure cruises and other more specialist travel groups. I also recruit guides for the cruise ships, such as *Sirius Cruises*, and... Well, I'm currently in a bit of a bind." Connor slid the cards across the table, waiting as Petra and Maratse looked at them. "If you don't mind me asking, where are you guys headed? I mean, if you're not on duty?"

"Spain," Maratse said.

"Okay," Connor said, with a nod. "You're going south."

"*Iiji.*"

"For a little sun?" Connor looked out of the window. "I get it. But just how far south are you willing to go?"

"I don't understand," Petra said. She picked up Connor's card. "Are you recruiting us? We're police."

Connor laughed, and said, "Stranger things have happened. Besides…" Connor leaned back in his chair. He ran his hand across the stubble of his chin as he looked at them. "You both speak several languages. You're young and presentable," he said, smiling at Petra. "And…"

"Rustic," Petra said, eyes twinkling as she took Maratse's hand.

"Yes," Connor said, with a laugh. "We could also say *authentic*."

"I like *rustic*," Petra said.

Maratse frowned as he looked at Connor then shifted his gaze back to Petra. "Rustic?"

"It means *cute*," she said, pressing her teeth into her bottom lip, stifling a smile.

"What about whales?" Connor asked. "What do you know about them?"

"Whales?" Maratse frowned.

"Yeah, Humpbacks, Blues, Southern Rights… My whale guy just bailed on me. My ice guy…" Connor paused. "That's not right, my ice guy *and* my ice girl, found another boat, and I'm left with some vacancies." He leaned over the table, drawing Maratse and Petra closer with a wave of his hand. "Like I said, I'm in a bind. You're going south…"

"To Spain," Maratse said.

"I know, but what if you went a little further?"

"How far?" Petra asked.

"Oh, say Antarctica? Is that far enough?"

"Hmm," Maratse said.

Petra took Maratse's hand. She squeezed it for a moment before turning back to Connor. "We're listening," she said.

Chapter 7

Qitu checked his smartphone, scrolling through the *arrivals* feed at Kastrup Airport, as Svea made three mugs of tea.

"It's hot," she said, waiting for Qitu to look at her before pressing the mug into his hand.

"*Qujanaq.*" Qitu slipped his phone into his pocket, pressed the mug to his nose and took a sniff of strong lemon and ginger tea. He smiled at Svea, then walked back to the wall of information – Kaama and Svea's *shared screen* – and gestured at the whole wall with his free hand. "Talk me through it again."

"Don't you have to get back?" Kaama asked.

"Maratse's flight is delayed, and Tertu is busy with her own things." Qitu took a sip of tea, before continuing. "I have time, and I promise to give you more information, when we get that far."

"Right," Kaama said, with a nod to Svea. "Go for it, girl."

Svea made a show of rolling up her sweater sleeves and tying her long blonde hair in a messy bun. It bounced on her neck as she pointed out each connection on the wall.

"We started here," she said, pointing to a thin newspaper article to the right. "It's a clipping from a Canadian paper about mining in Nunavut – the territory governed by the Canadian Inuit." Svea waited for Qitu to nod, and then tapped the article. "You probably know that the Chinese have been trying to buy mines in the Arctic, which is causing concern in Canada."

"Because of the shipping lanes," Kaama added.

"And the strategic importance of the Arctic," Qitu said. "If they buy a mine, they'll build a new harbour to ship out ore, or perhaps develop the existing harbour. It has nothing to do with what's in the ground. It's all about establishing…"

"A foothold," Svea said, before biting her lip. "Sorry. Couldn't help it."

Qitu smiled and took another sip of tea, nodding for Svea to continue.

"The Chinese are struggling to close the deal on the purchase of the mine in Canada, or any Western mine for that matter. It's automatically assumed that any Chinese company buying a mine is actually a front for the Chinese government. They can't seem to get around that, no matter how hard they try."

"So," Kaama said, as she took a step closer to the wall, "they try to find a friendly ear in the government or choose a friendlier country." She took a step back, gesturing for Svea to continue.

"If we go back a few years, then we find this man, Juatan Fortin," Svea said, tapping a yellowed article from an old Canadian newspaper. "Fortin used to work for Tomsen Mining in the Northwest Territory. He's

Canadian Inuit, and originally from Tuktoyaktuk, right on the coast in the very north, on the Beaufort Sea."

"Used to work in a mine?" Qitu said.

Svea nodded. "In 1999."

Qitu took a step closer to the wall. "That year sounds important, but I can't remember why."

"It's the year the MV *Xue Long* entered the Northwest Passage, stopping unannounced in Tuktoyaktuk." Svea paused to fix her hair as it unravelled.

"Just leave it, girl," Kaama said. "I like it like that."

Svea let her hair hang loose and then reached for her tea. She tugged at the string of the teabag, then curled both hands around the mug.

"The Canadians had a wake-up call when they discovered a Chinese ship in their waters. There are plenty of articles and opinion pieces about it," Svea said, with a nod to the wall. "We've got some of them here and the rest on the hard-drives."

"But what about Fortin?" Qitu asked. "Where does he fit in?"

"He doesn't," Svea said. "He disappeared."

"But he's on your wall. Why?"

"Because his body was found in his truck a few kilometres south of the mine he worked at. The medical examiner estimated he had been dead for three days when they found him." Svea tapped a print-out of an obituary from a northern magazine. "But according to the security logs at the Tomsen Mining gate, he was at the mine one day earlier."

"Meaning?"

"Meaning that if the medical examiner is right, and the security log is correct, Juatan Fortin was both dead and alive on the second of the three days."

"Around the same time that Fortin's body was found," Kaama said, continuing where Svea left off, "a local police officer shot and killed an illegal immigrant. The police officer was killed in the exchange. On the same day, Tomsen Mining reported a computer crash. They lost some data. This was 1999, before information was backed-up in a cloud or anything like that."

"The data they lost," Qitu said. "Was it sensitive or valuable?"

"Both, probably," Kaama said. She paused to check her computer, then added, "Tomsen Mining was successful in extracting ore in Arctic locations, working around the challenges of permafrost. They mined diamonds in Canada, but they sent geologists on secret surveys all over the Arctic, including…"

"Greenland," Qitu said.

"Exactly." Kaama opened another file on her computer. "It wasn't easy, but we scrolled through a tonne of minutes from company meetings… Svea even went to Canada, using her Swedish charm to get into the company records."

"It wasn't easy," Svea said, with a frown.

"You loved it, you big flirt," Kaama said. She grinned, and then turned back to her computer, waving Qitu over for a closer look. "They never bought it, but they were keeping close eyes on these locations in Greenland, looking at aluminium and gold. I think the idea was to step in and buy the companies if they started to fail, depending upon the results of their geology surveys."

"It's standard practice," Svea said, stepping around the back of Kaama's computer so Qitu could see her face. "Back then, and now. Small companies, from Britain, for example, apply for permission to mine in Greenland. Then they buy a failing company, drill for the purposes of exploration and hope to find something before the money runs out."

"And if they find something?" Qitu asked, knowing the answer, but curious to hear Svea's take on it.

"They know the big companies are watching them, so they hope to be bought out, preferably before they run out of money. Then they try to make a profit on the sale of the company, the equipment, and, more importantly, the mining rights."

"This is still going on," Qitu said. "In Greenland."

"Yes, in Svartenhuk," Svea said. "Something about a German exploration, looking for Alfred Wegener's diaries." Svea returned to the wall, pointing at an article printed from a German website. "Berndt Media," she said, then paused. "Who did you say was funding Nuuk Media Group?"

Qitu took a moment to finish his tea, and then

said, "Like I said, it's still going on. Berndt Media had a change of heart after the scandal in Greenland, and the events in Berlin. The company was made into a trust, and the money was diverted to interests that would make up for previous mistakes and indiscretions. NMG is funded by Berndt. Rights to land in Greenland were the prize they were seeking, but Maratse got in the way. And Petra too, both officially and unofficially, depending upon your sources."

"Maratse?" Kaama said. "The same Constable Maratse you mentioned earlier?"

"*Aap.*"

"You said he was retired."

"He did retire. He *is* retired. But it seems that trouble follows him around Greenland, and sometimes further afield." Qitu paused to check the arrivals feed on his smartphone. "They've taken off," he said. "From Kangerlussuaq. Svea?"

"Yes?"

"Tell me more."

"All right," she said. "If we go back to the British example. Simply put, a country like England gets approval to mine if they meet the different environmental and economic requirements, because they are considered allies. A British mining company is concerned with profit, not global strategy. But the Chinese, for example... Well, their intentions are suspect. It's not like the Russians – they already have an Arctic presence, and a lot of territory in the Arctic. But the Chinese are a near-Arctic state, in that they are desperately trying to gain that foothold to secure their Arctic position, without actually having any territory in the Arctic. We believe that the man in Canada, Juatan Fortin, was used to gain access to Tomsen Mining's information."

"Industrial espionage," Qitu said.

"Exactly. If the Chinese knew who Tomsen was trying to buy, and, more importantly, for how much, then they could outbid them." Svea shrugged. "It's quite simple really."

"Only it's not," Kaama said. "Because under the current geopolitical circumstances, and ever since the Canadians were shocked into taking a closer look at their northern borders, the chances of the Chinese ever buying a mine, or anything else for that matter, in the Arctic are very remote."

"Non-existent," Svea said, "now that the Americans have their eye on Greenland."

"They've always had their eye on Greenland," Qitu said.

"Yes, but now the ice is all but gone…"

Qitu pointed at the picture of Malik he had tacked to the wall when he first arrived.

"Greenland continues to have a complex relationship with Denmark," he said. "People like Malik have been stirring the pot and encouraging renewed nationalism. His first attempts at securing the populist vote backfired when he was suspected of murdering the First Minister's daughter." Qitu paused as Kaama and Svea exchanged curious glances. "But now, as a minister in the Greenland government, he's perfectly positioned to influence policies. It makes him a good target to be approached by foreign powers, especially as he has an appetite for various vices."

"Then you think he's been approached already?" Kaama asked.

"I think it's interesting that his friend, Levi Aaqqii, a man who has had two business ventures go bankrupt in the last three years, has recently come into some money."

"That's your interest in Levi? Bankruptcy?" Svea asked.

"*Naamik*," Qitu said, shaking his head. "Tertu is working on an ongoing investigation, involving torture and pornography accessed via the dark web. She's trying to expose the users in Greenland who accessed a particular site, and Levi's son's name came up in that investigation."

"You've talked to him?"

"We tried, but he left Greenland before we could meet him, and his current whereabouts are unknown. He has disappeared, and, given Levi's previous economic situation, it's unlikely he could afford to set his son up in another country without some kind of support."

"So," Svea said, as she started to connect the dots. "Levi Aaqqii comes into some money."

"*Aap*," Qitu said.

"He reaches out to Malik Uutaaq…"

"A friend from school." Qitu nodded.

"And now a minister in the Greenland government." Svea peeled a marker from the putty on the wall and made a note beside Malik's picture. "He's popular. And gaining influence?" She paused to look at Qitu, making another note as he nodded again. "But he needs money to run a campaign that might challenge the First Minister."

"He won't need much, compared to an American political campaign," Qitu said. "But Greenland is an expensive country, and very expensive to travel in. Malik will need cash if he's to visit all the towns, and the larger villages on the west coast. Even more if he goes east or tries to visit some or all of the settlements. He probably wouldn't even try, but if he did, he would win an election, just by turning up."

"And then Greenland has a First Minister…" Kaama said.

"Who dreams of independence."

"And lends a friendly ear to the Chinese," Svea said, tapping the blank piece of paper in the middle of the wall. "This Chinese man in particular."

"That's about right," Qitu said. "None of this is new. It's well known."

"Maybe," Kaama said. "But no one knows who the mysterious Chinese man is, but I'm betting he has something to do with Juatan Fortin's death. He might even have been aboard the *Xue Long* when it sailed into Tuktoyaktuk."

"So all we have to do," Svea said, "is find him and link him to Fortin's death."

"You're trying to make this into a twenty-one-year-old murder case," Qitu said. "Assuming Fortin didn't die of natural causes."

"He didn't," Kaama said, with a nod to the medical examiner's report. "He was poisoned with Saxitoxin."

"With what?"

"A neurotoxin, found in shellfish," Svea said, casting an apologetic smile at Kaama. "Sorry, I couldn't help it."

"But," Kaama said, after an exaggerated sigh. "The autopsy revealed that Fortin's last meal was reindeer meat, and potatoes. No shellfish of any kind."

Qitu stepped closer to the wall as Kaama and Svea continued their teasing. He followed the different marker lines connecting the articles and images, charting a course of failed acquisition by foreign powers seeking to gain a foothold in the Arctic. Given what he knew of Malik Uutaaq, his strengths and, ultimately, his weaknesses, Qitu understood the importance of confirming all the accounts and their sources, before publishing the article. Because if they could prove everything then they could expose China, right at the very moment they found their man in the Arctic, preferably sooner, if Malik Uutaaq was to be saved. While saving Malik Uutaaq was not high on Qitu's list of priorities, neither did he wish to see the man suffer. One way or another, Qitu felt Malik Uutaaq had suffered enough already.

Chapter 8

The inside of the Airbus 330-200 filled up quickly with passengers accompanied by the familiar sound of peeling Velcro and the tough zips of Arctic parkas. Maratse stuffed his police jacket and Petra's parka into the overhead locker, sharing nods and flat smiles with the passengers around him until he clambered over Petra to take the window seat.

"You don't want to sit here?" he asked.

"Nothing to see," she said.

"You can rest your head on the side to sleep."

"I've got you," Petra said.

"Hmm."

Petra plucked at Maratse's fingers until the passengers settled, exchanged pleasantries with the passenger in the aisle seat next to her, before tilting her head to catch the flight assistant's welcome, and an update on the delay.

"Arriving around midnight," Petra said, as the crew prepared for take-off.

"There'll be a shuttle to the hotel," Maratse said. "Copenhagen Towers."

"And after that, after the trial?"

"*Iiji?*"

Petra took Maratse's hand, held it in her lap. "What do you think, about what Connor said?"

"I think the plan was to go to Spain."

"Yes, but…"

"You wanted to go to Spain, and I want to be with you."

"I know, and that's sweet but…" Petra paused for take-off, leaning her head against Maratse's shoulder until the plane lifted off the runway and began the slow climb to cruising altitude. "It's just I think you would enjoy it."

"A cruise ship? I've seen enough of them."

"I know, but this is in Antarctica. You've never been there. It will be exciting. It's one of those once-in-a-lifetime opportunities, and I think we have to take it."

"You want to go?"

"I do."

"Okay," Maratse said. "We'll go."

Petra turned to stare at Maratse's face, her brown eyes growing larger in the dimly lit cabin interior, drawing him towards her as she waited, silent, patient, like a hunter on the ice.

"There," she said, as Maratse's lips twitched.

"What?"

"That smile." Petra flicked the tip of Maratse's nose with her finger. "You want to go. Admit it."

"I haven't had time to think about it, not really."

"*Hmm*," Petra said, in her best imitation of the retired police constable sitting beside her.

"Was that me?"

"Yes," she said, flopping back into her seat. She brushed her hair from her face with one hand, while fumbling with the tray-table with the other. "Just for that," she said, as the stewardess handed out the post take-off refreshments, "I'm stealing your pretzels."

"You always do," Maratse said.

"Yes. It's my privilege."

After the refreshments and the in-flight meal had been served, Petra settled in her seat, slipped one arm around Maratse's and pressed her head on his shoulder.

"Wake me just before we land," she said.

"*Iiji*."

Petra's hair, soft with the smell of coconut, tickled Maratse's cheek, purging all other thoughts from his mind as he settled on what was important – that they were safe, that the past was behind them, permanently. The trial would bring everything to a close, allowing them to settle, to make decisions about their future, a future that felt right. Maratse let those thoughts – the best he could ever have hoped for – sink deep into his body, spreading a sense of contentment that reminded him of the best moments on the ice, with a light wind, a disciplined team in front of the sledge, and a dusting of granular snow between the runners and the smooth black ice stretching across the fjord.

The thud of the Airbus' wheels onto the runway at Kastrup Airport, Copenhagen, jolted them both awake. Petra rubbed her eyes, for the better part of two minutes before she was ready to rise. They blinked their way through security and yawned into the luggage area. Maratse rested on the arms of the luggage trolley with Petra perched on the end, as they waited for Maratse's battered case and Petra's backpack.

"There," she said, pointing a lazy finger at the first piece of luggage, and again at the second as Maratse fetched them.

"Shuttle bus," Maratse said, once the trolley was loaded. Petra fell into step beside him as he pushed through customs, blinking again in the harsh light, until they spilled out into a flow of passengers in the main terminal.

"Constable Maratse," Petra said, as she read a sign in the hands of a short woman leaning against a pillar just beyond the press of people waiting to receive their friends and relations from the Greenland flight. "It's you."

"*Iiji*," Maratse said, as he turned the trolley towards the woman with the sign. He slowed to a stop, stepping around the trolley to shake the woman's hand. "Sergeant Ada Valkyrien," he said. "This is Petra Jensen."

"It's Sergeant, right?" Ada said, as she took Petra's hand.

"Yes," Petra said. Her lips curled in a curious smile as she took in Ada's appearance, the leather jacket, her close-cropped hair, and her long fringe.

"David's better half, I presume." Ada smiled. "Prettier too."

"Thank you," Petra said, cheeks flushing. She curled a loose strand of hair around her ear as Ada pointed to the parking area.

"I'll take you to the airport. Get you settled in."

"I thought there was a shuttle bus," Maratse said.

"There is," Ada said. "But God knows what's going on with that. It's parked right over there." She pointed at a medium-sized bus with steamed windows. "It's been there for three hours. Full of Chinese tourists. No idea what that's about." She took Petra's backpack and then nodded at a tiny Chevrolet tucked between two police patrol cars. "This is me."

Ada chatted as she drove through the wet Copenhagen streets, glancing at Maratse in the rear-view mirror each time she stopped at a traffic light.

"Just making sure you're awake," she said, grinning as Maratse sat clamped between the baby seat and the passenger door. He held Petra's backpack across his thighs, with one hand bracing his suitcase on top of the baby seat.

"How old is your child?" Petra asked, as Ada accelerated.

"Nikolaj is nearly a year old." Ada glanced at Petra. "He's with my mom. He's been there a lot lately. The investigation got a little crazy. Mom helped out, and she offered to keep helping, just until it was all over." Ada caught Maratse's eye. "The trial came a lot sooner than expected. It's good."

"Hmm," Maratse said.

"But what about you?" Ada turned to Petra. "Any children? Any plans?"

Petra pressed her hands to her thighs, hiding the scars between the joins of her fingers. "No plans," she said. "It's been…"

"Crazy?" Ada said.

"Yes."

"I heard about what happed to Fari Severinsen."

Petra pressed her lips closed, volunteering nothing as Ada waited for a response.

"He was shot at the hospital?"

"Yes," Petra said.

"And you were there?"

"We both were," Maratse said, leaning forward. "Fari attacked, he was shot. It's done."

"And the head of the *Makakajuit*, Greenland's most successful, if not Greenland's *only*, organised crime organisation is eliminated." Ada snapped her fingers. "Just like that."

"*Iiji*," Maratse said. "That's how it happened." He settled back in his seat.

Ada stopped at the next light, glanced at Maratse in the mirror, then pulled away as soon as the light turned green. She said nothing more before switching lanes and pulling into a side street.

"The hotel's just over there," she said, pointing at the sign for Copenhagen Towers.

Ada parked in a short-stay parking spot and turned the engine off. Petra reached for the door handle, but Ada stopped her with a light touch of her arm.

"I won't ask about what happened. I've seen the report, seen the statements from the Chief of

Police, the leader of the Special Response Unit...
I get it. It's done. I won't mention it again," she
said.

"That would be best," Petra said.

Ada turned to look at Maratse, and said,
"And not a word at the trial. They want
information about how Fari used the guards and
prison personnel, not about Fari himself."

"I understand," Maratse said.

He started to say more but stopped as the
shuttle bus from the airport bumped up the raised
curb, braking to a sudden stop outside the main
entrance to the hotel. A group of agitated tourists
steamed out of the bus, shouting at the driver,
slapping his arms with rolled up brochures as he
opened the rear doors to get at the luggage.

"Three hours later," Ada said, with a shrug.

Petra and Ada grabbed the luggage, before
tugging Maratse out of the back of the car. They
skirted the angry tourists, catching little of the
rapid Chinese curses hurled at the driver.

"Someone's in trouble," Ada said.

"Hmm." Maratse caught the driver's eye,
then moved on as the driver fended off another
brochure beating.

The staff in the hotel lobby kept one eye on
the group outside as Ada checked Maratse and
Petra into their room. The thick glass doors
suppressed the angry chatter, until the doors
opened, and the tourists burst into the lobby.
Maratse and Petra stood to one side as the group
surged towards the check-in desk. The concierge
stiffened as the first of the tourists switched to

English interspersed with occasional Chinese words as she complained about the wait at the airport.

Ada joined Maratse and Petra, handing Petra the key cards for their room, but with one eye firmly on the Chinese tourists.

"What do you think?" she said to Petra.

"They seem very angry."

"Yes," Ada said, flicking her head to one side as the driver entered the lobby.

The driver strode towards the Chinese tourists at the desk, pushing his way through the first ring in an effort to reach the spokesperson. He raised one hand as if to strike out, drawing Ada into the fray, as the tourists rallied to repel the driver. Maratse took a step forward, but Petra caught his arm.

"Wait," she said, with a nod to two men with hotel security badges stitched into their shirts. The men came out of a small side room a second after the concierge lifted her hand from beneath the desk. "Alarm button," Petra said.

Petra took Maratse's arm, drawing him away from the desk as the security men and Ada subdued the driver. Maratse turned his head, pausing as a slight figure in black with black bobbed hair, entered the security room.

"What is it?" Petra asked.

"A woman. I think." Maratse took a step towards the security room, pausing as the door clicked closed. "She went in there."

"Staff?"

"*Eeqqi*," Maratse said. "I don't think so."

He turned his head at a shout from Ada, then stepped back as the hotel security men helped Ada secure the driver on the lobby floor.

"David," Petra said, catching his arm as he took a step forward. "They've got this. We should wait."

"Hmm," he said.

He turned to look at the security room, frowning again as the door clicked closed, as if someone had just come out of the room. He looked along the corridor, towards the elevators, saw no one, then turned back to Petra, only to pause at the sound of elevator doors opening.

"David," Petra said. "That's Malik Uutaaq."

Malik Uutaaq stumbled out of the elevator, tripping over his feet as he reached out to the wall. He pressed his palm against the wall, resting for a second, catching his breath, before taking another step towards the front desk.

"I need help," he said, staring past Maratse and Petra, eyes fixed on the concierge. "I need an ambulance."

"Malik," Maratse said, taking a step forward.

"She's hurt," Malik said, as Maratse took his arm. "I went to my room, she was on the floor."

"Malik," Petra said, taking his other arm, as Maratse guided him to a chair. "Who's hurt?"

"Tipaaqu," Malik said. He swallowed, caught his breath, and said, "I think she's dead. She's dead in my room."

Chapter 9

The kettle whistled on the hotplate at the back of the workshop. Hong Wei looked up as the Danish mechanic, limping slightly from old age and a war wound from Afghanistan, lifted the kettle from the heat and poured two large mugs of tea. Hong Wei knew the mechanic would add sugar and milk to his tea, calling it *cheap chai*, while Hong Wei would take his black. The mechanic mumbled something about never liking tea, as he carried the two cups to the lounge area of the workshop, a more comfortable place for his customers, somewhere they could relax as he tinkered with their cars on the other side of tiny squares of thick glass, rising from a low brick wall to the ceiling. The mechanic set Hong Wei's tea on a round table beside the red leather armchair, while he plumped for the sofa.

"Thank you, Ole," Hong Wei said in English.

"You're welcome."

The men sipped their tea in silence, barely aware of the creak of hot water in the pipes from the apartments above Ole's workshop, content in each other's company. Hong Wei treasured these moments, small moments of calm with little more than the creaking pipes to disturb him. Ole, for his part, seemed content with the arrangement, receiving a comfortable sum of money in exchange for a few days' inconvenience a couple of times a year. In truth, as he admitted to Hong Wei, closing the workshop for a few days once in a while gave him a chance to rest, and the customers thought nothing of him closing for illness, or, during a flurry of days required by Hong Wei and his associates, a sudden break to visit a sick family member. The excuses were not important, and neither did Ole need to work to pay the rent. Hong Wei covered that. But a functional garage fitted the Chinese intelligence officer's needs better than an empty one, and so, Ole maintained a modest list of customers for the sake of appearances, and, as he would say, *to keep his hand in*.

Brief moments of calm. A cup of tea. The creaking of the pipes. A reprieve in which Hong Wei often closed his eyes, cup poised beneath his nose, as he thought. Once he had thought through the requirements of the current operation or operations, whatever time was left over he used to recall and examine his first major operation, and his first major mistake.

The steam filled the pores of the skin on his cheeks as he remembered the operation in Tuktoyaktuk, how he and Pān Tāo had sweated beneath the reindeer carcass, cursing the biting flies of the Arctic, as they left the cool air of the water, and carried the reindeer into the village. They had chosen a time when they believed the residents would be indoors, eating, drinking maybe – hopefully too drunk or too occupied to notice the strangers entering town, disguised as best they could be as hunters returning from a successful foray on the open tundra.

They were wrong.

Hong Wei's first mistake.

Blood from the kill and mud from the trail did little to hide their gait – too fast, or their eyes – too inquisitive, darting all over the place, from house to house, up and down the packed-earth streets. Even the stray sledge dogs knew they were fake, sniffing at their legs as they walked, pressing wet noses into their crotches when they stopped to get their bearings.

"That one," Hong Wei had said, directing Pān Tāo to a small dilapidated house with a nod of his head.

The reindeer posed a problem, suddenly, as Hong Wei and Pān Tāo carried the kill onto the deck of the house, shooing the dogs away with soft kicks – too soft for Arctic dogs – as children clumped in the road below the deck. They worried the dogs would chew on the carcass, and so they carried it into the house, drawing queried looks from the children, followed by gasps as Hong Wei dropped his quarter of the reindeer onto the floor just inside the screen door.

The operation was, in hindsight, doomed from the start, as Hong Wei focused on the looks but forgot the purpose. If they *looked* right, he surmised, then no one would question their purpose, something he chewed over with every cup of tea he shared with Ole in the mechanic's workshop. *Purpose*, he now knew, was tantamount to success. The purpose of an operation must be disguised for it to be successful. It wasn't enough to look the part. In fact, he now knew, *looking* the part often created more problems than intended.

But not anymore.

Now, since Tuktoyaktuk, Hong Wei was careful to disguise the purpose, choosing to operate in plain sight, while keeping his intent in the shadows.

"She's back," Ole said.

Hong Wei caught the flutter in his heart, stilled it with a long, slow intake of breath, and took a deliberate sip of tea. Only then did he open his eyes, smiling at Pān Tāo's daughter as she slipped onto the sofa beside Ole, just before the old mechanic excused himself.

"See?" Xiá said in Chinese. "Every time I come in; I scare him away."

"He's not scared," Hong Wei said. "He's showing you respect."

"Maybe." Xiá crossed her legs in the way she knew bothered Hong Wei, bouncing her foot to an irregular beat. He accused her of doing it on purpose, to which she would always appear shocked, as if she didn't understand, but they both knew he liked order, and she liked to upset it, as often as she could.

"What have you done?" Hong Wei said, with a glance at Xiá's foot.

"Exactly what you instructed. I have wiped the tapes. There's no record of you being in or near the hotel. The shuttle bus was a good trick."

"And you paid the driver?"

"Handsomely."

"And?" Hong Wei prompted Xiá with a wave of his hand.

"I cloned Malik Uutaaq's computer."

Hong Wei frowned. "But that's not all, is it?"

Xiá stilled her foot, and said, "There were complications."

"Such as?"

"A disturbance."

Hong Wei took another sip of tea – cold now, growing colder by the second, like the chill he felt creeping down his spine.

"But you resolved it?"

"I had to."

"Resulting in?"

Xiá teased her fringe, drawing her hair in front of her eyes, and dipping her head, if only for a second. When she looked up, she met Hong Wei's firm gaze with a fury of her own.

"I created an opportunity, but it must be exploited, soon, if it is to work."

"You acted rashly."

"No," Xiá said. "I reacted. Now it's up to you to turn my actions to your advantage." Xiá took a shallow breath before explaining, in detail, what she had done. She waited as Hong Wei closed his eyes, thinking. She watched him take sips of cold tea until the cup was empty and he opened his eyes to place it on the table. "You've thought it through," she said.

"Tipaaqu Jeremiassen could have been useful," Hong Wei said.

"She still is. Perhaps more so now." Xiá shrugged. "More predictable. Less ambitious."

"She's dead, Xiá."

Xiá shrugged again. "Like I said."

"But now we have to adapt our approach. We have to exert more influence, call in favours, release more funds."

"So?"

"Xiá," Hong Wei said, leaning forwards. "The more wheels you set in motion, the greater the chance someone will see them turning. We risk drawing more attention to ourselves."

"By offering our support to Malik Uutaaq? It's better this way. Now we can offer him whatever money we choose. He will be indebted to us as we help him out of a bad situation."

"You're assuming he's suspected of murdering his assistant."

Xiá's eyes sparkled as she smiled.

"I used his belt."

"What about his alibi?"

"Gone," she said. "Along with the surveillance tapes."

"You're forgetting something – *someone*."

Hong Wei watched Xiá as she feigned confusion. He knew she hadn't forgotten anything, but experience had taught him that it was sometimes necessary to goad her to get her to admit it. *Arrogance.* It was one of her flaws, something he neither appreciated, nor knew quite how to eradicate. He had learned to pamper Pān Tāo's daughter's quirks, just as she had learned to play on his guilt.

This is not about her father.

And yet, it was always about her father.

They both knew it. They both had to work around it.

And so he did – *always*.

"Come on, Xiá," he said. "You can't be that…"

"Stupid?"

Xiá turned her brown, almost black, eyes on Hong Wei, pressing him back into his seat, like no one else could, or would even dare, unless they too shared the pain of guilt and death.

"I was going to say *short-sighted*."

"I prefer stupid," Xiá said. "But, for the sake of humouring you. I have it all planned out. Malik Uutaaq will reach out to his friend…"

"Levi Aaqqii."

"Exactly." Xiá shifted position, kicking off her shoes and tucking her heels under her bottom, as if she were settling down to discuss the latest and juiciest gossip, not the planned assassination of a Greenlandic businessman. "I'll arrange a meeting." She looked up as Ole entered the lounge area, gesturing at the kettle in his hand.

"Tea?" he asked.

"Tea, bald tyres, and an hour of your time," Xiá said.

"I don't know," Ole said, turning to Hong Wei. "I don't get involved. That was our arrangement."

Hong Wei looked at Xiá, raising his finger as she started to speak, before addressing Ole. "I think I know what Xiá has planned. It won't take more than an hour, for which you will be well compensated."

"And it will be fun," Xiá said. She tilted her head to give Ole the benefit of her attention, swallowing him whole with the softest of looks, until he melted, nodded that he would help, and withdrew, quietly, back into the kitchen.

"Xiá," Hong Wei said, switching to Chinese.

"What?"

"You mustn't force Ole like that. Your looks, your..." Hong Wei paused to sigh. "Your sex is not a weapon that you can use again and again. Used wrongly, inappropriately..."

"Was I inappropriate?"

Hong Wei paused again, this time waiting for Xiá to answer her own question. When she didn't, he continued.

"You were right before. Ole *is* scared of you. You intimidate him. And now..." Hong Wei nodded his head towards the shadow of Ole in the kitchen. "You did it again."

"He needed encouragement."

"You suggested something more, with your looks, and your body."

"It's mine to suggest," Xiá said.

Hong Wei sighed again. "This is not the first time we've talked about this."

"And it bores me every time we do, *Fùqīn*."

"I'm not your father, Xiá."

"No? Then stop acting like one."

Xiá stood, brushed her cardigan flat against her thighs, then fixed Hong Wei with a look, one part venom, one part love, all defiance.

"I'm tired," she said. "It's been a busy night covering your tracks. I'm going to bed."

Hong Wei caught the glint in Xiá's eye and held up his hand for her to wait.

"What are you not telling me?"

"Nothing."

"Xiá," Hong Wei said. "Tell me."

"Okay," Xiá said, with an exaggerated sigh. "I saw Malik's calendar."

"And?"

"I saw a name that was familiar." Xiá smiled as Hong Wei leaned forward.

"Who?"

"Constable David Maratse," she said. "He's coming here, to Copenhagen."

"Maratse?"

"Yes. Maratse."

"Constable Maratse," Hong Wei whispered. "There's a name from the past."

Xiá twirled into a curtsy once then flattened her cardigan tails as she picked up her shoes. Hong Wei considered calling her back as she padded out of the lounge. If it wasn't for the mention of Maratse's name, he might have reminded her of her place, how he had provided for her, all but adopted her, certainly cared for and loved her her entire life.

But he didn't.

He let her go, just as he always did, whispering a silent promise to Pān Tāo that next time he would do better, followed by a curse that he had to die that day, that he never got to be the father Xiá needed.

No, he thought. *Instead, she got me. And now… Maratse.*

"Tea," Ole said, as he entered the lounge. He offered a Hong Wei a fresh cup – a *clean* cup, before sitting down on the sofa.

"Thank you."

Ole nodded.

"She's a handful," he said, as Hong Wei sipped his tea. "I have a daughter."

"Really?" Hong Wei lowered his cup. "You never said."

"Nothing to say." Ole turned the cup in his hands. "My life imploded after Afghanistan. I was one of the older soldiers. Too old to learn new tricks. I'd seen too much already. But then I saw a lot more. Couldn't handle it. Turned to drink – thought I could handle *that*. Turns out I couldn't. Which is when my wife took my daughter and left." Ole looked up. "This is all I've got. If you promise I won't lose it…"

"You won't. I promise."

"Then I'll help the girl," Ole said. "Just this one time."

Hong Wei smiled as Ole left, saddened by the thought that Ole was right, it would be *just the one time.* Xiá would have planned for that.

Chapter 10

Petra waved as Sergeant Ada Valkyrien entered the hotel restaurant, drawing her over to a window table, as far from the commotion in the lobby as was possible. Ada forced a tired smile onto her face as she sat next to Petra. She took a moment, as if deciding just how much she could tell the Greenlanders, before mouthing the words *fuck it*, and telling them what she knew.

"There's a body in Malik Uutaaq's hotel room. It's his assistant, Tipaaqu Jeremiassen. Malik's belt is cinched around her neck. There's not much sign of a struggle. It looks like she was taken at the door. Her killer must have been standing right behind it as she walked in."

"Her killer?" Maratse said. "Not Malik?"

Ada paused. "You know how it is. We can't know before the scene has been swept. But if I had to make a guess, I'd say he didn't do it."

"Based on what?" Petra asked.

"His demeanour," Ada said. "His panic. It's not just the alcohol, he's genuinely confused." She reached for one of the empty glasses on the table and poured herself a glass of water from the jug. The ice clunked as she poured. "He's scared," she said, after a sip of water. "He told us who he is, and I know why he's here, although

~ 107 ~

we hadn't met before tonight."

Petra caught the look Ada cast at Maratse, and said, "Why is he here?"

Ada waited for Maratse to say something, filling in the blanks when he didn't. "Malik Uutaaq made a public statement about the investigation into Vestsyssel Prison. He implied that there was an undercover informant passing on information to the police…"

"Me," Maratse said.

"And that's why…"

"Fari Severinsen came looking for you," Ada said. She shrugged. "Perhaps I know a little more than I let on, but," she said, when Maratse started to speak. "I don't need to know any more. What's done is done. But the situation with Malik… It's interesting."

Ada finished her water and stood. She checked the time on her smartphone, slipped it back into her pocket, and then nodded in the direction of the lobby.

"I have to get a few statements before they finish their shift. It seems that I've caught this case now, at least until it gets taken from me."

"What is it?" Petra asked, as Ada frowned.

"It's just all the video has been wiped. Everything from the hotel cameras – the ones here, in the restaurant." Ada pointed at the camera tucked into the corners of the room. "The corridors, lobby, all entrances – everything is gone from about six o'clock this evening. Security says there's an automatic backup every morning at three o'clock. Apparently, that's when they have more bandwidth. But there's nothing to back up tonight."

"Where's the computer?" Petra asked.

"The one with the video feed?" Ada turned her head towards the lobby. "In a room right behind reception."

"David saw a woman by the door, just when the fight started."

"A woman?"

"*Iiji*," Maratse said. "Short. Dark hair. Dark clothes."

"And she went into the security room?"

"*Imaqa*. Maybe. I never saw her come out."

"Well, if you remember anything." Ada stuffed her hands into the pockets of her leather jacket, flapping the sides like tiny wings as she thought. "Other than that there's nothing more you can do, apart from get some rest. You're all checked-in." Ada turned to Maratse. "We don't need you before Friday morning. So, relax, enjoy the city, and I'll pick you up on Friday."

"And Malik?" Maratse said.

"We'll take him down to the station. Hold him overnight, see what he can tell us."

"We know him," Petra said. "If we can help, we'd like to."

Maratse looked at Petra, saw the soft light reflected in her eyes. He took her hand as she slid it across the table.

"He's suffered a lot, already," Petra said. "I'm willing to move on, to forget about certain things."

"What things?" Ada asked.

"Malik thinks you have to speak Greenlandic to *be* Greenlandic." Petra shrugged. "It's just something going on back home."

"*Piitalaat*," Maratse whispered, with a smile.

"Okay then," Ada said. "I have to go. See you Friday, after breakfast."

Petra waited until Ada left the restaurant before squeezing Maratse's hand. "Breakfast," she said. "I'm starving."

"It's after midnight."

"But early evening in Greenland." Petra stood up. "Come on. We slept on the flight. We'll find somewhere. Then sleep late. Explore Copenhagen in the afternoon."

Petra stood, pulled Maratse to his feet, then led him out of the restaurant. She paused at the sight of Malik being helped into the back of a police patrol car, then led Maratse onto the street in search of food.

Sunlight pressed through the windows to wake Petra and Maratse. The curtains were pushed to either side, just as they were in most houses in Greenland, rarely closed, the whole year round, as if the light was too precious to hide. Petra brushed her hair from her face, prodding Maratse in the chest until he woke. He opened one eye, parting his lips in a toothy grin as he looked at Petra's hair – wild like black solar flares curling and bursting from her head.

"Get up," Petra said, leaning over to kiss Maratse's nose. "Breakfast. Shopping."

"More breakfast?" Maratse frowned as Petra

slipped out of bed. She pulled the top sheet with her, wrapping it around her body, securing it in a loose knot above her breasts.

"Brunch," she said, with a shrug. "We're on holiday."

Maratse watched Petra pad around the bed and into the bathroom. He lay back on the pillow at the sound of Petra turning on the shower. Thoughts of Malik in the back of the police patrol car buzzed through his mind, punctuated with brief images – like fire shadows cast on the snow, or the side of a walled tent – of the small woman in black as she entered the security room. He was sure of it now. Whoever she was, she had entered that room when hotel security was preoccupied with the clash in the lobby.

Preoccupied.

Maratse closed his eyes.

Distracted – more likely.

Warm water dripped onto his face and he opened his eyes, smiling as Petra leaned over him, her wet hair brushing against his cheeks.

"What are you thinking about?"

"Nothing," he said.

"*Hmm.*"

Maratse frowned. "What does that mean?"

"I have no idea," Petra said, pushing Maratse to one side to make space to sit. She had swapped the sheet for a towel, revealing more of her legs. Maratse pressed his hand on Petra's thigh, felt the rough scoring of the stick-and-poke tattoos on her fingers, as she brushed his hand with her own. "It could mean many things, *Constable*," she said.

"Like what?"

Petra laughed. "Like what? *Hmm*, where to start?"

Petra began her list, drawing confused smiles from Maratse as she listed the range of emotions she packed into his grunt.

"Depending on the situation," she said. "Your mood. How hungry you are. How tired you are. Of course, it's very economical."

"Economical?"

"Sure," Petra said. "Like a whole vocabulary rolled into one word."

Petra took her hand from Maratse's to smooth her hair into a wet ponytail at the back of her head. She plucked at the loose strands on either side, until Maratse shook his head, reaching for her fingers, letting the strands fall to either side of her face.

"It's not like I'm calling you simple," she said. The corners of her mouth twitched in the beginnings of a smile. "But what everyone else thinks…"

"I don't care what anyone else thinks,"

"No?"

"*Eeqqi*," Maratse said, with a slow shake of his head.

This new Petra reminded him of the old one, before she aged, if that even made any sense. The more she healed, the younger she became, close to her true age, not the age forced upon her through trauma and sadism. No, this was the Petra he remembered, the one who supported him through *his* trauma, the one who made him whole. The Petra he fell in love with, never knowing he could.

"*Piitalaat*," he said.

"Yes?"

"Breakfast."

Breakfast was brunch, in a small café just off the main pedestrian shopping street, *Strøget*, in Copenhagen's busy tourist area. Petra chatted through a plate of *huevos rancheros*, teasing Maratse over his simple tastes in coffee, then taking his hand, holding it as she worked her fork around her eggs. They took their time, Petra leading the conversation, compensating for Maratse's grunts with comments on the winter clothes worn by the tourists, how she could spot the Danes among them – wearing uniform black winter jackets, and how Maratse might, possibly, if he cared to even consider it, choose a new jacket for the holiday.

"What's wrong with my jacket?"

Petra took a breath, held it, then slowly blew out her cheeks, as if just contemplating where to start might exhaust her. She settled on the obvious.

"It's a police jacket."

"*Iiji.*"

"Well, you're not…"

"I'm retired," Maratse said. "I retired early."

"I know." Petra nodded. "And I know it's important to you, but…"

Maratse waited for the *but*, knowing that she had a point, but curious too at his own need to preserve at least one part of his previous life, before his own trauma, at the hands of the Chinese man in the mining camp, forced a change of circumstances, a new life, new challenges, and the series of unfortunate events that followed, equally traumatic in their own way.

Petra's *but* never came. A deep American voice cut through the chatter as Connor bumped his way around the café to their table in the window.

"I saw you from the street," he said, with a nod to Maratse. "I saw your jacket. Knew it was you."

Petra rolled her eyes, waiting for Maratse to say something, but the smile on his face was enough. The jacket stayed.

"Have you had time to think about my offer?" Connor asked, pulling out a chair.

"We're just finding our feet," Petra said. "We had a bumpy landing."

"Really? I thought it was quite smooth."

"*After* we landed," Petra said, swapping a look with Maratse.

"And I have to do something on Friday."

"But you're done after Friday?" Connor paused to order a coffee. "Strong, no cream," he said, before turning back to Petra and Maratse. "I mean, you can fly on Saturday... if you wanted to?"

Maratse nodded. "I think so."

"And...?" Connor dipped his head, looking from Maratse to Petra, waiting for a signal. He settled on Petra, and said, "It's down to you, I think. I can't read the Constable."

"Not many people can," Petra said. "But we're still interested."

"Interested enough that I can book your flights to Tierra del Fuego? Actually, the ship is in port in Ushuaia, Argentina. I just like saying Tierra del Fuego."

"Argentina?" Petra said.

"And then Antarctica," Connor said. "It's the chance of a lifetime. Plus, you'd really be helping me out. The guests – our passengers – are a nice bunch, mostly late sixties, early seventies. They are pleasant, adventurous, and they have deep pockets."

"Deep pockets?" Maratse said.

Connor nodded. "They tip well."

The waitress returned with Connor's coffee, giving Petra a chance to switch to Danish, drawing a final decision from Maratse.

"I'll enjoy it," she said. "I don't have to go to Spain. I just want to get away. Not Greenland. Not Denmark. Somewhere new, with you, where I can forget about everything." She tugged at Maratse's fingers. "Even in Denmark, the past follows us. Look at Malik. That happened within a few hours of us arriving here. If we're going to escape things, to really get away, we have to go far away." Petra laughed as a thought crossed her mind. "The opposite pole is pretty far, David. It should be far enough."

"Okay, we'll go," Maratse said. He turned to Connor and switched back to English. "We accept," he said. "We'll come with you to

Tierra..."

"*Del Fuego,*" Connor said. "Fantastic. I'm pleased. Only, I won't be coming with you. I have to scout for the next cruise – more cancellations. But I'll have all the travel arrangements made by the end of the day. If you give me your email, I'll send them to you, plus the contracts, everything." Connor settled back in his chair, bumping the chair of the young Chinese woman all in black behind him. He turned to apologise, then reached for his coffee, lifting it in a toast, as he said, "Really. This is great news. You're gonna have a great time."

Chapter 11

The walls of the courtroom were neither green nor grey. They were devoid of adornment – wearing nothing that might stir a feeling, whether positive or negative. The interior of the room was not designed to inspire or conspire. It was, in both form and function, meant solely for the facilitation of truth, the pursuit of justice, and the satisfactory result of expedited process, at a fair tempo, weighted accordingly to the nature of the case. Maratse, sitting as comfortably as his new shirt, smart trousers, and thin formal jacket allowed, considered himself lucky that he was required for one day only, and that his testimony would be brief. Shorter, in fact, if he concentrated, rather than let himself be absorbed by the green grey walls, transporting him to somewhere considered by many to be just as bleak, were it not for the life Maratse knew was to be found there.

"Mr. Maratse," the prosecutor said, drawing Maratse back into the courtroom, away from the sea ice, which was disappointing, in that in his mind's eye, he had seen movement, something obscure but of intense interest.

"*Iiji.*"

"If you will continue, in Danish."

"Yes," Maratse said.

"In your own time."

"Which part?"

"Start with the doctor." The prosecutor paused to check his notes. "Salmonsen."

"He was cleaning up," Maratse said.

The prosecutor pressed his lips into a thin smile. "Cleaning up?"

"Kaakajik was on the floor. Salmonsen had given him something. I was sedated."

"But still conscious?"

"*Iiji*," Maratse said, and then, "Yes. Still awake."

"And what did Salmonsen say?"

"He told me he was going to take his own life, to prevent him testifying."

"He said that? Those very words?"

Maratse shrugged. "It was obvious."

"In your drugged state it was *obvious* to you that the doctor intended to commit suicide..."

"He injected himself with an overdose," Maratse said.

"In front of you?"

"Yes."

"And what else did he say?"

Maratse glanced at Petra sitting in the row of seats reserved for the press and public. "He said he had a message from Fari Severinsen. He said I was not going to die, because he wanted me to suffer."

"Frederick Severinsen wanted you to suffer?"

Maratse turned back to the prosecutor and nodded.

"Please confirm, Mr. Maratse."

"Yes," Maratse said. "Fari wanted me to suffer. He told Salmonsen to tell me he would find Piitalaat…"

"Sergeant Petra Jensen, a police officer in Greenland," the prosecutor added.

"*Iiji.*"

"And?"

"I couldn't let that happen."

"But things were already happening, Mr. Maratse. There was a riot in the prison. Events were spiralling out of control, and yet you were in the doctor's surgery."

"He was cleaning up," Maratse said.

"And Erinaq Sinngertaat? What about him?"

"He worked for Fari."

"But he was a prison guard – personally assigned by the warden of Vestsyssel Prison to keep an eye on you."

Maratse nodded.

"What are we supposed to make of that?"

"I don't understand the question."

"You don't…" The Prosecutor sighed, reframing the question. "Sinngertaat was assigned to you. Did the warden have any connection to Frederick Severinsen?"

"Not that I was aware of." Maratse turned to look at Ada, before adding, "I wasn't actually in the prison for a very long time."

"No," the prosecutor said. "But in that very short space of time, you were stabbed, enrolled in an undercover police investigation, witness to, if not the instigator of, a prison riot, present at the moment Salmonsen killed himself, and, also present at the scene of Frederik Severinsen's death." The prosecutor flicked through to another page in his notes. "Shot by a high calibre bullet from a hunting rifle."

"*Iiji.*"

"Mr. Maratse…"

"Yes," Maratse said. "He was killed with the bullet from a rifle."

"In self-defence?"

Maratse frowned. "Fari Severinsen never *defended* himself. He always attacked, in the shadows, at the end of a telephone line. His threats were enough to make people take their own lives."

"And why was that, do you think?"

"Because they were never threats. They were promises. If he said he was going to do something, he did it, or had someone do it."

The prosecutor smirked. "Thank you for that rather loquacious response. Quite unexpected. But, let me ask this – you were given this impression in the short time you were interned at Vestsyssel Prison."

"Yes."

"After all the events that occurred."

"Yes."

"Following a series of violent events that occurred prior to and were in fact responsible for your subsequent incarceration – cut short, I might add, in return for your testimony today."

Maratse shifted in his seat and turned his head to give the prosecutor the benefit of his full attention. "What are you asking?"

"Asking? Not so much. I am wondering however… In fact, one could say I find it quite curious, that the past year of your life has been so eventful."

"If I could change that," Maratse said. "I would."

"I believe you."

"And today?"

The prosecutor closed his notes. "Do I believe what you said today? Is that what you're asking?" He tapped his fingers on his thick folder of notes. "What you've said today, together with your written statement, fits with what I expected you to contribute to this case. What happens after that will be determined at a later date. But what I think you're asking is if you will be required to return," he said, smiling thinly before gesturing at the walls. "You're not comfortable inside, are you, Constable?"

"I'm retired."

"I know. But that's not what I asked."

"I prefer to be outside."

"Then you'll be happy to know that we're done. No matter how curious I am to know more about the events prior to this case, you are not on trial, Mr. Maratse. We'll just have to save those stories for another time."

"Hmm."

Maratse waited for a nod from the bailiff, before leaving the courtroom, taking one last look at the walls, searching for that elusive shadow, the *thought* of something that had distracted him.

But it was gone, lost in the moment, then expelled by Petra's body as she wrapped her arms around his neck, pressing her cheeks to his, and then tugging him out of the courtroom, into the January sun that had, momentarily, beaten back the winter rains.

"It's done," she said. "We're free."

"You are free," Ada said, as she joined them on the steps outside. "Although," she said, brushing her fringe to one side as she looked at Maratse, "there's something going on in there."

"It's his thinking face," Petra said. "He'll grunt in a moment."

"Hmm?" Maratse said, looking up.

"See?"

"Yes." Ada smiled. "I get it now." She shook Petra's hand, exchanging complements and promises to keep them informed about Malik. "He's a curious one," she said, as she shook Maratse's hand. "Still hasn't said much at all. Still in shock. But we're ready to help him when he comes out of it. Right now, he's volunteering to stay at the station. Very strange."

"Can we talk to him?" Petra asked.

"Not a good idea," Ada said. "With the greatest of respect, from one colleague to another." She hiked her thumb at the courtroom behind them. "You're free of one thing, don't get mixed up in another."

Petra took Maratse's hand, nodded once, before changing the subject. "We'd best get going, anyway," she said. "We need a few more things before we leave."

~ 122 ~

"You're leaving tomorrow?"

"For Tierra del Fuego," Petra said.

"South America?"

"Argentina," Maratse said, returning to the conversation.

"Is it winter down there?"

"Summer," Petra said. "I think. But we're going on from there." She bit her lip to stifle an excited giggle. "To Antarctica."

"What?"

"As guides on a cruise ship." Petra pulled one of Connor's business cards from her pocket." We're filling in for someone. It's crazy, but we *have* to do it."

"Absolutely," Ada said, as she looked at Connor's card.

"Keep it," Petra said, as Ada handed her the card. "We've got another."

Ada slipped the card into her pocket, tugging at her jacket as a cold breeze lifted wet leaves from the pavement. Ada fiddled with the broken zip until she could pull it to her chin. "That's it. I have to pick up Nikolaj." Ada smiled, waved, and then left them to it.

"David?" Petra said. "You're very quiet."

"I'm okay. Just…"

"Lost in your thoughts?"

"*Iiji*," he said, squeezing Petra's hand. "I want to change, then we can go shopping."

"Pity," Petra said, as they walked towards a row of taxis parked on the street outside the courtroom. "I rather like this look."

The remainder of the day in Copenhagen disappeared in a blur of shops, several breaks for coffee, and a prolonged trip to the bookstore, resulting in another coffee for Petra as Maratse shuffled his way along the shelves of science fiction.

"I still don't know how you read that stuff," she said, when he was finally finished.

"It's an escape."

"But what about when you're on the ice? Isn't that an escape?"

"It's different." Maratse tucked the books into a bag at the checkout. "I don't need to imagine anything out there. It's all in front of me. But in a room in a house," he said, as they walked out of the shop, "I need distraction."

"But not internet."

Maratse shook his head. "No time."

"No time?" Petra laughed, tugging at her collar as the damp Copenhagen air chilled her more than the dry cold of Greenland. "It's not about *time*," she said, and then, "What's a smartphone girl like me, doing with a luddite like you?"

"Luddite?"

"I read about them – on the internet."

"And?"

"People who reject technology. Well, more than that. They were protesting how machinery was taking over, taking their jobs, so they sabotaged it."

"I don't reject technology," Maratse said, as Petra took his hand. "I appreciate outboard motors…"

"You *appreciate* outboard motors?" Petra smiled.

"*Iiji.*"

"That's it," she said, stopping abruptly, and jerking Maratse to a stop.

The streetlight above them lit Maratse's face, reflecting in his brown eyes, highlighting his furrowed brow in a soft white light.

"What?" he said.

"I've decided. As crazy as it sounds, I *must* stay with you for the rest of my life."

"Piitalaat?"

"No, I'm not proposing, *this* girl still wants some old-fashioned things in life, but when you tell me that you *appreciate outboard motors*. Well, that's the last straw. I can't take it anymore. I just have to have you."

Petra, with her January-blushed cheeks, her brilliant gaze, and loose strands of her hair twisting in the winter breeze, reached out for Maratse, pulling him close.

"Piitalaat…"

"Shush."

Petra pressed her lips to his, oblivious to the tourists, the shoppers, the just-finished-work employees, and everyone else who brushed past them. She sealed herself to Maratse, kissing him through the sudden stream of tears carrying a host of emotions and memories – the sweet and the torturous.

"We're finally free," she whispered, pulling her lips ever so slightly away from Maratse's.

"*Iiji.*"

"And I feel… *whole* again."

Maratse reached up to brush the tears from her cheeks with a rough thumb.

"I'm glad," he said.

The stream of pedestrians washed around them, like the waters flowing around a rock in a river, trapping Petra and Maratse in the downriver eddy. Regardless of what Maratse might have seen in the blank spaces of his mind, and ignoring events to which they were not connected, even he could feel the change, that things were flowing in the right direction, flowing downriver, heading south. Perhaps south was where they were supposed to end up, and he said as much, drawing excited nods and soft, tear-laden kisses from Petra. The world around them moved in one thick flow of bodies, while Petra and Maratse stopped, safe within a bubble of time, of their own creation, something they might even admit that they deserved. Finally. That life was about to turn in a new direction.

"But I'll need your help," Maratse said, pulling slowly away from Petra.

"With what?"

"Whales," he said, taking her hand, as they prepared to step out of the street eddy.

"You know all about whales," she said.

"I know a little about whales. I know a lot more about ice."

"So, tell them about ice." She plucked at his fingers as they walked back to the hotel. "Connor knows who we are. He knows who he has hired.

Besides, we're not getting paid. It's a holiday with a few hours in between when we talk about life in polar regions. You'll be fine," she said. "We're both going to be fine. From now on. Forever."

"*Iiji,*" Maratse said, pushing shadows from his mind – the old, and the curious shadow of the slight woman in black he thought he had seen watching them from a shop window – before shrugging and stepping into the future.

Chapter 12

It had taken much of the previous day to set up, between shadowing Maratse through the streets of Copenhagen, but as the afternoon dark turned into the black winter evening, she was ready. Ole was ready, and slightly less nervous than he had been when switching the tyres on Levi Aaqqii's car. It bothered Xiá that the old Danish mechanic had fretted about time, that he wouldn't have enough, when she had assured him – repeatedly – that he had as much time as he needed, that she would make sure of it. And she did, enticing Levi with an urgent business call that he just had to take, during which she used software to change the sex of her voice, together with sufficiently juicy details about expected profits compared to next to no investment. A win-win arrangement, she had assured him, without giving any real details, or making anything more than vague commitments. If anything it bothered her that Levi was so readily duped, especially when Ole knocked on the window of his van, drawing her out of the shadows and into the passenger seat, clamping her hand over the microphone as Ole whispered that he needed more time.

"Stubborn nuts," he had said, adding something more about the last time Levi's car had been serviced.

Xiá had waved him away, then returned to her beanbag seat in the back of Ole's van, apologising for the interruption, before feeding Levi another line of potential profit. Beyond that, another part of her brain was relishing the next stage of the plan, the more unfortunate but equally necessary stage that Hong Wei regretted but understood. Xiá tapped the corner of the cool box with her foot as she wound up the call with Levi, just as Ole signalled he was done with the tyres. Xiá stepped out of the van and switched to her encrypted phone, telling Hong Wei that it was time to call Levi, as Ole rolled Levi's tyres into the back of his van, slid the door closed and climbed in behind the wheel. Xiá finished her call, slipped a GPS tracker under the bumper of Levi's car, then joined Ole in the van.

"Nearly done," she said.

"I don't like this."

"Ole," Xiá said, pressing a slim hand to his cheek. "It's all right. It'll soon be over. I just need you to drive to this location, here."

She turned the screen of her phone to show him the route she had plotted to an intersection crossing the E20 motorway, one junction before the airport turnoff. After rush hour she knew that the traffic was light, and that Levi would be suitably compelled to drive fast. The only thing she hadn't planned on was that it would be dry. No rain.

It was unfortunate. One might even say *unlucky*.

But, she mused, *I never plan on luck.*

Xiá turned to look through the seats into the back of the van. The bicycle was just visible, as was the square can of oil, she had strapped to the pannier rack on the back.

"Let's go," she said, as Hong Wei confirmed with a cryptic text that his follow-up call to Levi ensured that the Greenlander was suitably motivated to meet him at the agreed intersection.

Of course, Hong Wei was already on his way to the airport hotel, ready to receive Xiá once she was finished for the night.

It will be a long night, she thought. The corners of her mouth curled in anticipation, and she patted the thin tube she had tucked inside a hidden pocket in her cycling jacket.

Ole pulled out of the parking lot, adjusting his mirror and flicking on the lights as he pulled out onto the road.

The one part of Xiá's plan that Hong Wei had not approved involved the bicycle.

"Too dangerous," he said. "I can't let you do it."

"Don't smother me. I'll do it, and I'll do it well."

"Your overconfidence…"

"Will be my undoing?" Xiá sighed, adding a theatrical rolling of her eyes as Hong Wei tried to finish his sentence. She didn't let him. "Is that something you used to tell my father? Or was it you who was overconfident?"

"Xiá…"

"What? That's not fair?"

"I was going to remind you that I was your superior."

Xiá didn't have time for that, not since the day Hong Wei had begun to tell her what truly happened to her father, as much as he could that wasn't redacted. It was, on reflection, Hong Wei's second biggest mistake, the first being the day he recruited her for the *Guoanbu*, Chinese intelligence. She had often wondered why, and, when he didn't volunteer an answer, she simply guessed that it was a misguided way of keeping her close and keeping an eye on her. Of course, she later understood that it was guilt over her father's death that made Xiá Hong Wei's personal project, and it was that same guilt she turned against him.

"Unlike you, or my father, I am not overconfident," Xiá said. "The operation is planned; every eventuality is covered. It will be complete exactly one hour after you call Levi, arranging to meet."

"You're very sure of yourself, Xiá."

"Yes," she had answered – her last words before leaving the workshop with Ole. She knew Hong Wei would worry about her, and a part of her was grateful that he did. But she wasn't so naive to think that Hong Wei was so preoccupied with her that he had no time for other thoughts. Not at all. Xiá knew that ever since she mentioned Maratse's name, a part of *his* brain was working, scheming, and plotting how to make best use of that new information, something that allowed her to carry out her own operation.

Exactly as planned, she thought, as Ole pulled into a bus stop and helped Xiá with her bicycle.

"Wait for me here, at the gas station," she said, tapping the screen of her smartphone. Ole nodded once, but his eyes lingered on the screen as a small blue dot flashed as it moved up the road highlighted on the map.

Xiá watched the dot, waiting for it to draw nearer, before securing the phone to the clip on her handlebars. Ole drove off. Xiá waited, eyes on the screen, then, once Ole was out of sight, she punctured the oil can with two sharp stabs of a screwdriver. The oil glugged out of the can as Xiá swerved an erratic course along the road, in to the kerb, then out to the white dotted line in the middle. Xiá waited for Levi's GPS tracker to close the gap, took a breath, then lurched across his path forcing him to slam on the brakes as she stood on the pedals, blessing her bicycle childhood, and accelerating out of the way of Levi's car.

She heard the clamping of the brakes, the shudder of the tyres, and the sweet sound of Levi's car bumping up and over the kerb, crashing through the thin vegetation, and then down the embankment onto the motorway below.

Xiá leaped off the bike, slashed the tape securing the oil can to the rack, and tossed the can to one side. She walked the bicycle along the side of the road, towards oncoming traffic, noting the blip of Levi's tracker, and the crazy swerves it made on the map, followed by the sudden forward movement, together with a crash of metal and glass. Xiá looked up, as one might, at the sound of something heavy crashing at speed into something else. A truck, perhaps. She decided not to look, just to trust that it was done, that the operation was over.

Almost, she thought, as she leaned the bicycle against a signpost, locking it there with a D lock through the frame. Judging by the number of bicycles she had seen locked in similar places about the city, she guessed it would be there for at least two weeks.

Xiá slipped the keys into her pocket, then tapped the tube tucked inside her jacket one more time.

"Hey," she said, as she opened the side door of Ole's van. "Hungry?"

"What?"

Xiá reached into the back of the van and tugged the cool box to the door.

"I bought us a treat," she said. "From that shop on the corner, close to the workshop."

"*Atlantis*?"

"That's the one." Xiá pulled out two sandwiches wrapped in greaseproof paper. The image of two Greek pillars with sea fronds and a lobster was stencilled on the top of each. "Crayfish, or *crawfish*, if you prefer." She pressed one of the sandwiches into Ole's hand as he walked around the side of the van. "There's beer in the box," she said, gesturing for Ole to sit inside. Xiá got in behind him and pulled the door closed. "Better safe than sorry." Xiá grinned in the tiny yellow glow of the interior light.

Ole found a blanket, spotted with dried paint. He threw it over Levi's tyres and sat down. Xiá handed him a beer.

"Did you hear the crash?" she asked, turning her head at the distant sound of a siren, approaching fast.

Ole shook his head. "I didn't *want* to hear it. I kept the windows closed and turned up the radio."

"Smart," Xiá said.

Ole fiddled with the string wrapped around the sandwich, cursing the knot, as if someone had tied it tighter than usual. Xiá said nothing as she put her sandwich in her pocket and reached into her jacket. She pulled out the slim metal tube, then took the N100 face mask she had hidden in the cool box. She turned her back on Ole as she slipped the mask over her mouth and nose. Then, at the sound of Ole's first bite, she primed the tube.

It was a simple device with a carbon dioxide cartridge, the firing button was hidden beneath a safety cap. With the cap removed Xiá turned to face Ole and pressed the button, releasing a small cloud of wet vapour into the mechanic's face. Xiá slipped the cap and the tube into her jacket, grabbing the wrapper from Ole's sandwich as he fought for his last breath. She removed the mask as she rolled the door to one side, pulling it off her head as she stepped out of the van.

Xiá slid the van door all the way until it locked, bunched the mask into her jacket pocket, and then walked purposefully towards another bus stop, just beyond the gas station.

She took a deep breath of brisk January air as she arrived at the stop, relieved that she could, and exulted that she had completed another mission with Saxitoxin without killing herself. She had used less than a gram of it but knew that eleven grams was considered enough to kill 40,000 people. *An extraordinary number,* she thought. *Even for me.*

Xiá caught the bus to the airport, ignoring the *no eating* sign, as she sank her delicate teeth into her crayfish sandwich, throwing defiant glances at the driver as he stared at her in the mirror. She got off the bus shortly after, splitting the tube into four parts, and depositing them in four different locations. She kept the sandwich wrapper – a small souvenir for a job well done.

"You're well?" Hong Wei said, as he opened the hotel door.

"Of course," Xiá said, as she stepped inside the room.

"And the operation?"

"Smooth, but deliciously messy." Xiá flopped onto the bed nearest the window. She kicked off her shoes as Hong Wei pulled a chair from beneath the desk to sit opposite her.

"Xiá," he said.

"What?"

"I need you to listen."

Xiá propped herself up on her elbows, tilted her head to one side, and stared at Hong Wei.

"I'm listening."

"I have a use for Maratse. He's your next mission."

"Really?" Xiá opened her eyes wide in mock surprise. "So *that's* why I've been following him for the past two days?"

"Xiá... Please."

Xiá tilted her head as she studied Hong Wei's face. "It's personal then – you and Maratse."

Hong Wei nodded.

"It's always personal, Xiá," he said.

Chapter 13

"We have to move him," Ada said. She reached for the clipboard to sign for Malik Uutaaq's transfer out of the station cells and into Blegdamsvej Prison. She nodded to a constable to open the cell door, watching as he entered, then waiting for him to come out. Ada stepped to one side for a better look into Malik's cell.

"He won't come out," the constable said.

"Well, that's not an option, is it?" Ada walked to the cell door and leaned against the frame. "Malik? What's going on?"

"I didn't do it."

"You've said that already. But until you have an alibi, someone who can vouch for you, then we have to work with what we've got, and right now, all that we've got suggests that you are involved, and we need to act on that. It's up to you and your lawyer to demonstrate otherwise."

Ada took a moment to study Malik, noting the light in his eyes, sharper than before, and the urgency in his voice. Gone was the slur of confusion, alcohol, and terror. The twenty-four hours seemed to have helped Malik Uutaaq regain a sense of reality, and a better grasp on the situation.

"There is someone," Malik said, looking up.

"Someone who can vouch for me."

"You've remembered or…?"

"Remembered," Malik said.

"Who then?" Ada stepped into the cell. She pulled out her smartphone, her thumb poised over the keypad displayed on the screen as she waited for Malik to give her the number.

"I don't know the number." Malik leaned forward to point at the raised workstation positioned between the cells. "It'll be in my phone."

"What's the name?"

"Levi Aaqqii. He's a businessman. He lives here in the city. I met him for dinner…" Malik stopped talking as the constable walked over to Ada and whispered in her ear.

"You're sure?" Ada said.

The constable nodded. "It's the name, like the jeans. It was his car we pulled off the motorway last night." The constable lowered his voice, and said, "It was in pieces. So was the driver."

"Okay." Ada slipped her phone into her pocket and beckoned for Malik to follow her. "Let's grab a coffee."

"What's happened to Levi?" Malik asked, as he followed Ada out of the cell.

"You'll need your shoes," Ada said, steering Malik to the officer on duty at the workstation. She waited for Malik to slip his shoes on, watching him as he tied his laces. He was taller than she imagined a Greenlander would be, although most men and women towered over her. Ada nodded as Malik stood and then waved at the officer. "I've signed for him. I'll keep an eye on him and take him to Blegdamsvej."

"Alone?"

"He's a minister of the Greenland government," Ada said. "I'll take my chances. I'll let you know when we leave the building." Ada pointed at the door, waited for Malik to acknowledge her, then nodded for him to follow.

"What happened to Levi?"

Ada stopped at the security door, waiting for them to be buzzed through. "Was he a friend of yours?"

"An old friend."

"You were close?" she asked. The door clicked and she pushed it open.

"Not really. He contacted me, just recently. Tipaaqu…" Malik stopped to take a breath. He waved Ada away, nodding that he was okay. "She set it up," he said, as he recovered.

"The meeting with Levi?"

"*Aap.*"

Ada led the way to the canteen, pausing once in a while as Malik slowed, but keeping the pace steady, drawing him away from the cells, hoping that the distance might loosen him up. Regardless of the evidence – Tipaaqu's body *was* found in Malik's room, his belt *was* wrapped around her neck – the lack of camera footage bothered her. The hotel security team said it had been wiped, deleted, but neither of them could explain who might have done it, or why. Those two security men, as far as Ada was aware, were the only two people who had access to the computer.

Unless, she thought, *it was Maratse's ghost.*

Either way, Ada believed Malik Uutaaq deserved a break, and perhaps a coffee at a quiet table – not an interview room – might help him remember more than he had already volunteered.

"Have a seat," she said, as they walked into the canteen.

Ada pointed at an empty table in the corner, furthest from the door. She waited for Malik to sit down before buying two coffees. Ada set them on the table as she sat down, sliding one mug into Malik's hands. She set her own coffee to one side, then pulled out her smartphone, setting it on the table between them. Ada turned on the voice recorder app, finger poised over the slider to start recording, waiting until Malik nodded.

"It's just easier if we have it documented," she said, as Malik took a slurp of coffee. "But I should tell you, before we begin, that Levi Aaqqii is dead."

"Dead?"

"A collision on the motorway. I don't have all the details, but the constable you met in the cell confirmed it."

"He's dead?"

"Yes."

Ada gauged Malik's reaction, curious to see how he might react to a second death to which he was connected.

"We had dinner…" Malik's face paled.

"Yes," Ada said. "When was that?"

"You know when it was."

"Yes, but if you say it, if I record it, then I

can check it."

"Wednesday."

"Okay. And Levi made the reservation?"

"*Aap*."

"And it was just the two of you?"

Malik opened his mouth to speak, and then stopped, lips parted, as if someone had turned off the power.

"Malik?"

"Just the two of us," he said. "Levi and me."

"You're sure? Only, you paused just then."

"I had to think."

"About what?"

Ada glanced at the app on her phone, relieved to see the timer was progressing, that the app was recording. Malik's pause seemed significant, and Ada wondered how she might steer him back to that moment, especially as he seemed to gain more confidence with each sip of coffee.

"It was just Levi and me," Malik said. "We had three courses, and lots of wine."

"And coffee, at the end of the meal?"

"*Naamik*," Malik said, after another pause. "Just wine."

"Okay." Ada tapped her fingers on the table. She looked at Malik, noted his renewed composure, and decided on a different approach. "I thought this chat would help you, and I can see you're thinking more clearly now, so how about we catch up again, after I've checked with the hotel?"

"Catch up?"

"Yes, for another chat. Of course, you'll be

transferred to custody at Blegdamsvej Prison."
Ada lifted her hands off the table, patting the air
as if she was slowing traffic. "Just for the rest of
the afternoon. Until we get things sorted. I'll have
someone drive you over but be sure to ask about
legal representation as soon as you arrive."

"Why?"

"Because you're going to need a lawyer,
Malik."

Ada chewed on the few details of the case she
knew to be fact as she drove to the hotel. Tipaaqu
was dead, murdered in Malik's room. He had
presented himself in the lobby. Ada snorted at the
word *presented*, as if he was arriving on
appointment, and announcing himself to the
receptionist. *Or the concierge,* she thought, as she
recalled checking Maratse and Petra into their
room, then responding to the tussle in the lobby,
to which the hotel security responded.

Ada put a mental bookmark on her thoughts
as she arrived at the hotel and parked her car. She
locked it with two clicks of her key fob,
reminding herself that she needed new batteries,
before flashing her identity card at the hotel staff
member shouting at her to move her car.

"Police," she said. "I'll only be a minute."

Ada didn't wait for a response but allowed
herself a brief smile of satisfaction at her tiny
abuse of power, as she entered the hotel.

That's how it starts, she thought, slowing as
she approached the front desk.

Ada reached for the bell to call for assistance,

only to pause at the sight of a Greenlandic man walking towards the door. Copenhagen Towers, she mused, seemed to be *the* place for Greenlanders to spend the night in the city, but this particular Greenlander seemed a little out of place, even more so when he was joined by a woman with pink hair and what looked like black tusks protruding from her skin just below her lower lip. Ada followed them to the door, shoving aside her more rational approach to policing, and choosing to follow a sudden and intense curiosity.

"Excuse me," she said, as she stepped out of the hotel.

The woman with the pink hair turned, then tapped the man's arm, bringing him to a stop so that Ada could catch up.

"I'm a police officer," Ada said, reaching for her card. The woman scowled and Ada was quick to add, "No, you've done nothing wrong. I just…"

"Yes?" the man said.

"It's a little crazy," Ada said. "But I just have some questions." She frowned as the man stared at her lips, then continued, preferring his stare to that of his companion's. "Are you staying at the hotel?"

"Visiting."

"Visiting a guest?"

"And looking for someone, yes," the man said.

"A Greenlander?"

"*Aap.*"

"Okay." Ada brushed her fringe from her

face as a sudden breeze caught it. "One more question, and then I'm done."

The man waited, focused on her lips, while the woman continued to stare. Ada dismissed it as a simple, if not pleasant, distrust in the police – nothing personal, just a perk of the job.

"What did you want to ask?" the man said.

"If you were meeting Malik Uutaaq?"

"Why?"

"Ah, I can't tell you that. Sorry."

"But if I said *yes* you could?"

"If you said *yes*, then I might have more questions."

The man looked at his watch, then turned to the woman, whispering something in what Ada guessed was Greenlandic. The woman gave Ada a last scathing look – a warning, perhaps – and then squeezed the man's arm before walking away. The man watched her go, before turning back to Ada.

"My name is Qitu Kalia," he said, offering Ada his hand. "I'm deaf, so I lip read. If you have questions, you have to look at me."

"I do have questions."

"As do I." Qitu smiled. "I should tell you, I'm a journalist."

"Right…"

Qitu nodded at the hotel door, and said, "But if you still want to talk, I'll let you buy me coffee."

Ada bit her lip, taking a moment to think just how many coffees she had bought lately, how that fit with her monthly budget, food and clothes for

Nikolaj…"

"Or I could buy *you* a coffee," Qitu said.

Ada laughed. "I'm that transparent?"

"I read more than lips, officer…?"

"Ada Valkyrien, Sergeant."

"And you want to know about Malik Uutaaq?"

"Yes."

"Or about the people following him?"

Ada caught the smile on Qitu's lips and wondered if she was being played, only to realise she didn't care. It appeared that the case she had stumbled into had just become more interesting.

As if I didn't have enough on my plate, she thought, only to remind herself that it was Saturday, and the Vestsyssel Prison case would reconvene on Monday.

"Let's go inside," she said.

Qitu led the way, giving Ada a chance to observe him, the confidence with which he ordered coffee, turning his head slightly to catch the barista's questions about strength, cream, and sugar. Simple things that she took for granted. Only, as it turned out, the coffee was the only simple thing about Qitu Kalia and the story he had to tell her.

Ada listened as Qitu volunteered information about his investigation, how he considered Malik Uutaaq to be a person of interest to foreign agents.

"The Chinese?"

"*Aap.*"

"But we're talking about Greenland," Ada

said.

Qitu shook his head. "No, Sergeant, we're talking about a strategic island in the middle of an area which is the subject of increased political posturing. You see Greenland as a part of the Danish empire." Qitu smiled as Ada started to protest. "I could have said *realm*, but I chose empire."

"Why?"

"Because that's how the majority of Danes still see Greenland. What you don't see, is a self-governing state with dreams of economical and political independence. Malik Uutaaq is at the forefront of that dream, leading the way in many ways."

"And you support him?"

"I neither support nor oppose him. I wish to remain objective."

"But why are you telling me this?"

"Because," Qitu said. "After the events of Thursday night, I think he's being set up."

"And your investigation?"

"Has uncovered evidence of Chinese interest in Greenland and in Malik's associates."

"Levi Aaqqii?"

"*Aap.*"

Ada's coffee cooled in the tall glass as she considered her next move – how much she could say, and what she should keep to herself. *But as long as Malik Uutaaq is saying nothing...*

"You're wondering if you should tell me about Levi's death. Aren't you?" Qitu shrugged. "I'm a journalist, and I have friends in the city.

We heard about Levi's *accident*."

Ada frowned. "You think it was planned?"

"I'm saying it's an interesting coincidence."

"Hold on a second," Ada said, as her smartphone started to ring. She turned to one side to answer it, blocking her face from Qitu's view.

"You have to go?" he said, as Ada finished her call.

"Not really." Ada slipped her phone into her pocket. She looked at Qitu, licking her top lip as she thought, mouthing a silent *fuck it*, before she spoke. "Malik Uutaaq should have been transferred to Blegdamsvej Prison – extended custody."

"And?"

"I told him to ask for legal counsel when he got there."

"And? Has he found a lawyer?"

"Yes," Ada said. "An expensive one. Malik Uutaaq is no longer in custody."

Chapter 14

Malik stared at the slip of paper in his hand, barely registering the traffic on the nearby stretch of motorway, or his taxi pulling away from the kerb. He looked up at the wave-formed lid-like roof of *Royal Arena*, Copenhagen's prime multifunctional stadium just south of the city centre. The vertical slats, like a massive industrial blind turned on its side, and the wave effect reminded him of *Katuaq*, Greenland's cultural centre in Nuuk, albeit on a much larger scale. He checked the time on the paper, crumpled it into his pocket, and walked towards the main entrance.

A short but distinct shout turned Malik's head before he reached the main doors. Malik adjusted course at a wave from a man wearing a workman's helmet and a fluorescent safety vest over a set of overalls. He had a second helmet under his arm and presented it to Malik as he approached.

"Put the vest and the helmet on," the man said, in English.

"I'm supposed to meet someone inside."

"Not without these. Put them on."

Malik tugged the helmet onto his head and slipped his arms inside the vest as he hurried to keep pace with the man striding ahead of him, leading him to a side door busy with activity.

"In there," the man said. "On the right. Stick to the wall."

The man walked away before Malik could ask anything more of him. He took a step forward, stopped at a shout, and stepped to one side, out of the way of a small forklift truck ferrying a pallet of wood flooring into the arena. An empty forklift exited the side door, just as the first entered. Malik moved to the side, kept to the right, and walked inside.

The scale of the arena and the activity inside it threatened to distract him, if it wasn't for the mystery surrounding the location for his meeting with Hong Wei, and the terse instructions his new lawyer had given him. As he worked his way along the inside wall of the arena, Malik realised that he knew next to nothing about the terms of his release, if he even had been released, or if he was on some kind of special parole. Then there were the recurring thoughts of Tipaaqu, the sight of her face, pale but swollen, as if she wore a tight collar around her neck. *Or my belt,* he reminded himself, a second before the squeezing sensation in his gut, that same feeling he got every time he thought of Tipaaqu.

"Mr. Uutaaq."

Malik looked up.

"Over here," Hong Wei said, with a wave from a seat on the second row of the first balcony of seats. Malik climbed the stairs, and then worked his way along the row to sit beside the

Chinese man.

Malik started to speak, but Hong Wei stopped him with a gentle wave of his hand.

"Take a moment," he said, his English piqued with the hint of an oriental accent. "Observe."

Malik looked down on the workers below. He watched them lay a section of wood flooring, taking their time with each length of wood, measuring, appraising, then measuring again before moving on to the next section.

"Each piece of wood," Hong Wei said, "takes three minutes to place. Perhaps five seconds more, or five seconds less, but no more than that. These men are professionals." Hong Wei gestured at all the workmen involved in laying the floor. "But those two men, and that one woman, are the ones with the specific skills. They will get the job done. They determine the time it will take. They alone have a complete grasp of the project duration. The budget, well, that's in other hands, more specialists. A project manager, if you will. He, or she, will have made it their priority to understand the function of each and every person on the team, from the delivery driver, to the forklift driver, to the men positioning the flooring, the three specialists measuring and observing the placement of each piece, and the cyclists who will race in this arena one week from this very day, if not the very hour." Hong Wei checked his watch.

Malik waited.

"Do you like bicycle sports?"

"What?"

"Cycling." Hong Wei gestured once more at the arena. "When I was a child, to own a bicycle was to embrace freedom, to be a revolutionary. My parents' generation used bicycles to transport munitions when fighting the Japanese. I was fortunate to avoid that particular struggle. But consider the bicycle. A machine with moving parts, yet easy to repair. Pedals can be replaced with branches bound together with string. The tyres can be stuffed with grass when the inner tube is punctured. The chain, perhaps, with its many links is the weakest link, but also relatively easy to mend, to replace, or to do without entirely. The bicycle will still function without its chain. Even when it cannot be pedalled, it can still be pushed. Of course, such a bicycle will never race in an arena such as this, but neither does it have to. Provided it can still perform its most basic function, it's still serviceable, useful, not to be discarded."

Hong Wei's voice tapered to a whisper, drawing Malik in closer, until his ear was but a hand's width from Hong Wei's lips.

"You, Mr. Uutaaq, are my bicycle. Do you understand?"

"Yes."

"You are a simple man, with few moving parts. And yet, still you manage to get yourself into difficult situations. I have gotten you out of them. Perhaps you are struggling to come to terms with recent events. And yet, if we continue with my bicycle metaphor, you might say I have fixed your deflated tyres. I have repaired your pedals, and, with your chain still intact, you are able to maintain a course, heading in a specific direction, towards a specific goal. I determine that goal, Mr. Uutaaq, and I manage all the parts of the project to achieve it." Hong Wei pointed at the two men and the woman supervising the positioning of the flooring. "Once, you might have been equal to those three people, but now, you are the man laying the flooring and adjusting it at their discretion."

"Yes," Malik said, filling the pause with what he assumed Hong Wei expected him to say.

"If that man did not listen to his supervisors, if he misaligned the flooring leaving the slightest of kinks in the surface, catastrophe would ensue, and he would likely lose his job. Now, while the world might quickly recover from a bicycle crash, no matter how spectacular, the world will not be so quick to recover from any mistakes that *you* might make." Hong Wei raised his voice just enough to give his words even more edge. "There will be no kinks, Mr. Uutaaq. There will be no accidents. You will do precisely what I say, when I say it."

"I will," Malik said, suppressing the thought that he really had no alternative.

"And in return, I will make sure you are serviceable. While it might feel like you have grass in your tyres to begin with, I will reward progress and accomplishments with new inner tubes, new pedals, oil for your chain." Hong Wei paused for a soft laugh. "Forgive the metaphor, Mr. Uutaaq. Let me be blunt, you won't want for

~ 152 ~

anything. And neither will your son or your daughter – her name is Pipaluk, I believe."

"Yes."

"And even your ex-wife, Naala, will be rewarded, if that's your wish."

Malik nodded, convinced that it was the right thing to do, that it was expected, but also fully aware that he was trapped, and each affirmative response made it more difficult to escape.

"This arena," Hong Wei said, "is world class. And yet bicycles are raced the world over. Some races are more obscure than others, tucked away in remote corners of the world. Greenland is an obscure race, made even more so by the teams competing for it. They do not like to draw attention to their race." Hong Wei flicked his slim finger at the workers below. "The prize for the athletes competing in *this* race is money and fame. The prize in the race for Greenland is the arena."

Malik flinched as Hong Wei stood. He kept his eyes on the Chinese man's face as Hong Wei took a simple mobile phone from his pocket and handed it to Malik.

"You have a chequered past, Mr. Uutaaq. Not all of which has been your doing, but nonetheless, you are associated with a number of distasteful events. More recently, your name has been attached to a murder – another one. Your second, I believe."

"I did not murder Tinka Winther, and I did not murder…"

"Tipaaqu Jeremiassen?" Hong Wei smiled. "I

~ 153 ~

know. And, as the first suspicious murder proved, the people of Greenland are very forgiving. But will they forgive you a second time? Time will tell, but I'll do my part to help them forget, and to help you secure your rightful place in the Greenland government. But I won't tolerate failure, Mr. Uutaaq."

Malik clutched the mobile, and said, "I understand."

"Good. Expect my text." Hong Wei dipped his head curtly, just once, and then walked away, leaving Malik alone on the second row of seats on the first balcony in *Royal Arena*.

The activity below Malik stopped just after midday, after Malik had been there for at least half an hour, following Hong Wei's departure. Malik guessed the workers were on a break and pushed himself to his feet, slipping the mobile into his pocket as he walked along the row to the stairs. He balled his vest into the helmet and left both on a pallet as he walked out of the arena. He walked towards the road, wondering if he should take a taxi back into the city, or the metro. The lack of taxis on the road, and the proximity of the metro encouraged him to take public transport, and he bought his ticket just minutes before the next train.

Malik turned Hong Wei's words over and over in his mind, curious that the Chinese man should know so much about him, and oblivious to the dark-haired woman watching him from where she stood just a few metres further along the platform. When the train arrived, Malik stepped into the nearest car, the woman followed him, weaving her way through the passengers until she stood close by, close enough for Malik to notice her perfume – something musky, subtle, but just strong enough to lift his head.

"Hi," she said, parting her lips in a moist smile, sending another soft wave of perfume Malik's way as she brushed loose strands of hair away from her brilliant blue eyes.

"Sorry," Malik said. "I don't know you."

"I know." The woman gave a slight shrug.

Malik paused, suddenly curious, but curbing his normal course of action – his playbook. Step one would be to engage in light conversation, a prelude to the next step, to gauge the woman's interest. She looked to be in her mid to late twenties, an age Malik appreciated for the thirst and hunger of youth, together with just enough experience to make things interesting. But these were not normal times, as the twinge in his gut reminded him. And there was something about the woman's eyes. There was a thirst, but behind that, something else flickered, something Malik couldn't quite put his finger on.

And yet.

This is the metro, he thought. *A public space. She's just a passenger. A Dane – probably a student. She doesn't have to work for him.* Malik's forehead creased as he continued the thought. *She doesn't have to be a test.*

"So many thoughts," the woman said. She pressed her thumb to Malik's forehead, flattening his frown with the soft touch of her skin. "What's going on in there?" She lowered her hand as the train slowed to a stop at the next metro station.

"I just…"

"Yes?" The woman's fringe slipped over her eyes as she tilted her head to one side, smiling, waiting for his response.

"Sorry," Malik said. "This isn't me. It's been a tough few days."

"Then I know exactly what you need." The woman slipped her arm through Malik's as the train stopped and the door slid open. "There's a bar, just outside the station."

"I don't know," Malik said, pulling back, resisting.

"But I do," the woman said. "Let's go, Malik."

Chapter 15

The woman's grip was strong, but as they stepped out of the metro train something caught her eye. Malik felt her fingers relax around his arm and he made the most of it, breaking free as he lurched for the steps. The past few days had been one trial after another, one more desperate situation in which he, Malik Uutaaq, a government minister, was taken for a fool, a patsy, someone to take the fall and to keep falling until he hit rock bottom. As he wheezed up the stairs – two at a time – Malik could almost feel that rocky surface, the bottom of a steep granite well, scraping at the heels of his shoes.

No more.

Not again.

I'm done and the world can go fuck itself.

The thought made him smile, made the last few steps, and the push through the crowd possible, almost fun, something he could enjoy if it wasn't for the sound of the woman racing up the steps behind him.

If he had thought about it, he might have noticed her athletic appearance – not just slim but toned. Then there was that look in her eyes, beneath the surface. It wasn't anger, although the momentary narrowing of her eyes could easily have been some form of latent aggression.

There wasn't time to speculate. A quick glance over his shoulder showed that she was gaining – now just an arm's length from grabbing his jacket.

He felt her fingers twist around the loose material in the small of his back. Malik kept running, ignoring the pain in his chest as he loosened the zip, shrugging his arms out of the jacket as he pushed forwards. The woman cursed as she pulled Malik's jacket off his body. He kept running, spurred on by a euphoric burst of energy, the result of one simple evasive trick.

His next wasn't so successful.

Malik pushed through the crowd at the metro entrance and raced to the taxi at the front of the rank, sliding into the side of the car as he pushed a younger man out of the way. Malik clawed at the door handle, slipping his fingers inside, trying to yank it open, only to feel someone grab his shoulder and twist him away from the door.

"That's my cab," the man said, but Malik didn't hear him, the sound of the woman approaching was like the onrush of a train, slamming into him, rolling the three of them onto the ground. "What the fuck?"

The man rolled onto his feet and took two steps towards Malik, but now that she had Malik, the woman wasn't going to stop. With one knee on the pavement, and her right hand cupped around Malik's throat, she swept her left leg in a low arc, felling the man before he took another step.

"Stay down," she snarled, as she stood, tugging Malik onto his feet, pushing him forwards away from the line of taxis.

"Listen…" Malik said.

"Save it. You've been enough trouble already."

"But I don't know you. I don't know what you want."

"You'll find out."

Malik stumbled as the woman pushed him ahead of her. It started to rain, and his shirt soaked up the first few drops falling from an increasingly dark sky. Light from the oncoming traffic glittered with prisms of yellow and white, reflecting off the wet surface of the road as Malik shivered. His flight was over, and there was little fight left in him. Whatever there might once have been was now stripped from him – first with Tinka's death, and now Tipaaqu's. He couldn't run, and he couldn't resist, and nor did he seem ever likely to get a break. His political career had turned into one long series of misadventures, and he wondered at the root of it all, wondered where he could place the blame.

Nivi Winther.

The name of Greenland's First Minister pushed its way to the front of his mind, even as the woman, her hand gripping his arm once more, started talking. He ignored her, concentrating on Nivi, as he recognised the true source of his pain and misfortune. It wasn't as if *she* hadn't suffered, he wasn't so blind to ignore that. *But this has to stop,* he thought, again, only vaguely aware of the woman talking to him, asking him questions – urgently now, with an added tone in her voice that finally made him stop and look at her.

Which is when the second woman caught up with them.

Malik stumbled as the Danish woman pushed him away. He thought about running, but stopped, as if caught in the headlights, as a Chinese woman – shorter than the Dane, more familiar – slid a curved blade from the inside of her sleeve and slashed at the Dane.

The fight spilled into the street, as the Dane danced away, almost tripping over the kerb, then recovering, slapping the hood of a car as it braked to a sudden stop within a metre of slamming into her. The Chinese woman slashed again, forcing the Dane further in the street, into the oncoming traffic – both sides, two lanes each way. A bus jerked to a stop, brakes hissing as the Dane bounced off the driver's side. The Chinese woman paused, fingers curled casually around the handle of her knife as she tugged a black elastic band from her wrist and tied it in her hair, pulling back her fringe. She glanced at Malik.

"Stay there," she said. "Stay *right* there."

Malik froze, eyes locked on the Chinese woman, convinced she must have been sent by Hong Wei, almost laughing as he realised he had been right all along, that he *had* been followed. But then the Dane pulled a gun from inside her jacket, and Malik took the only course of action he had left.

He ran.

Malik stumbled as he heard the first shot. And again when he heard the second, followed by the splinter of glass as the bullet creased the front window of the bus. Screams followed the crack of the bullets, followed by sirens, the older two-tones, and the newer sharp phase blasts that reminded him of the movies. But still he ran, through the rain, until the shadow of a tall office building on the corner of a street offered shelter beneath the overhanging entrance, a chance to catch his breath.

The sirens shuddered to a stop, but the blue emergency lights continued flashing, like long fingers reaching out for Malik, piercing cars – through the front windshield and out of the rear. The light was blinding, and Malik closed his eyes, taking another breath, planning his next move.

Into the city, he thought. *Back to the hotel... grab my things. Get on a plane back to...*

Malik opened his eyes as someone pressed their palm into his chest, pushing him backwards, against the glass wall of the office building.

"She's gone," the Danish woman said. "The police scared her off. Now..." The woman paused for a breath, long enough for Malik to see that she was bleeding, that her other hand was pressed to her side, inside her jacket.

"She got you."

"Yes, Malik," the woman said. "She *got* me. But now, if you don't have any more objections, it's time to get you off the street."

"What about the police?" Malik tried to move, to see around the woman, but she held him steady, flat against the glass door, as she slipped her bloody hand inside her jacket pocket. Malik caught a glimpse of the pistol and said nothing more.

"It's Fenna," the woman said, as she held the phone to her ear. "I'm on foot. Use my tracker and come pick us up."

"Your name is Fenna?"

"That's right," she said. "Now we know each other's name, we're practically friends. So, Malik, do me a favour, and act like one, eh?"

"I don't understand."

"You don't have to. Just don't fucking run again. All right?"

Fenna took her hand from Malik's chest, raising her finger as if to say *don't test me*.

Malik didn't.

He waited as she took a step out into the street. He watched as she zipped her jacket and hid her bloody hand inside her pocket.

"Come," she said, with a brief wave at Malik.

"Where are we going?" he asked, as he fell into step beside her.

"Somewhere safe."

"Is it safe?"

Fenna turned her head to look at him. If he looked beyond the wet strands of hair plastered to her cheek, the spots of blood around her mouth, he could see that same glint of something hard in her eyes.

"What you're really asking," she said, her

voice pitched above the rain and the noises of the street, but no louder than that, keeping him close if he wanted to hear the answer. "Is if you're safe with me."

"Yes," he said, braver now, but cold again, almost cursing himself for thinking that wherever she was taking him, he hoped it would be warm.

"This way," she said, as a dark blue van flashed its lights, and pulled alongside the pavement. The side door slid open and Fenna pushed Malik inside.

The interior of the van was dry, but not much warmer than the street. Malik settled on a tarpaulin folded behind the driver's seat, as a man helped Fenna out of her jacket. He watched as Fenna unbuttoned her bloodstained shirt, slipping her left arm out of the sleeve and letting the shirt hang as the man inspected the knife wound – a deep slash beneath her ribs – before tearing a bandage out of its wrapper and pressing it to Fenna's side.

"Hold that," he said, as he reached for a roll of duct tape.

"Tape? Really?" Fenna said, cursing the man as he nodded.

Malik watched, fascinated by the sight, as the van stopped and started in early evening traffic. When the man was done taping Fenna's bandage to her side, she slipped her shirt off completely, tossing the bloody rag into the back of the van and then pulling her jacket on. Malik caught a last glimpse of Fenna's bloodstained sports bra, before she zipped her jacket closed, and then settled on her knees in front of him.

"My name is Fenna Brongaard," she said. "I'm an intelligence officer."

"For the Danes?"

Fenna paused. "Yes, in a manner of speaking."

"And what do you want with me?"

The man beside Fenna laughed, stopping when Fenna gave him a look.

"I think you can do better than that, Malik," she said. "I think you know already, and it's probably best if you just start talking."

Malik swallowed, taking a second to think, before blurting out, "That woman. Is she…"

"Dead?" Fenna shook her head.

"I heard shots." Malik glanced at Fenna's jacket, peering into the gloom, convinced he would see the bulge of a handgun at her side.

"She's alive," Fenna said. "And by now she's reporting back to her handler."

"Her handler?"

"The one in charge." Fenna sank back onto her heels, giving Malik a little more space, perhaps even a little more freedom to think.

She waited.

Malik thought back to his meeting with Hong Wei in the arena. He tried to remember the face of the young woman in the hotel restaurant, the one Hong Wei kept hidden in the shadows. *To follow me, or to protect me?* Malik struggled with the answer, but the struggle with what to say next was harder, as he weighed up who might have his best interests at heart, and who could offer him the most protection.

"You're thinking again, Malik," Fenna said.

"Yes."

"You're trying to make a decision, trying to decide the right course of action." Fenna brushed her wet hair to one side. "Take your time. Just be sure you make the right decision."

Fenna clicked her fingers at the man, then nodded as he pulled two bottles of water out of a backpack. He gave one to Malik and the other to Fenna.

"Drink," Fenna said, as she unscrewed the cap of her bottle. "It's not poison."

Malik drank, long gulps, just like he did after one of Tipaaqu's workouts.

Tipaaqu.

Malik saw her face, pre-death, saw her bright, intelligent eyes, heard her sharp combative *take-no-shit* tongue.

What would Tipaaqu do?

"All better now?" Fenna asked, taking the bottle from his hands.

Malik frowned as the van started to sway in traffic. He leaned forwards to stare at the bottle in Fenna's hands, wondering if he had seen her take even a single sip of water. She had said it wasn't poison, but then why did he feel so drowsy all of a sudden?

"Wow, okay," Fenna said, steadying Malik with a hand on his shoulder as he started to rock. "You're a little sleepy, Malik. It's going to be okay. We're going to get you home."

"I don't know who he is," Malik said,

frowning as the words seemed sticky on his tongue.

"That's okay, Malik. I'm sure you'll remember. Sooner than you think."

Malik barely felt Fenna's hands as she guided him onto the floor of the van.

"That's it," she said. "Let's take him home."

"Yes, home," Malik slurred, before the dim light from the street blinked out.

Chapter 16

Ushuaia. Tierra del Fuego. Argentina. Petra ran her fingers over the words as their flight neared its final destination. She said the names aloud in her best Spanish accent with what she thought was an appropriate South American twist. She giggled at her attempts – louder and longer when Maratse tried.

"You're giggling," he said.

"I was," Petra said, catching her breath. "Now I'm laughing."

Maratse let the tourist brochure fall into his lap as Petra apologised, waving her hand in front of her face, wafting reconditioned air at the tears streaming down her cheeks.

"It's good to hear you laugh," Maratse said.

"I'm so sorry."

"I'm not."

Petra's eyes shone as she bit her bottom lip. She took Maratse's hand, squeezed it, then smiled at the passenger sitting next to him.

"Is it your honeymoon?" the woman asked in English. The faint crow's feet around her eyes stretched as she smiled, knocking years off her age, as Petra's smile and laughter bridged the gap between their cultures.

"Maybe," Petra said, with another squeeze of

Maratse's hand.

"Oh, that's wonderful," the woman said. She leaned forward, acknowledging Maratse with a brief dip of her head, before beckoning for Petra to move closer. "You must go to the lighthouse, just outside the city."

"The lighthouse?"

"Yes, yes, its name is Les Eclaireurs. It is the lighthouse at the end of the world, the most perfect place to say *te amo!*"

"*Te amo?*"

"Yes, yes." The woman took Petra's hand in hers, clasping it between warm, dry fingers. "You look him in the eyes," she said, lifting her chin, acknowledging Maratse once more, before forgetting him again, pulling Petra close. "When you have his attention – a pretty thing like you should always have his attention. But when you stand there, look him in the eyes, take his hands, and you say..." The woman waited.

"*Te amo.*"

"Yes." The woman smiled, clapping Petra's hand between her own. "You tell him that, then this *maybe* honeymoon will become the real thing." She lowered her voice to a conspiratorial whisper. "He doesn't stand a chance. You know it, yes?"

"I think so."

The woman let go of Petra's hand, nodding as she slumped back in her seat.

"And you," she said, with a gentle slap of Maratse's thigh.

"Hmm?"

"No, no," she said. "Not that. You must say the same to her." Another slap, and a pointed nod directing Maratse's attention to Petra. "*Te amo.* Say it with feeling. Try it."

Petra pressed her hand to her mouth, hiding another laugh, but her eyes shone when Maratse looked into them.

"Piitalaat…"

"Yes?"

"*Te amo.*"

"Yes," she said, as the woman let out a short sigh.

"The lighthouse," the woman said, as the captain announced they would be landing soon. "As soon as possible."

Petra took one step out of the pine, metal and glass airport and stopped to catch her breath. Beyond the shuttle buses and taxis, across Beagle Channel, and pinched in a long line at the base of the snow-capped mountains, the city of Ushuaia glittered in the late-January sun.

"It's like home," she said, pointing at the mountains, then pinching Maratse as she remembered the population of the city, one more fact she had read in the brochure. "The city has the same population as Greenland," she said. "All of Greenland, in one city. With mountains, and…"

Maratse smiled as Petra paused for another breath.

"Lighthouses," he said.

"Yes, and lighthouses." Petra grabbed

~ 169 ~

Maratse's hand, pulling him closer to the shuttle buses. "This is just what we needed. We are exactly where we need to be right now. It's like home, but different. Familiar, but so strange," she said, turning her head at another burst of Spanish as loved ones met each other outside the airport building. "We did the right thing," she said. "Better than Spain."

"You're sure?"

"Sure?" Petra pointed at the mountains. "Just look at that. Even you can relax here."

"*Iiji*," Maratse said. "I think so."

"You think? *Gah*! You're impossible, but," she said, gripping his jacket and pulling him towards her. "*Te amo*." Petra wrinkled her nose. "Even with the jacket."

Petra let go of Maratse as they heard someone call his name. She turned to look at the row of buses, before catching the eye of a short, wiry man with sunburned skin standing beside a pickup truck with a large cab.

"Mr. Maratse and Ms. Jensen?"

"Yes," Petra said. "That's us."

"My name is Alasdair Donne," the man said, as he took Petra's backpack. "I'm the mechanic on the *Admiral Chichagov*. The captain sent me to pick you up."

"The captain sent you?"

"Aye, well," Alasdair said with a smile. "I had an errand, and I fancied a trip into the city. So, anyway, here we all are." He dumped their luggage in the bed of the pickup. "First time in Argentina?"

"First time in South America," Petra said. Alasdair opened the passenger door and she climbed in. Maratse took one of the seats in the back.

"Well, you won't see much of Ushuaia. We sail the day after tomorrow. But your first night is in a hotel close to the water. So, you'll get a flavour of the city."

"And a lighthouse?" Maratse said, drawing a smile from Petra.

"Ah, Les Eclaireurs Lighthouse, of course. There's a boat that takes tourists to the lighthouse, more than one I'm sure. Just ask at the hotel. They'll fix you up."

"And we're free to do that?" Petra asked. "We're not needed on the ship?"

"Not before Monday." Alasdair shrugged his shoulders as he started the car. "I'd make the most of it, if I were you."

"You're a mechanic?" Maratse asked, as Alasdair drove behind a shuttle bus along the road around the bay and into the city.

"That's right. But I mostly work on the small stuff, outboard engines, tracked vehicles. I don't have anything to do with the ship's engines, or the helicopter."

"Helicopter?" Petra said.

"Sure. We've got a Chinese Harbin Z-9. It's basically a Eurocopter. Slim and fast, tuned for polar climes." Alasdair slowed to a stop for a traffic light. "Speaking of which," he said, with a look at Maratse in the back and Petra sitting beside him. "You're from Greenland?"

"Yes," Petra said.

"So, this," he said, gesturing at the mountains through the windshield, "will all be familiar to you?"

"It looks familiar," Petra said. "But this is our first time so far south."

"Right, well, I can tell you that it can be just as unstable, twice as cold, and if we're unlucky, crossing *Drake Passage* can be a real son of a bitch, if you'll excuse my Spanish."

"My Spanish isn't very good," Maratse said, with a smile at Petra. "But you're talking about rough seas?"

"Oh aye, you can say that again."

"I hadn't thought about that," Petra said, as Alasdair shifted into first as the lights changed.

"You don't sail well?"

"I can get a little seasick."

"The doc will fix you up if it gets rough," Alasdair said.

He spent the next few minutes pointing out places of interest as they drove into Ushuaia. The pretty colours of the buildings brought back more memories of Greenland, albeit in a different style, with a more American feel to them.

"*South American*," Petra whispered, reminding herself with a soft pinch of her skin that this was all real, that they were at the very ends of the earth, a very long way from home.

The long flights, including the required changes along the way, caught up with them, suppressing the excitement of being in another country, and forcing them to stay alert, just a little while longer as Alasdair dropped them off at the hotel, confirming that he would return to pick them up before they sailed. They checked in. Petra did the talking, sliding their passports along the desk, then turning to Maratse as he reminded her to, "Ask about the boat."

"After we've found our room," she said.

"Hmm," he said. "Too tired then. Ask now."

"No need," she said, as the receptionist slid their keys and a welcome folder into Petra's hands. Petra tapped the cover of the folder and smiled. "Boat timetable included."

"The next boat leaves in one hour," the receptionist said. "A short excursion, back in time for dinner. Shall I add you to the list?"

"*Iiji,*" Maratse said.

Petra nodded. "That means *yes.*"

The brochures tucked inside the folder described the lighthouse as the *perfect location for outdoor romantics.* Petra's hair flowed behind her head in the sea breeze as she pressed her back into Maratse's chest, tugging his arms around her as they bounced through the light chop of the waves on the way to the lighthouse. Maratse pointed out the penguins, to which Petra replied that they were too pretty to eat. The sea lions on the rocks, on the other hand, inspired comments about food, how hungry they were, how the boat trip had been a good idea, but now all they could think about was dinner.

"Piitalaat," Maratse said, as the tourist boat bobbed close to the shore, and they looked up at the red and white striped lighthouse.

"Yes?"

"*Te amo*," he said.

"I know."

Petra pressed her head against Maratse's shoulder, ignoring the wind whipping her hair around her face. The tang of salt and seaweed drifted off the rocks, mingling with the hunting and fishing smells ingrained in the fibres of Maratse's jacket, lending another familiar sense of home to the southern scene before them. The tourists filmed the lighthouse from every angle, reminding Petra that they needed a camera, that maybe her smartphone wouldn't suffice.

"I don't know why I didn't think of it," she said.

"Take a picture anyway."

Petra pulled out her phone, stepping forward as Maratse held her shoulders, just enough to compensate for the rocking of the boat.

"How about I take one for you?" said one of the tourists, lowering his own camera as he walked across the deck towards them.

"Thank you," Petra said, pressing her phone into the man's hand. Petra pulled Maratse to the railing, pressing him backwards as the man took one photo, and then another when Petra suggested he turn the camera upright.

"That's my new wallpaper," she said, thanking the man as she flicked through the photos. Petra turned the screen towards Maratse, pointing out the smile on his face, and laughing at the strands of her hair she could see tickling his nose in the photo. "Perfect."

"Hmm," Maratse said, punctuating his grunt with a smile.

The ride back to Ushuaia took in more sights along the seafront, with interesting facts about the mountains, the Andes, Patagonia, and the history of the area, including a passionate account of the war with the British over *Las Malvinas*, also known as the Falkland Islands.

More facts, more sights, and the gentle rise and fall of the boat riding the tide back to Ushuaia, tugged at Petra's eyelids, pulling them closed as she sat, her collar zipped tight beneath her chin, and Maratse's arms wrapped around her body.

Maratse took long deep breaths of the sea air as he enjoyed the mild temperature, the sight of the mountains, and the snow catching the lingering rays of south polar sunshine. He would have travelled to Spain, without complaint. He knew he would go wherever Petra wanted. But despite his initial scepticism, following her to the end of the world, at least, the very bottom of the world, seemed like the perfect way to begin their life together, putting the past behind them, laying old ghosts to rest.

He took another deep breath, watching Petra's body rise slightly as he filled his lungs with sea air.

Those ghosts were gone.

The past was finally behind them.

Maratse dipped his head to kiss Petra on her forehead. "*Tea amo*," he whispered.

"*Te*," Petra said, lifting her hand to stroke Maratse's cheek. "But, *yes*, I love you too."

Chapter 17

Xiá dumped her knife in the canal as she mingled with the tourists enjoying Copenhagen's waterside in Nyhavn. She lingered at the back of a group of Chinese businessmen and women, smiling when they glanced at her, pressing forward when the guide signalled that they were about to walk on to the next location. She joined them on the canal boat, feigning innocence and acting lost when the Chinese guide queried her lack of ticket.

"I must have lost it," she said, timing her response to the moment when the canal boat driver signalled he was ready to leave.

"Well," the guide said. "Don't lose it again." He stepped back to let Xiá onboard, flushing at the smile she gave him.

The group huddled together on the brightly coloured plastic bench seats, zipping their insulated jackets, and cupping their hands around paper mugs of coffee and tea. Xiá nodded her thanks and took a coffee. She blew on the surface, staring straight ahead, seemingly oblivious of the guide pointing out the various attractions on both sides of the canal. The group turned their heads one way and then the other, rubbing the shoulders of their shiny jackets together. The sound made

Xiá think of shifting sands in the Taklamakan Desert, and the operation she led to find an Indian agent supposedly hiding there. Her first mission, and the first of many tests Hong Wei designed for her to assess her strengths and to eradicate her weaknesses.

And now, she wondered. *What will he think when I tell him that the Dane has been drawn into the open?*

No matter the trust Hong Wei placed in Xiá, she knew he told her only as much as she needed to know for each operation. She often wondered, and suggested, that if she knew more of the *bigger picture,* then she might be better able to anticipate than simply react to every situation.

Hong Wei's reply had been frustratingly evasive.

"Beijing tells me what I need to know," he had said. "And I tell you…"

"Less," she said.

"I tell you everything required for the operation."

"But not enough to get the most out of it."

"That's for me to decide."

"Is that what you told my father?"

Her father.

It was the one weakness Hong Wei had failed to eradicate, but it was *his* weakness. It was Hong Wei's guilt that turned any mention of Xiá's father into a weapon she could use, and *did* use, at each and every opportunity. The memory of her father bound her to Hong Wei, just as he was in turn bound to her – her protection, her career, and her legacy.

Or my father's legacy?

Xiá knew her father had fallen from grace in the eyes of the Chinese Communist Party, and Hong Wei's reluctance to talk about it suggested that there was more to their last operation than he was ever going to tell her.

But he will, before the end.

Xiá imagined the *end* to be close. But whether it was this mission or the next depended upon the goals of the operation, something only Beijing and Hong Wei knew for sure. But they could only act on the information *she* provided them, and Xiá knew she had something of interest, a bargaining chip that she could use to get another morsel of information out of Hong Wei.

The canal boat bumped against the black oak beam of the next dock, and Xiá followed the group off the boat, up the timber ramp and back onto the streets of Copenhagen. They had travelled less than a kilometre – just around the block from Nyhavn to the new opera house – but far enough for Xiá to believe she could now return to the street and make her way back to Hong Wei's hotel room.

She walked across wet cobbled streets, using the reflective windows of shops and offices as mirrors, tilting her head when necessary, to avoid the glare of copper lights and candles in the coffee shops, casting warm inviting colours onto the street.

The windows revealed no shadowy figures

behind her.

The cafés were full of shoppers, tourists, and business folk, seeking warmth and chatter at the end of a winter dark January, on the cusp of an equally dark February. Xiá resisted the temptation to join them and walked on.

"Stay at your present location," Hong Wei said, when Xiá called from her secure phone. "I'm coming to pick you up."

He arrived shortly after she called, pulling up to the kerb as she shivered on the pavement. The rear passenger door on the passenger side of the black SUV opened and Xiá climbed inside. The driver pulled away from the kerb a second before she closed the door.

"Report," Hong Wei said, as Xiá settled onto the back seat.

"Where are we going?"

"The airport." Hong Wei tapped the leather seat between them, prompting her, as he said, "We don't have much time. I have been summoned to Beijing. You will be flying south."

"South?"

"I'll tell you more as soon as you have finished your report."

Xiá looked at the driver, catching his eye in the mirror, wondering if he was new, or just one of Hong Wei's many operatives he kept hidden from Xiá.

"You can trust my driver," Hong Wei said.

"Really? I don't know him."

Hong Wei sighed, and then looked at his

watch. He leaned forward, ordering the driver to pull over. "We have an hour," he said, gesturing for Xiá to get out of the vehicle. "You really must learn to trust me, Xiá," Hong Wei said, as he buttoned the front of his knee-length black wool overcoat.

"I do," she said. "Just not your driver."

Hong Wei sighed a second time, then nodded at a café on the corner of the street. They started walking towards it. "What you really want is to ask me more about your father, and you don't believe I'll tell you anything unless we're alone."

Xiá shrugged. "If that's what you think."

"I don't *think* it, I *know* it. You have traded operational information for information about your father a lot, of late, but this must end soon."

"I'll stop when you tell me the whole story," Xiá said, as they reached the café. "The truth," she added, before they stepped inside.

Hong Wei found a quiet table at the back of the café. He waited for Xiá to begin her report when she joined him with their drinks, nodding slowly when she didn't.

"All right," he said, speaking low in a soft Cantonese. "Juatan Fortin was already drunk when Pān Tāo and I entered his house. We took the reindeer inside – a mistake, too curious – but then we left shortly after, thinking nothing more of it as we took Fortin and his truck south along the Inuvik-Tuktoyaktuk Highway."

"You needed his identity card," Xiá said.

"Yes. But we took him with us, pretending we were friends in need of a ride, when there was too much activity around his house. I mentioned the children watching us – they brought older children with them, teenagers. Some of them were drunk, all of them were too noisy. They asked too many questions, calling in through the screen door, entering the house until Pān Tāo, your father, stopped them."

"How?"

"He told them to go away, but..." Hong Wei paused. "He had an accent, and no words of Inuktitut, only English..."

"With an accent."

Hong Wei removed the tea bag from his cup and put it on the saucer. "Also," he said, wiping spots of tea from the table with a napkin. "The teenagers saw Pān Tāo's handgun, poking out of the waistband of his jeans. They shouted *robber* at him, then *thieves*, convinced Fortin was in trouble. We heard doors banging, and that's when we left, taking Fortin out to his car, trying to convince the children and their older siblings that we were friends, waving our pistols when we couldn't. It was a difficult moment, but we left the village in Fortin's pickup."

"You were followed?"

"By one of the villagers, also in a pickup. Your father drove, while I crawled into the back. I fired at the truck behind us and the driver stopped. We kept going."

"And the mission?"

"Was still on. We had Fortin's identity card. We had Fortin, and we decided that even if the villagers called the local police, or even the

RCMP, we would be far away, and their story would be just another wild Friday night story. Nothing special. Nothing credible."

"Was it Friday?" Xiá asked.

"What?" Hong Wei looked away as he shook his head. "I don't remember."

Xiá wondered at that but saved the thought for later. She sipped her tea as she waited for Hong Wei to continue.

"Pān Tāo started to get tired. You must realise, these roads are very long and unfinished. The pickup bounced all the time. We had to change one tyre just a short way out of the village. It probably needed changing before we got there."

"And Fortin?"

"Sobering up. We tied him up and put him in the back, under a tarp."

"And then you drove on."

Hong Wei nodded, then took a sip of tea.

"Your turn, Xiá," he said.

Xiá considered how much she knew of her father's last operation. Hong Wei's narrative had taken them out of Tuktoyaktuk, further down the highway, closer to their destination. There was a body in the back of the pickup. Xiá didn't believe the story was over, but neither did it appear that Hong Wei was ready to reveal more.

Not yet, anyway, she thought. *I need to give him my report.*

Xiá placed her cup on its saucer, and began, starting with how she followed Malik, as ordered, from the arena to the metro station.

"Which is when I saw her," she said.

"You saw Konstabel Brongaard?"

"Konstabel?"

"Her previous rank," Hong Wei said, waving the question aside. "Continue."

"There was a van following Malik. As soon as he entered the station, Brongaard got out and followed him."

"Just her?"

Xiá nodded. "The rest of the team stayed inside the van. They pulled away. I went down into the station."

"And took a train…"

"To the next stop, which is when she saw me."

"When you got out?"

Xiá nodded. "She saw me, reacted, and Malik took his chance and ran." Xiá smiled at the memory. "I followed them."

"At speed?"

"Casually," Xiá said.

"And yet, there are police reports of shots being fired," Hong Wei said, as he stared at Xiá. "A bus window was shattered; the driver was injured." Hong Wei traced his finger down his cheek. "Glass injuries."

"From safety glass?"

"And maybe the bullet. It's not important, Xiá. The point is that you engaged Fenna Brongaard in public."

"With a knife. *She* pulled the gun."

"Because you forced her to."

"Yes," Xiá said. "Drawing her out of the

~ 184 ~

shadows. Just like you wanted me to."

Hong Wei paused for another sip of tea. Xiá watched his face, knowing that she was right the second she saw corner of his mouth twitch upwards.

"I did what you told me to do," she said.

"Yes."

"But now she has Malik. I saw her team take him away in their van."

"It was to be expected."

Xiá frowned as Hong Wei distracted her with a glimpse of another piece of the larger puzzle.

"Don't worry about Malik," Hong Wei said, as she started to speak. "The situation is changing now, rapidly."

"Because Brongaard is exposed?"

"And the Canadians," Hong Wei said.

"She's not working for the Danes?"

"She stopped working for them a long time ago – relatively speaking. No," Hong Wei said. "The Danes are relatively new to this game, although, they are passionate. Which isn't surprising when you consider how much they and their friends have to lose."

"But what about the Canadians?" Xiá leaned forward over the table. "This is connected to my father, isn't it?"

"There are many things connected to Pān Tāo, Xiá. And I'll tell you more, when the time is right. But first, you must fly south. Listen carefully. Here are your new instructions."

Xiá sipped her tea as Hong Wei talked, suddenly curious that she should travel so *far* south, extending her area of operations to the very end of the world.

Chapter 18

Maratse pressed his face to the passenger window of Alasdair's pickup and stared up at the *Admiral Chichagov*. The old Russian icebreaker, with its black hull and red and white superstructure, complete with rusty tears around the square salt-streaked windows. The icebreaker looked its age when compared to the sleek and forward-angled, white and silver-lined cruise ship berthed on the opposite side of the tourist dock, reaching out from the port of Ushuaia. Alasdair parked just beside the ramp leading from the dock to the *Admiral Chichagov*'s deck.

"Aye," he said. "She's a bit of a beast."

"We can't take that one?" Petra said, as she cast a short, but longing look at the modern cruise liner opposite the icebreaker.

"You could," Alasdair said. "But you'd have to sail north from here. This is as far south as a ship like that can sail. She's too pretty for where we're going."

"Hmm," Maratse said.

"What's that, mate?"

"It means he likes the ugly one," Petra said. She opened the passenger door and stepped out onto the dock.

"She's named after an old Russian admiral,"

Alasdair said, as he and Maratse joined Petra. "Chichagov was an explorer. He went looking for the Northeast Passage in the mid-1700s. Didn't find it. But he did find an English wife on retirement. Which, all things considered, was probably a lot more fun than freezing his nuts off in the Arctic. If you'll excuse my crassness," he said, with a dip of his head towards Petra.

"You're excused," she said.

"And what about the engines?" Maratse asked. He turned his head to look at the stern, noting the flat helicopter pad with the Chinese helicopter lashed to it, before following the black hull down to the waterline.

"She's triple-screwed, diesel electric," Alasdair said, tracing his hand from the stern to the bow as he talked. "Cruiser stern – with the helicopter pad, as you can see. The hangar is in front of that. The engine room is in the middle. She's got four decks – the ones you can see above the main deck. A deck forecastle, with the smokestack behind it." He pointed at the black-lipped and red-ringed white smokestack. "You can still see the shadow of the old hammer and sickle of the USSR." He paused for a moment, as if there was more to tell, before moving his hand over the deck, dropping down towards the bow pointing at the low and sprawling buildings of the city. The mountains of Tierra del Fuego looked down on the port from where they stood, just outside the limits of the city. "Icebreaker bow," he said. "Where the muscle is."

"How thick?" Maratse asked.

"She's got a Russian ice class LL2," Alasdair said, with a scratch of his head. "So, she can break ice up to two metres thick. The captain likes to avoid icebreaking if possible. In fact, the general idea is to avoid the ice, putting in at ports like Rothera – where the British Antarctic Survey have their research station. That's about as far south as we'll go. But then we go east to South Georgia Island." Alasdair laughed. "You'll see plenty of penguins on this trip."

"We'll try not to eat them," Maratse said, still studying the ship.

"What?"

"He's joking," Petra said, turning her head to look at Maratse. "Although, he's not good at jokes so…"

"How long is the ship?" Maratse nodded at the bow.

"One hundred and thirty-five metres long, twenty-six metres wide, and forty-five from the keel to the top of the smokestack." Alasdair scratched his head once more, searching the last numbers. "Oh, and twenty knots maximum speed – but that's when she's really cooking. Just two knots when breaking ice. And that," he said, with a wave to a stocky woman with long red hair fashioned into a messy bun walking down the gangplank, "is about the limit of what I know about the ship. But here's the captain. I'll leave you to it," he said, as the captain approached. I've got a couple more errands before we sail."

"Thanks Alasdair," the captain said, as she greeted Maratse and Petra. "Off again?"

"Yes, Captain," Alasdair said, as he climbed back into the pickup. He waved once before reversing along the dock until he could turn. The captain watched him leave before introducing herself.

"Elina Mäkelä," she said. "I do prefer crew to address me as Captain, especially in front of the passengers. But if I invite you for a meal, then please, call me Elina." The light from the sun bursting through the clouds reflected in her deep blue eyes. "That's the formalities, let me show you my ship. And you'll want to see your cabin, of course."

"We left our bags in the pickup," Petra said, turning to where Alasdair was parked. She saw Maratse's battered suitcase and her own backpack tucked onto a pallet beside several boxes of fresh fruit.

"I'll have one of the crew bring them onboard," Elina said. "If you'll follow me."

Petra took one last look at the aggressive lines and polished curves of the modern cruise ship before taking Maratse's hand and following the captain onto the icebreaker.

"Connor told me you were coming," Elina said, glancing over her shoulder as she talked. "He said were you quite the catch."

"I'm not sure about that," Petra said, speaking quickly in anticipation of Maratse's grunt. "We were in the right place at the right time."

"You're being modest, I think," Elina said. She stopped and turned as they stepped onto the deck. "Connor knows people, and, more importantly, he knows how to satisfy our passengers. To be sure, they would expect experts on Antarctica to tell them about the history, the geography, the flora and fauna. But they also appreciate authenticity. Now, there are no indigenous peoples of any kind in Antarctica – just scientists, carpenters, and pilots, etc. The passengers have been told about the changes in hospitality staff – guides, for example. And from what I've heard, even before meeting you, the passengers' response at having genuine Inuit on their cruise – detectives no less – has offset any concerns they might have had. You will likely be the stars of the show," Elina said, with a smile, "at least, after they have finished taking photos of the ship, and photographing everything that moves in and on the water." Elina paused again as she looked at Maratse's old police jacket. "Of course, authenticity is one thing, but you will be expected to assume the role of guides, and we have rules regarding attire."

"Hmm?" Maratse said.

"Attire," Elina repeated, flicking her finger at Maratse's jacket. "Comfortable but smart clothes inside the ship. Jackets, salopettes and an inflatable life preserver when on deck. And you'll be expected to wear drysuits beneath your jackets if you go on any excursions."

"Excursions?"

"In the RIBs, the rigid inflatable boats. We use them to get from the *Chichagov* to the islands, or even for whale spotting. We have three, but one of the outboards needs a new part. I hope Alasdair finds it, or we'll have to sail without it." Elina gestured at the door leading into the superstructure. "A quick tour to the bridge, then I'll have one of the crew show you your cabin."

Petra whispered to Maratse in Danish, something about clothes, and wondering if they still had time to buy him a new jacket before sailing.

"Hmm," Maratse said, as they followed the captain inside the ship.

The corridors smelled of bleach and the faint smell of diesel.

"Which you'll get used to," Elina said, as they took the stairs to the bridge. "And if you get seasick, then I suggest you talk to Madhu Rao, the ship's doctor. His sickbay is on deck one. We passed it on the way in."

The captain stopped outside the bridge, as if preparing them for something special. She flashed a smile, then opened the door, gesturing for them to walk ahead of her. While those of a more technical bent might have been stunned by the array of instruments, the radio station, the chart station, and the captain's chair, Maratse and Petra walked straight to the windows, staring at the sun-bleached snow caps of the mountains.

"It doesn't matter where we are," Elina said, as she joined them. "The view from this bridge is stunning. You must come as often as you like. Of course, there's only space for so many, so we have one rule. In fair weather, passengers have priority. If there are more than four guests on the bridge, non-bridge staff leave to make room for more." Elina walked to the side of the bridge to pour three mugs of coffee. "In bad weather," she said, handing Maratse and Petra a mug, "the bridge is restricted. As is the open deck. The *Chichagov* might be an old ship – laid down in 1973 and completed in 1975, I believe – but she has modern aspirations and adheres to the latest health and safety regulations. If you are instructed to remain in your cabin, you can bet there's a good reason to do so."

Elina looked at Maratse and Petra over the lip of her mug as she took a sip of coffee, waiting for them to nod or say that they agreed, that they understood, continuing when they did so.

"But I think that's as far as I'll go with the rules," she said. "If in doubt – ask."

"We will," Petra said.

"Now, if you'll excuse me," Elina said. "I have some things to attend to. Feel free to stay on the bridge and enjoy your coffee." Elina placed her mug beside the coffee machine on her way out. She paused at the door, and said, "I might have forgotten to say this, but *welcome aboard*." She left shortly after.

"What have we done?" Petra said, as soon as they were alone.

"What do you mean?"

"All these rules. And the guests." Petra gestured at the captain's chair. "All their expectations…"

"Piitalaat," Maratse said. He put his mug

down and took her hand. "Remember who you are."

"A police sergeant…"

"*Iiji.*" Maratse smiled. "Not just any police sergeant. You are from Greenland. You said, when we arrived, this city reminded you of home. We could be in Nuuk. We *are* at home. Connor told the captain he had hired Inuit guides. Then let us *be* Inuit. We don't have to pretend. We just have to be ourselves."

"David?" Petra said, casting a quizzical glance at his coffee mug, as if it had been laced with something stronger.

"Hmm?"

"What just happened?"

"What do you mean?"

"I mean, you just gave me a pep talk."

"*Imaqa.*"

"No, not *maybe*, you definitely did."

Maratse shrugged, and said, "Did it work?"

"Yes," Petra said, putting down her mug so that she could take both Maratse's hands. "Incredible but true. You just made me feel so much better."

"You were in doubt?"

"I was." Petra sighed. "I still have doubts. I still doubt myself, wondering if I can do the things other people think I can do. Even wondering if I can do the things I know I used to do."

"I don't doubt you, Piitalaat."

"But you would say that."

"I *do* say that." Maratse frowned. "I just did."

"I know."

"And do you believe what I say?"

"I believe that you mean it."

"Good," Maratse said. "That's all you need to know."

Petra leaned forward to kiss Maratse's cheek. "There is something else I believe," she said, wrinkling her nose.

"What?"

"The captain was right about your jacket."

"Piitalaat…"

"No," she said, with a shake of her head. "We're going to find you another jacket. A crew jacket, like the one Alasdair was wearing."

"But I like this jacket," Maratse said.

"It's disgusting, David. And it has been for a very long time."

"It's authentic." Maratse turned to follow Petra as she walked off the bridge. "We were hired to be authentic, Piitalaat."

"That's true," she said. "But you heard the captain, they have very strict Health and Safety standards. We have to follow them."

"Piitalaat…"

"Follow me," she said, as she climbed down the stairs, heading for the lower decks, in search of a new jacket.

Chapter 19

The smell of bacon and the spit of fat in the frying pan woke Malik. He opened his eyes, blinking away the residual sluggishness, rubbing at and pinching the sleep from his eyelashes, as he struggled to remember a chase, a van, and a woman – young and tough.

She had a gun.

Malik remembered the gun.

He remembered being cold and wet, slammed against the glass door of an office building, then shoved inside the back of a van. He drank something – a bottle of water. The van had moved, like he was on a boat.

That was all he could remember.

Not the thin duvet covering his body, or the bed, the white papered walls with the pastel blue sailing motif repeated in a diamond pattern around the room. He lifted the duvet, curious to see that he was still fully clothed. A glance over the side of the bed revealed his shoes arranged neatly on the hardwood floor at the end of the bed. The only thing missing was his jacket, but then he remembered losing that in the chase.

Malik looked up as Fenna appeared in the doorway.

"Breakfast," she said. "Be quick. Before it

gets cold."

She left as quickly as she had appeared, drawing Malik out of bed with the promise of food and an explanation. He was not dead, but he was hungry.

Malik left his shoes in the room and padded into the tiny hallway. He recognised the constraints of a summer house, smaller than a normal house, and common in tourist areas and especially along the Danish coast. He heard the soft crash of surf nearby and blinked into the sun reflecting off the surface of the sea, as he stepped into the kitchen cum dining room, the heart of the summer house. Fenna served bacon and eggs from the pan onto a plate of toasted bread.

"No ketchup," she said, gesturing for Malik to sit down. "And no drugs."

"What?"

Fenna pointed at a glass of orange juice beside Malik's plate. "We drugged you in the van. That's why you're feeling a little sluggish. It's the after effects. Food helps, and then a bit of fresh air, when we walk along the beach."

"Where am I?"

"Just outside the city. You can see the wind farm out there. It's the one close to the airport. You'll hear the planes too."

Malik sat down at the table and Fenna joined him, sipping at her juice before talking.

"Do you remember me?"

"*Aap*," Malik said, with a nod of his head.

"I told you I worked in intelligence. I'm Danish, or I used to be. Now I work for the

Canadians, a charming woman called Meredith, to be precise. She has some questions for you, and I'm the one she sent to ask them."

"The Canadians?"

"Yes," Fenna said. She picked up her cutlery, then pointed at Malik's breakfast with the tip of the knife. "Eat. Before it gets cold."

Malik watched Fenna eat the first few mouthfuls of bacon and toast, before picking up his knife and fork. He glanced around the kitchen, half expecting a team of thugs or police to come bursting into the summer house, perhaps even through the patio doors opening out onto the deck. But nothing happened. He heard nothing more than the scrape of Fenna's cutlery on the plate, the crunch of toast beneath her teeth, and the sea surf on the beach.

"It's just you and me, Malik," Fenna said, pausing to fetch the coffee. "Eat."

Malik cut a corner off a wedge of toast and broke the surface of the egg with it. He ate, slowly at first, before succumbing to the groans in his belly and tucking into his breakfast. Fenna poured coffee in two mugs, and they ate in silence, until the plates were empty, and the coffee mugs were drained.

Fenna pushed back her chair and stood, nodding towards the bedrooms as she took Malik's plate and cleared the table. "You'll need your shoes," she said. "And you can borrow a jacket from the rack."

"We're going somewhere?"

"Outside, on the beach, as soon as you're

ready." Fenna paused to look at Malik, holding the plates in both hands. "We both want answers. The sooner you grab your shoes and a jacket, we can begin. Okay?"

Malik nodded. He left the kitchen, returning with his shoes and taking a jacket on his way. Fenna opened the patio doors and stepped outside, zipping her jacket as she waited for Malik.

"I always forget that winters are colder in Denmark than Greenland," she said, as Malik joined her on the deck. She closed the door, stuffed her hands into the deep pockets of her jacket and started walking along a narrow sandy path that led to an equally narrow beach, littered with small pebbles and mussel shells between stretches of dark sand recently leached of water. Malik walked alongside Fenna as soon as the beach widened.

"You know I'm a minster in the Greenland government?"

"Yes," Fenna said. "Currently in Denmark to attend a criminal trial. Until certain unfortunate events, including the death of your campaign manager. We've reached out to your colleagues, to the ministry, and explained that you are in shock, and have taken some compassionate leave until further notice."

"They believed you?"

Fenna moved away slightly to negotiate the remains of a driftwood pallet, nodding as she returned to Malik's side. "Yes, they believed us. I think you'll agree that our story is easier to believe than the alternative – that you were spirited out of custody by a fancy lawyer, financed by a secretive, and most likely foreign individual, before being chased through the streets of Copenhagen…" Fenna paused, before adding, "by me."

"There was another… woman," Malik said.

"You saw her?"

"I heard shots. I saw you were bleeding." Malik glanced at Fenna's side, remembering something about a bandage and duct tape.

"And do you know who she is?"

"*Naamik*," Malik said. And then again, with more feeling as Fenna stopped to look at him. "No. I don't know her."

"That's a pity," Fenna said. "Neither do we."

The beach narrowed at a path where the water deepened in a channel dividing the plots of summer houses. Fenna stepped onto the bridge, stopping in the middle to rest against the railings. She nodded for Malik to do the same.

"The woman who attacked me is Chinese," Fenna said. "Most likely an operative with Chinese intelligence – an assassin, probably."

"Assassin?" Malik said, paling at the thought, and not just the chill breeze blowing inland from the brisk waters of Øresund, the strait between Denmark and Sweden.

"Maybe that's a bit of a stretch, but considering her skills, it's likely. Anyway," Fenna said, "the more interesting question is why she was following you, and who sent her?"

"I don't know," Malik said.

"Okay," Fenna said, with a nod. "See, I don't believe you. And the reason I don't, is that you haven't asked why *I* was following you, or how I even knew where to find you. It wasn't chance that led me to the metro station, bumping into you, Malik. I know you met with someone at *Royal Arena*. I'm pretty sure I know who you met with."

Malik looked away as Fenna's eyes bored into his.

"You met a Chinese man, didn't you?"

Malik turned to look out across the sound. He rested his elbows on the thick wooden railing and leaned into it. "Yes," he breathed, drawing Fenna across the bridge to stand beside him.

"His name is Hong Wei?"

"*Aap.*"

"He bailed you out of custody."

Malik nodded.

"And in return, he asked you to do something for him. Malik?"

"Yes," he said. He turned his head to look at Fenna, holding her gaze before looking back across the water, idly wondering if he would be safer in Sweden, if he would be safe anywhere. "He wants me to speak in favour of foreign investment in Greenland."

"Chinese investment?"

"*Aap*," Malik said. "Obviously."

"He's done it before," Fenna said. "The mining camp at the top of Nuuk fjord. You know of it?"

"A little."

"It was exploratory, supposedly. A small step towards a greater investment, a mining town. A *Chinese* town in Greenland."

Malik pushed off the railing and looked at Fenna. "And what's so wrong with that? Eh?"

"It would be a foothold for China, in Greenland…"

"And in return they promised a new airport, a new port." Malik started counting off his fingers. "They would improve infrastructure, improve health services…"

"Greenland already has excellent health services," Fenna said.

"Spread across the country. The Chinese could build better medical centres, closer to the settlements."

"And who would staff them? Greenlanders?"

"Maybe."

"Or Chinese?"

"Does it matter? The people would benefit."

"And the Chinese would call the shots, Malik. They would dictate what you can and cannot do."

Malik clenched his jaw, and then said, "Denmark does that already."

"But you're free, Malik. No one tells you what you can say, or even think. Do you really believe that China is interested in your people? The minerals in the earth? The oil in the seabed? Or is it just your location?"

Fenna let the last question sink in, turning away from Malik as the breeze grew stronger, teasing her hair into witch-like wisps dancing in the wind.

Malik said nothing. He clenched his fists inside his pockets, as familiar thoughts of independence and control seethed through his mind. He knew people thought he was politically naive, that his first campaign – when he refused to speak any language other than Greenlandic – was divisive and infantile. *But they don't understand. They choose not to listen.* There was a rising tension in Greenland that Malik understood and was ready to exploit, but to do so required investment. And there was the rub, he could do nothing more for his country without money.

"The Chinese will pay," he said.

"Because they want to be an Arctic player," Fenna said. "It's not about you, or Greenland, its infrastructure, or even its politics. It's about global strategy and strategic power. You must understand this, Malik."

"What I understand, is that without new investment, Greenland will stagnate. Sure, plenty of money is thrown into culture, and tourism. But we can't eat culture, and if the tourists disappeared, how will we put food on our table?"

Malik paused, curious at his own words, as if the recent events had forced a change in his attitude, causing something to click. He almost laughed, almost felt a renewed sense of political vitality and willpower.

Almost.

Until he remembered where he was, and that he was just a puppet with lots of different hands pulling his strings.

"You know about Hong Wei," he said.

"Yes."

"And you know what he wants from me."

Fenna turned to look at Malik, nodding when she caught his eye.

"What about the Canadians? What do they want from me?"

"Nothing," Fenna said.

"Then why…"

"They don't want you, Malik. They want Hong Wei, for something he did a long time ago, way before you and I ever got involved." Fenna sighed, and said, "We're both pawns in this game. Other people are moving us around this great chessboard." Fenna pointed out across the sound. "You can bet our neighbours are following developments."

"The Swedes?"

"Swedes, Finns." Fenna shrugged. "Americans. Everyone."

"But you work for them. Why?"

"Because," Fenna said, turning to look at Malik. "At least if I'm involved, I can maybe make a difference."

"That's all I want to do," Malik said.

"Really?"

Malik thought for a moment, wondering just how much he believed that, only to realise that it felt good to say the words, that for the first time he meant them. While the house, his car – the big American import, his fancy clothes, the latest smartphone, his kids' iPads – all the perks that wealth afforded him, there was something more. Something he might even fight for, or, at least, work hard to achieve.

Harder than I usually do.

Fenna shifted her position, and Malik noticed the curious look in eyes as she looked at him.

"What?" he said.

"I think I believe you," Fenna said. "The only question is, how do we convince everyone else?"

"You mean Hong Wei?"

"Among others – journalists, for example. But yes, mostly him." Fenna pulled back her sleeve to check the time on her watch. "We need to get moving, and you need to make some decisions."

Malik listened as Fenna began to outline the next steps they both needed to take.

"Hong Wei knows I have you. He knows who pulls *my* strings. But he's not the only one who can help you, Malik. You've left quite a trail in your wake, including a police investigation, and some curious journalists…"

"The media?"

Fenna bit back a laugh. "A murder, followed by an accident – your business friend."

"Levi?"

"Dead on the motorway," Fenna said. "Lots of things point at you. I can tidy them up, just like Hong Wei can. But I need to know that you understand what you must do in return."

"You want me to work for you."

"Actually, I want you to work for both of us – Hong Wei, and me."

"But you said he knows…"

"Of course he does. You just have to prove your loyalty, make him think that you're still his puppet, but, secretly, you work for me."

Malik looked away, staring into the wind, feeling the bite of it on his cheeks. "How do I do that?"

"I'll help you, Malik. Just as soon as you're onboard." Fenna tapped Malik's arm and pointed back to the summer house. "I'm going to make some calls, and more coffee. I'm going to leave you here to think."

"To think?"

"To make a decision," she said. Fenna pointed in the other direction. "Or to run away. Now's your chance, Malik. Think about it."

Malik watched as Fenna walked away, heard the crunch of her boots on the mussel shells. He took a long deep breath of salty air, closed his eyes and pictured his children. Whatever he did next would affect them. Everything he had done affected them already, but this next decision felt more final than any of those that came before.

"Fuck," he said, as he stared into the wind.

Chapter 20

Xiá fumed on the long flight south to Tierra del Fuego. The PhD material she had loaded onto her tablet prior to leaving Copenhagen was dry in comparison to the thoughts that occupied the other part of her mind since leaving Danish airspace. While there were some snippets of interesting information concerning research at Chángchéng Zhàn, known as the Great Wall Station, and the second Chinese Antarctic station, Zhōngshān Zhàn, on the opposite side of the continent, Xiá was preoccupied with Hong Wei's obsession with Fenna Brongaard. Between expedition reports of unsuitable ships getting stuck in unexpected ice, Xiá found that she too was obsessed with Fenna, and smiled at the first strike she had landed on the foreign agent, wondering if she would get the chance to strike again. Perhaps her next strike would be a fatal one?

"You have drawn her out," Hong Wei had said, during their last hour together. "She must make the next move."

"She already has," Xiá had said. "She has Malik. That was her move. She will turn him."

"Malik Uutaaq is a simple man, Xiá. She will no doubt convince him that he must work for her, that it will be in his best interests. And when we bring him back into the fold, he will tell us the truth, that he has been approached and encouraged to spy on us. Fenna Brongaard will school him in that vein, trusting that he will be better equipped to lie with the truth than conceal a lie."

"Then what is the point?"

"The point is not *who* but *how*."

Xiá remembered Hong Wei's smile, the one he used when he thought he was teaching her something new. She had returned the smile he expected her to respond with – a curious curling of the lips suggesting a subtle blend of interest, curiosity, and confusion. She knew he found it endearing, but secretly she longed for the day when she could erase that smile from her tacit vocabulary, and wipe Hong Wei's own smug and patronising grin from his face.

"The pieces on the board," Hong Wei said, continuing. "Are less important than how they are being played. Sometimes, as in the case of Malik, several players can use the same piece. In chess, a piece is not played until the player removes their finger from it. In this case, with Malik, the last person to touch him might think they are in control, but the important thing is not who touched him last, but how heavy an impression their finger placed upon him. Fenna is just another piece on the board, and someone has her finger on Fenna, moving her from one place to the next."

"Her?"

"Meredith – no last name," Hong Wei said. "Canadian. Her operation is gaining strength and influence, releasing more funds as she secures more wins. This game we play, Xiá, is on many levels, one of which is ensuring enough wins to deprive our opposite numbers of their funding. These are the subtleties you must learn if you are to succeed me."

That last comment had thrown her, and the tail of it lingered as she flew south.

Xiá took a break from the history of Chinese polar research, asked for tea when the stewardess served drinks, stirring it to a bitter dark brew as she stirred her thoughts – just as bitter, but darker, much darker.

So much of her active service was spent in the shadows, cleaning up Hong Wei's activity, and creating opportunities, that Xiá was now more comfortable in the dark than the light. She entertained dark thoughts, allowing herself to imagine a variety of scenarios, including vengeance for what she believed she was about to learn, just as soon as Hong Wei revealed the last parts of the puzzle surrounding her father.

Unlike the name *Hong Wei*, her father, Pān Tāo, was not revered within the circles of power. His was a name to be cursed, associated with a failed operation and a very public stink that had followed Xiá through her adult life, from the minute Hong Wei had selected her for special training, to the present day. Xiá understood that Hong Wei smoothed the path for her, opening doors that were otherwise closed, and approving applications that would never have been entertained were it not for his endorsement. Her life belonged to him, and without him, she would remain in the shadow, regardless of his tantalising hints of succession.

No, she thought. *None of my achievements amount to much without his signature. Nothing I do will ever erase the deeds of my father, unless...*

The thought was not a new one, and it distracted her – in the past, and on the flight south, when she should have been cribbing for her fake PhD, just enough to sound knowledgeable, more than the layperson. Xiá's assumed identity – carefully orchestrated by Hong Wei – was supposed to provide her access to the ship, its passengers and crew, and one person in particular.

"Constable David Maratse."

Xiá noticed a flicker of something dark in Hong Wei's eyes when he said the man's name.

"He's the key to throw Fenna Brongaard off kilter."

"To what end?"

"To distract her and discredit her, and thus allow us to manipulate Malik further, to turn him once more, and cement our position in Greenland."

"Killing her would be easier."

"Yes, Xiá, you're right. But that's not the purpose here. See the whole board, remember each piece. If you killed Fenna, she would be replaced. Who do you think is more beneficial to us? An intelligence officer making decisions based on emotion, or a replacement who has no obvious weaknesses?"

"Until we find them."

"And how long will that take, do you think?"

Xiá didn't have an answer, but she felt the time was worth it when compared to the time taken to fly south, to fill her mind with what she considered useless trivia, before infiltrating a civilian operation, and setting a trap that may or may not succeed.

It's a waste of time. But until I can decide what to do with my time, I'm stuck with it.

Xiá picked up her tablet, and zoned out for the rest of the flight, forcing herself to read and repeat each time she felt the flicker of independent thought spark a potentially interesting new angle in her quest for independence.

Independence.

The thought almost made her smile.

It seemed to be a common theme, and a cause pursued by at least half of the people with whom she had crossed paths recently, herself included.

Xiá asked for more tea, stirring it as she stirred her thoughts.

She changed clothes as she changed airports, swapping her preferred slim black outfit for the clumsier and less streamlined attire better suited to a timid but enthusiastic polar scholar. Xiá pulled loud coloured clothing from her bag, mixing the bright red of her thin duvet jacket with the insect green of her puffed trousers. She curled her hair with adult pigtails, pressed big glasses onto her face, and pulled a surgical mask over her mouth. The last item was common enough in China's big cities, but it made her stick out in the airport. Until the world adopted the face mask as a necessary evil, it would remain a Chinese tourist fashion item, something Xiá could exploit.

Two more flights and a dash to a taxi, delivered her onto the dock in Ushuaia to be met by one of the crew of the *Admiral Chichagov* – another ugly boat, like the *Xue Long*, to add to her family's history with ugly boats. Xiá shook the thought from her mind as she greeted the crew member with a suitably timid shake of the hand.

"I'm sorry," the young man said, as he greeted Xiá. "We don't actually know your name, only that you're a last-minute replacement for…"

"Guo Guìyīng," Xiá said, adding another layer of accent to her English. "She is ill. My name is Xiá."

"*Just* Xiá?" the man asked.

"Yes," she said. "It's easier for you. Easier for me."

"Okay, *Xiá*, my name is Luukas Aalto. If you leave your bags here, I'll have someone pick them up and bring them to your cabin. But right now the captain is introducing the hospitality staff to the passengers." He checked his watch. "We can just make it before they break for dinner."

"I have to meet them now?"

"If you don't mind." The man paused, as if thinking about how to fit Xiá's presentation into the schedule.

"I don't mind," Xiá said. She remembered her mask and tugged it off her face, fixing the young man with a shy but generous smile.

"Great. Follow me."

Xiá slipped the face mask into her pocket and followed Luukas up the gangplank. She noted the turns to the lecture room, its proximity to sickbay, and the number of passengers arranged on the seats filling the first two thirds of a tiny auditorium. Xiá paused at the door with the crewman, until the captain waved her down onto the stage. She glanced at the two Greenlanders on her way down, recognising Maratse from the description Hong Wei had provided. She had expected him to at least have a walking stick, considering what Hong Wei said had been done to him, but the retired police constable seemed strong, despite his obvious discomfort standing on a stage in front of thirty passengers. Xiá guessed that the woman standing beside Maratse was the police sergeant, Petra Jensen, but there was little time for observation, as the captain introduced Xiá the second she reached the stage.

"As you know," the captain said, addressing the passengers, "there have been several changes in hospitality staff for this cruise. You've already met Petra and David, but now I'd like to introduce…"

"Xiá," Xiá said, as she greeted the captain.

"From the Polar Research Institute of China in…"

"Shanghai," Xiá said. "I'm on loan from

Shanghai."

"Yes," the captain, said, as she presented Xiá to the passengers. "Xiá will be holding two lectures during the cruise, which you can attend in person, or watch from the comfort of your cabin. As with all the lectures, there will be a playback feature, as advertised in your brochures and travel material. Anyway, together with our Greenlandic staff, and Seamus, our glaciologist," she said, gesturing at the tall, thin man standing beside Maratse, "I'm confident we can answer all your questions."

"I have a question."

Xiá suppressed a curse as a large white-haired man pushed himself out of his chair and looked at her. She considered an appropriate and polite rebuff, to give her time to respond, perhaps later, over dinner, but the man turned instead to look at Maratse.

"You're our whale expert," the man said.

"I know a little bit about whales," Maratse said. He nodded at the man, but glanced at Xiá, giving her a look that made her think she recognised him, until the passenger diverted his attention.

"You said in your presentation, that you were a former policeman."

"A constable," Maratse said.

"And a hunter."

"*Iiji*, I hunt, when I have the time."

"So, you hunt whales?"

Xiá noted a ripple among the passengers, a scratching of jacket shoulders, a shifting of heavy boot tread on the deck.

"I have been on a whale hunt," Maratse said.

"I wonder," the captain said, as she took a step forward. "If I might interrupt and remind everyone that dinner will be served from seven o'clock, which is just ten minutes from now, if you wanted to get ready."

The passengers shuffled their feet, making ready to leave, but the man questioning Maratse raised his voice, encouraging the passengers to remain in their seats, and sending a tiny thrill of excitement through Xiá's body as she saw a potential opportunity arise, something that would complement what she knew Hong Wei was arranging in Beijing.

"I'll finish my question," the man said. "Lord knows I've paid enough for Phyllis and me to take this cruise. So, if you please, I'll ask the constable, one more time, if he hunts whales?"

The captain glanced at Maratse and took a step back when he nodded that it was okay.

Xiá watched as Maratse blinked in the lights pointed down at the stage, then wished she was still wearing her mask as a smile played across her lips. She couldn't remember ever seeing someone look so uncomfortable, and, after another quick glance at the passenger asking the question, someone who seemed so determined to get an answer.

Perfect, she thought, as Maratse answered with an affirmative nod followed by his potentially inflammatory answer.

"*Iiji,*" Maratse said. "I hunt whales."

Chapter 21

Hong Wei relaxed in the white leather sofa tucked into a black and white bookshelf booth of the Hotel Kapok in Beijing. He ignored the scheduled reminder that flashed on his smartphone, choosing instead to finish his tea, to take one last look at Sun Tzu's thoughts on the use of spies, focusing on the *doomed spies*, and the art of doing things openly for the purpose of deception. It wasn't the first time he had done things in the open to elicit a response and achieve a hidden goal, but this time, reading Sun Tzu's words for perhaps the thousandth time, the word *doomed* bothered him, especially when he considered his use of Xiá, and the consequences of doing things openly.

A second flash on his smartphone screen, together with a muted vibration, prompted Hong Wei to leave the booth, to walk out of the exit, and take the short walk south to the Ministry of Public Security headquarters. The whole building, he knew, was full of spies. To use Sun Tzu's terminology, one might call them *surviving spies*, but Hong Wei knew he was twisting the old master's words. The spies within the Ministry of Public Security were not returning spies, bearing enemy secrets, rather they were *old* spies, having survived the transformation of the Chinese intelligence agency and resisted absorption into the Ministry of State Security. The sheer tenacity of political strong-arming of China's surviving spies impressed Hong Wei, but that same tenacity made him wary, particularly so when he saw the names of the men with whom he was scheduled to meet. While true friends within the industry of espionage were rare, it was Hong Wei's experience that they often fell behind, and the higher he progressed in the ranks, the less he could trust them.

I have no friends or allies here, he thought, as he entered the building. *None.*

The security checks were brief but thorough, as Hong Wei was processed into the building. The young woman escorting him to the meeting was suitably mute, resisting all of Hong Wei's attempts at light conversation, briefed, no doubt, on the dangers of letting even the slightest information slip to the spy from the Ministry of State Security. Hong Wei smiled at the woman's silence, taking note of her appearance, without her name, filing her potential for recruitment in his mind for a later date. She stopped outside a dark mahogany door and nodded for Hong Wei to enter.

The room was dark, lit only by a screen at the far end, revealing the podium at which Hong Wei assumed he was expected to stand. He shut the door behind him, noted the horseshoe seating arrangement of the tables and chairs arranged to face the podium and the screen, and then waited, standing at the podium, curious to see who would enter the room first.

Hong Wei suppressed a sigh when a side door opened, and an old man shuffled into the room. He recognised the captain of the *Xue Long*, guessed that he was now well into his eighties, but reminding himself that the old man's shuffling gait was purely a physical degeneration of his body, the captain's mind was still sharp.

Fuelled by pride and hate.

"Wén Hai," Hong Wei said, as the captain took a seat at the table on Hong Wei's right. "Such a pleasure to see you. How long has it been?"

"You know how long it has been."

"Ah, yes, twenty-one years."

"Almost," Wén Hai said.

"And your health?"

"Save your complements, Hong Wei." Wén Hai laughed. "Instead, ask yourself what I'm doing here. Focus on that."

"That's very charitable of you, Captain. Are you looking out for me?"

"Far from it," said a younger man, as he entered the room.

Hong Wei switched his focus from the old captain to the smartly dressed man, late thirties, with an ambitious stride and a confident smile. The man paused at the captain's chair, whispered something in his ear, drawing a smile, then proceeded to the table on Hong Wei's left – a classic seating strategy, forcing Hong Wei to turn his head back and forth when they spoke, as if he was watching tennis.

"I asked Wén Hai to attend this meeting," the young man said, "as he's the only person who has had the fortune – or misfortune – to have been with you on an operation. All the other operatives and agents, that I'm aware of, have conveniently disappeared. I assume that they are either under deep cover, involved in current operations of licensed skulduggery…" the man paused, as if waiting for Hong Wei to comment. "Or," he said, continuing as he sat down, "they are dead."

"Conveniently," Hong Wei said.

"What's that?"

"I was just confirming what you were thinking."

"You can read my thoughts?" the man leaned back in his seat, gesturing with open palms. "Incredible. And if true, this will be a rather quick hearing, as you already know what I am about to ask, and the answers I expect you to give."

Hong Wei smiled, enjoying the man's arrogance, wondering how to play him, but choosing to stall as he did so.

"I might be able to read your thoughts," Hong Wei said. "But I do not know your name."

"That's disappointing." The man returned Hong Wei's smile, and said, "You can call me Jié."

"Very well," Hong Wei said. "How should we proceed?"

"With a clarification, perhaps," Jié said. "You are inside MPS headquarters, which has no doubt alerted you to the fact that we are fully aware of your counterintelligence operation. As you know, counterintelligence still falls within our remit, and, to be frank, we are concerned that you have run this operation as far as you have, over quite some time, without approaching or consulting us." Jié held up his hand as Hong Wei started to respond. "This oversight calls your loyalty into question and has raised some concerns about your professionalism and your health."

"My health?"

"Your mental health. To be precise, the degree to which you have displayed nepotism in your recruitment of certain individuals. And..." Jié stopped Hong Wei with another brief wave of his hand. "A degree of narcissism, to which I have asked Wén Hai to be present, to comment on both counts."

"He was very sure of himself when I first met him," Wén Hai said, drawing a flat smile from Hong Wei. "He assumed he had seniority over me, my command, and thereby instructed my crew and officers to do his bidding."

"The mission..."

"Failed," Jié said.

Hong Wei turned his attention to Jié. "On some accounts, maybe. But the overriding goals..."

"Resulted in a death."

Hong Wei sighed, resisting the urge to look at his watch, to see just how long it had taken before Pān Tāo's name was brought up.

Not very long, he thought, only to frown as the captain mentioned another name.

~ 220 ~

"Zhāng Min," he said.

"Who?"

"You don't even remember?" Wén Hai shook his head. "Lieutenant Zhāng Min."

"Yes?"

"You ordered him to prevent the *Xue Long* from entering Tuktoyaktuk."

Hong Wei took a moment to think, as he remembered the young lieutenant.

"It was important that the *Xue Long* stayed out of the way…"

"She was already visible," Wén Hai said. "A few hours wouldn't have made any difference. But you impressed upon the young lieutenant, how important it was that he be the one to make a stand in the event that your orders were disobeyed."

"For the sake of the mission."

Wén Hai's voice crackled as spat his next words at Hong Wei, clenching his wrinkled fists as he said, "You told him to disobey his captain. You told him to commit mutiny."

Hong Wei waited for the old captain to recover, steeling himself when he didn't.

"I had him shot," Wén Hai said. "You forced me to kill a promising young lieutenant."

"Well," Jié said, as the captain glared at Hong Wei. "That's two Chinese deaths then." He stood and walked to the captain's table, offering the older man a glass of water, before helping him to his feet. "Thank you, Captain. I think I have enough for now." Jié waited for Wén Hai to shuffle to the door, closing it behind him, gently but firmly before turning back to Hong Wei. "You didn't know about the lieutenant, did you?"

"No."

"But neither does the captain need to know about Pān Tāo, at least no more than he might have read at the time." Jié gestured at the chair the captain had sat in. "Sit, please. I'll call for refreshments and have someone turn this damned projector off."

Hong Wei sat down at the table, curious about Jié's change of tack, analysing it, as he did the man's posture and tone of voice as he called for refreshments to be brought to the room.

"Ten minutes," he said, as he sat down at the middle table of the horseshoe, turning his chair towards Hong Wei, crossing his legs. Hong Wei noted the expensive socks, the newly buffed shoes, and the cut of the man's trouser hem. Everything was precise, as were his words. "Xiá," he said. "I know who she is."

"Pān Tāo's daughter."

"Yes." Jié nodded. "You took her in, following the death of her father."

"I kept an eye on her."

"And recruited her when she came of age."

"Yes."

"Hence the charges of nepotism."

"She's alert, has a quick mind. She learned fast, faster than many other promising candidates."

"I'm sure she did. In fact, I know so. I have seen her records."

Hong Wei shrugged, and said, "Then what is

the problem?"

Jié paused as an aide entered the room with a tray of tea. He smiled as the aide presented them with delicate cups and saucers, pouring a rich tea – lightly brewed – into both cups before leaving. Jié took a sip, before continuing.

"Given what I know about the events surrounding Pān Tāo's death, and the fact that Xiá was only recently made aware of your involvement, I would say you have timed the release of that information, and have fuelled the young lady's commitment, asking her to do many impossible tasks, and relying on her hunger for information to keep her suitably motivated."

"Xiá doesn't need motivation," Hong Wei said.

"No?" Jié placed his cup and saucer on the table. "Then why not tell her everything? Why not tell her the truth?"

Hong Wei settled in his chair, tilting his head to one side as he observed the young MPS officer.

"Are you questioning my methods?"

"Obviously," Jié said.

"Do you disapprove?"

"Beyond keeping us in the dark?" Jié shook his head. "Not particularly. From the little we have gleaned from the reports you have submitted; it seems that you are close to placing a mole inside the government of Greenland…"

"One who can be manipulated."

"We approve," Jié said, with a smile. "But you are playing a second game, drawing out the

Canadians, and potentially creating an incident."

"Potentially?" Hong Wei frowned. "You're not thinking of what happened in Copenhagen?"

"A minor scuffle, albeit with guns…"

"One gun," Hong Wei said. "Xiá used a knife."

"And arranged a car crash – particularly inventive, though a little demonstrative."

"She has flares of passion," Hong Wei said. "Her creativity…"

"Could be her undoing." Jié waved his hand. "But that's not what concerns us. We are concerned that in drawing out the Canadians, goading their operative, you risk drawing attention to an old case, the death of your partner, and the murder of Juatan Fortin."

"It won't get that far."

"We are not convinced."

"You want me to stop?" Hong Wei leaned forward, pinching his fingers. "We're this close. Everything is in play."

"It's too dangerous."

"Why?"

"You're using civilians."

"What?"

"The Greenlander. This *constable*. I've read earlier reports from Greenland. You've met him before."

"Yes."

"You tortured him, in front of the Canadian's agent."

"Konstabel Fenna Brongaard."

"Yes, her. Except she was working for the

Danes, at that time. But either way, you are pushing her to a limit that might be beyond your control."

"You've profiled her?"

"We've compiled a report. It's our opinion that you are going too far with this one."

"I am destabilising her investigation."

"To what end? To disguise the placing of a mole in the Greenland government?" Jié snorted. "This is too extravagant. It's unlike you to act like this. You've made it personal."

"She's too close. She'll expose our intentions, expose the mole." Hong Wei gauged the look on Jié's face, trying to anticipate the outcome of the meeting, perhaps even his future in intelligence.

"We can create a new mole."

"Not as flawed as this one. He's easily manipulated, and he holds a powerful position, with the potential to lead the government, if played correctly."

"We're not convinced."

"Then let me convince you."

Jié took a sip of tea, grimaced, then placed his hand around the pot. "Cold," he said. He leaned back, focused on Hong Wei.

Hong Wei waited.

"All right," Jié said, after a minute of silence. "How does this play out?"

"The Canadians – Konstabel Brongaard – took Malik."

"Yes?"

"She thinks she has turned him. She will have

promised to look after him, to clean his tracks, just as we did, but there she has the advantage of certain access unavailable to us."

"You're using her to erase Malik's trail."

"The public one, yes."

"And then?"

"Malik will feel free. Confident. He will come to me. I'll offer him plenty of money. But he will be careless, because he thinks Fenna will protect him." Hong Wei smiled. "She will prove that, bolstering him, making him overreach. But when I destroy Fenna, and the Canadian operation, he will be more vulnerable than ever before."

"And to do this…" Jié said. "You're going to use this constable – Maratse?"

"Yes."

"Because of his relationship to Fenna?"

"Because she feels guilty," Hong Wei said. "She will go out of her way to make amends. To protect him, and to seek forgiveness."

Hong Wei looked away. He closed his eyes, picturing a dusty Arctic road, a loaded pistol, and his hand wrapped around the grip, finger on the trigger.

"Hong Wei?"

"Yes?" Hong Wei said, looking up sharply.

"I just want to be sure, about that last thing you said, about *guilt* and *seeking forgiveness*."

"Yes?"

"We're talking about the Dane, Fenna Brongaard, aren't we?"

"Yes," Hong Wei said. "Absolutely."

"Okay," Jié said, as he stood. "Proceed."

Hong Wei remained in the room as Jié left. He resisted the urge to blink, knowing that if he did, he would see the moment he pulled the trigger, and the face of the man he killed in the Arctic, twenty-one years ago.

In the short time he had observed Jié, his face, his posture, his words, Hong Wei knew enough about the man to know how perceptive he was. They both knew that Hong Wei's last answer was a lie. But what bothered Hong Wei most, while he waited for word from Xiá, was why Jié had allowed the operation to continue. Clearly there were more pieces on the board, and more people moving them than even Hong Wei was aware.

Making it all the more important to succeed, he thought, bracing himself as he blinked, and the pistol fired.

Chapter 22

Maratse gestured for the man to sit, waiting until he did so, and then looked at Petra. They had been here before. As Greenlanders, it wasn't uncommon for people to question them about their lifestyle, traditions, and culture. But whales and the hunting of whales were difficult subjects to discuss. Always. He swapped looks with Petra, hoping he could convey as much with his eyes as she suggested he did with his grunts. She returned the look, then took a tiny step back, nodding as she did so, suggesting *I'm right here, always.* Maratse smiled, and then turned back to the passenger.

"What's your name?" he asked.

"William Bennett. And this is my wife, Phyllis."

Maratse smiled, before addressing William directly. "You have some questions?"

"Yes."

Maratse nodded. "Ask whatever you want, only I might struggle in between, with my English." Maratse waited for William's first question, bracing himself for an onslaught, while snatching glances at the Chinese scholar standing at the far end of the auditorium's stage, the one the captain introduced as Xiá.

"Why do you even need to hunt?" William asked. "Our last cruise was in the Arctic. You have supermarkets."

"In most of the towns and villages," Maratse said. "That's correct."

"So, you have all the food you need."

"Most of the year, but in the settlements, and even the more remote towns, the shelves start to empty around December and into the new year, before the supply ships can return, when ice and weather conditions allow."

"And that's why you hunt? Because you run out of food?" The creases on William's forehead suggested he was struggling with the concept. "You can just fly your food in."

"We could, when the weather is good. And then an apple costs a dollar or more. We can't grow fruit and only a few vegetables in Greenland, mostly down south. Traditionally, the minerals and vitamins we needed came from whales, along with the meat and fat. Hunting is a part of our history, now it's a part of our culture."

"But to kill an animal when you don't need to is just selfish and arrogant." William clenched his fists by his sides. "Such beautiful creatures."

"Hmm," Maratse said, as he took a moment's pause. The passengers in the auditorium fixed their gaze on him, as the lights seemed to grow stronger, hotter.

"Do you eat meat?" Petra said, taking a step forward.

"Piitalaat..." Maratse whispered.

"No, David, he just called us selfish and

arrogant."

"I'm sure it wasn't directed at you personally," the captain said, taking a step forward.

"Personal or not," Petra said. "I'd like to hear if William eats meat."

"Yes, I do," he said.

"From the supermarket?"

"From the store, that's right."

"What part?"

"Of the store?" William shrugged. "The meat section." He turned around to look at the passengers behind him, drawing a few smiles from those passengers who were not fixed on Petra and Maratse.

"I meant, what part of the animal," Petra said.

"A steak," William said, turning to look at her.

"From a cow?"

"Obviously."

More soft laughter.

"And if I had a picture of it," Petra said. "Could you point to the part of the cow where the meat for your steak came from?"

"Well…"

"And if I asked you what the cow had fed on, could you tell me?"

"Grass and grain… feedstuffs from the farmer," William said.

"What's on the grass?"

"What?"

"Fertiliser? What chemicals?" Petra paused, but not long enough for William to answer.

"What's in the *feedstuffs*? Do you know?"

"Of course not…"

"Piitalaat," Maratse said, softly.

"He called us arrogant, David. But what's more arrogant than not knowing where your food came from, or how it gets there, how it's killed, gutted, skinned…"

"Piitalaat." Maratse took her hand, squeezing it, just briefly, before she excused herself, walking, then running out of the auditorium.

William waited until she was gone, and then said, "I fail to see the comparison. My meat is bred to be eaten. Your whales are free creatures, wild. They should be protected and preserved, not shot by people who can afford to buy meat from the store."

"But that's the difference," Maratse said. "One of the differences, at least. Not everyone in Greenland can afford to buy meat from the store, not without help. When the hunter catches a whale, the family – several families – eat for a week, longer even. The dogs have food. The bones and the *soqqaq*…" Maratse paused, then made a filter with his fingers.

"Baleen," said one of the passengers.

"*Qujanaq*," Maratse said, drawing a smile, even as he glanced at the door, forcing himself not to go after Petra, not without finishing the discussion.

"The baleen and other parts of the whale can be made into jewellery, bringing in more money. But when the whales don't come, then the hunter doesn't eat. His children get thin, and the dogs even thinner. Maybe the ice doesn't come, and the winter seas are more dangerous, less predictable. Hunting a whale to feed his family is not an easy task for the hunter."

"You're romanticising it," William said. "It doesn't change anything."

"This is not about love," Maratse said, frowning as he realised he had missed something. "It's about living in and being a part of the environment. The hunter's children know what part of the whale they are eating." Maratse looked at the door, then stepped off the stage. "I have to go," he said, ignoring any further comments from the passenger.

Maratse jogged up the centre aisle, oblivious to the look Xiá cast at him, or William's accusation that Maratse and his *friend* had insulted him. He found Petra on the deck, hands pressed to the thick metal railings, wind blowing her hair across her face. Maratse called out her name, then approached, slowly, pressing his hand on hers as he reached the railing.

"I don't know why I reacted that way," Petra said. "Maybe I'm not as *healed* as I thought I was? I don't know."

Maratse stepped closer. Petra plucked at his fingers as she rested her head on his shoulder.

"But when he called you selfish…"

"It doesn't matter…"

"But it does," she said, turning her face towards him. "He has no idea who you are, what you've done, for so many people… and for me. How dare he?"

"It's not his fault," Maratse said. "He doesn't know us, what we've been through."

"But he called you arrogant."

"*Iiji*." Maratse shrugged. "It's okay."

"It's *not* okay." Petra sniffed back a stream of tears. "I didn't think it would be like this. I didn't think we would have to face something like that."

"You're a police sergeant," Maratse said. "You've faced a lot worse."

"This is different," she said. "You know it is. But maybe I've changed? Maybe I can't go back to work? What if I can't do my job? What if I'm broken?"

Maratse pulled her close, looking for the words, something to soothe her. If anything, even though he would never wish it, it was easier to help Petra when she was too traumatised to think. There was no room for self-doubt when she didn't have the strength to think. Maratse couldn't *just* hold her anymore, it wasn't enough to be by her side, to be physically present, now Petra needed words as much as she needed love, and on the deck of the *Admiral Chichagov* Maratse worried, suddenly, if he even knew the right words to help her.

"We can go home," he said, quietly. "We're still in port. We can leave."

"No," Petra said, straightening up. She pulled her head from Maratse's shoulder, corralled her windswept hair with her fingers, then forced a smile on her face. "We're here. I want to see the ice, to see Antarctica. Maybe we'll skip dinner, but breakfast, once we're underway, I'll be better." She squeezed Maratse's hand. "I can do this."

"We'll do it together."

"Sure," she said. "Although, don't ever pretend your English isn't good enough." She pointed in the direction of the auditorium. "I heard you in there. Everybody did. You're getting better."

"Hmm," Maratse said.

Petra rewarded him with a soft thump on his arm and kiss on his cheek.

"Come on," she said. "Let's find our cabin. We can do damage maintenance in the morning."

The *Admiral Chichagov* slipped away from the dock in the early hours of the morning, bathed in a prolonged summer light as the captain nosed the icebreaker's bow towards *Drake Passage*, the stretch of water between Cape Horn and the South Shetland Islands. Petra had told Maratse that it was named after Sir Francis Drake, the Englishman who circumnavigated the world centuries earlier, reading aloud from one of her many brochures. Maratse filtered the information, remembering only that *Drake Passage* allowed for better crossings even in poor conditions, with more room for manoeuvring when wind and ice threatened vessels sailing to Antarctica.

He spent an hour on the deck as the ship left the port of Ushuaia. He left Petra tucked up in her bunk, adding his blanket to hers before leaving the cabin. If he still smoked, this would have been the time to do it, as the wind freshened, and he felt the intoxicating pull of the sea. There was ice in the distance, both familiar and reassuring. Maratse leaned into the railing, curious at the thrum of the engines rumbling through the deck, through the soles of his boots, and vibrating gently through his body. He heard someone walk along the deck, and saw the Chinese woman pause at the door leading inside to the cabins. She held his gaze when he looked at her. Maratse experienced that same feeling he had had when he first saw her in the auditorium, that there was something familiar about her.

But not the glasses, he thought, as he waved, curious to see if she would join him.

Xiá stared at him for a few more seconds then disappeared through the door without another look.

"Hmm," Maratse said. He checked his watch, then decided he would return to the cabin, that there would be more sea ahead of them, and that Petra needed him.

Piitalaat.

Maratse had stopped counting the number of times he had needed her. They were together now. They could *need* each other as much as they wanted, for the rest of their lives. The thought brought a smile to his lips, even as the confusion of being *together* and the *rest of their lives* was still something he had yet to fully comprehend.

It might be love, he thought. It was, perhaps, the best explanation.

Maratse headed for the door, only to slow as he heard it open. He half-expected to see Xiá step out onto the deck. A change of heart, perhaps, and another chance for Maratse to try and remember where he had seen her before. But the woman who stepped through the door was older – a passenger who couldn't sleep, or was curious about the ship's sudden movement.

"It's you," the woman said, as Maratse stopped at the door.

"Phyllis?" he said.

"That's right. And of course, I know your name. William has been cursing you all night, taking off like that, running after that rude woman."

"Piitalaat," Maratse said.

"What?"

"It's her name."

"I don't care," Phyllis said. "I don't even want to know. I tried convincing William that we could just leave, that he'd been insulted, that we had grounds for a refund – a *full* refund, mind you."

"Hmm…"

Maratse wished Petra was with him, that *anyone* was with him, or even that he was dealing with a drunk – several drunks – on a Friday night in a remote Greenlandic town, anything but trying to deal with a *Phyllis* on the deck of an icebreaker nosing into *Drake Passage*. It was almost absurd, after all he had been through, all he *and* Petra – mostly Petra – had been subjected to, that an angry passenger's wife could disarm him so easily.

"Is that all you've got to say?"

"*Iiji*," Maratse said, with a nod of the head. Really, he *had* nothing more, not knowing where to begin, where he was going, only that he wished he was back in his cabin right there and then, not duelling with Phyllis, something she seemed particularly capable of.

Xiá rescued him, turning his head as she opened a door behind Phyllis – too fast for Phyllis to see her, but enough to realise somebody was behind her.

"What's that?" she asked, as Maratse excused himself, brushing past her, no longer concerned about who Xiá was, only that she had just saved him.

Chapter 23

Petra was the first to wake, peeling back the covers and slipping out of the bunk. She had tugged Maratse into the tiny bed once he returned to the cabin, pressing him against the bulkhead as she curled into his body. They made the best use of the available space, ignoring the top bunk, preferring, and needing the touch of each other's bodies. As Petra pulled on her clothes the knocking on the door grew louder, stirring Maratse, and compelling Petra to return to the bunk, dipping her head to kiss his nose, then pulling the blankets over him.

"I'll answer it," she said, as she picked her way around their boots to the cabin door.

"Sorry about this," the captain said, peering around Petra as she searched the room. "Is David with you?"

"I'm here," Maratse said, lifting his arm from under the blanket and waving.

"Could you get dressed?"

"*Iiji.*"

"And meet me – both of you – in my quarters." Elina nodded at the crewman waiting by the door. "This is Luukas. He'll escort you."

"He'll *escort* us?" Petra said, with a glance at Luukas. He avoided her eyes with a dip of his head, drawing more questions into Petra's frown, and an evasive retreat from the captain as she backed away from the door.

"I'll explain when you come up."

Petra formulated another question, but the captain was gone, tramping along the narrow corridor and up the stairs before Petra could ask it. Petra looked at Luukas, waited for a response, then stepped back inside the cabin and closed the door when he refused to look at her.

"This is weird," she said, as Maratse pulled on his jeans.

"We'll find out soon enough," he said.

"Yes, but we've got an escort."

"Which is what?"

"Like a guard, or something."

"Hmm."

"David," Petra said, as she finished dressing. "Did anything happen last night?"

"After the auditorium?"

"Yes."

Maratse pulled on a t-shirt, shaking his head as he pushed it through the hole. "I went for a walk when we pulled away from the dock."

"And nothing happened?"

"I talked to William's wife." Maratse slumped in the chair to pull on his socks and boots. "She wasn't very pleasant."

"Neither was her husband."

Maratse shrugged and then brushed his teeth, glancing at Petra in the mirror as the frown in her forehead deepened.

"I don't like it," she said. "It doesn't feel

right."

"Then let's find out," Maratse said.

He thumbed at her frown, kissed her cheek, then took her hand, leading Petra out of the cabin. Luukas fell in behind them, following them along the corridor and up the stairs, three flights, to the bridge. He squeezed past Maratse and Petra to knock on the captain's door, standing back against the bulkhead to let them through as the captain called for them to enter. Elina gestured at a small table by the window and waited for Maratse and Petra to sit. She nodded for Luukas to close the cabin door before joining them at the table.

"There's been an incident," she said, looking at Petra first, and then Maratse. "It's delicate, and, quite frankly, alarming."

"What is?" Petra said.

"A man is dead, and the circumstances are, to be blunt, suspicious."

"Who?" Petra took Maratse's hand, squeezing it beneath the table.

"William Bennett," Elina said. "The same passenger David and you had an argument with, in the auditorium last night."

"Dead?" Maratse said, frowning as he tried to recall the man's age, if he had any visible health issues.

"His wife, Phyllis, found him flat on his back, collapsed, when she returned to her cabin." Elina poured three glasses of water from the jug on the table. "This was early this morning. She was on deck when we left the dock." Elina paused to look up. "She remembers seeing you, David, on the deck. She spoke to you."

"*Iiji*," Maratse said. "I remember."

"After that, perhaps five minutes later, she returned to her cabin to find her husband on the floor. She had to push the door open, pushing back his feet so that she could get in."

"And why are we here?" Petra asked.

"That's where it gets complicated. And then," Elina said, following a deep breath, "even more complicated."

"How?"

"Phyllis was in shock when we were alerted. The doctor, Madhu Rao, was called. He pronounced William dead, and we moved the body to sickbay. He's there now, pending the next move, which will be freezing the body before returning to port."

"We're turning around?"

"We were," Elina said. "Until we got the news – the complications." She took a sip of water, gestured for Maratse and Petra to take their glasses, and then continued. "The *Admiral Chichagov* is registered to a company in Ukraine. This means, in practice, that on a ship in international waters, the laws of the country in which the ship is registered apply. If it had happened at the dock while still in port, then the laws of Argentina would apply, as far as I know."

"But Ukraine..." Petra said.

"No," Elina said. "That's where it gets complicated. We've known for a while that the ship's owners were keen to sell. It's not unheard of for a ship to change hands while at sea. Unusual in this line of work, but ships are meant to be on the move. If a company could only sell a ship when it was docked..." Elina shrugged. "It's impractical."

"What are you not telling us?" Petra asked.

"It's the complication," Elina said. "The new owners are Chinese."

"And?"

"They don't want us to return to Ushuaia. We've been ordered to sail within helicopter range and send our helicopter back to the mainland to pick up a Chinese investigator."

"To investigate William's death?"

"Yes."

"Because it's suspicious?"

Elina nodded, and then added, with a glance at Maratse, "Because David was seen in the corridor near the Bennetts' cabin."

"David was?" Petra said, turning to look at Maratse.

"I was coming back to our cabin," he said.

"Which is probably true..."

"*Probably*?" Petra twisted in her chair to look at the captain. "What are you saying?"

"I'm just saying that Phyllis reported seeing Maratse on deck, and then he was seen outside William's cabin."

"By whom?"

"I'm not at liberty to say," Elina said. "But two people reported seeing David near William's cabin shortly before he was found dead. The doctor confirms that William's body was still warm when he arrived. He estimates his death to be within an hour of David being in the corridor."

"An hour?"

"His best guess."

Maratse reached for the glass of water and took a sip as Petra fired questions at the captain. "Piitalaat," he said, quietly, then louder, taking her hand. "It's okay, Piitalaat."

"It's not *okay*, David. She's accusing you of murder."

"I'm not accusing David of anything, but I have been ordered to take the necessary steps as required by the investigator."

"The Chinese investigator?"

"That's right, according to the international law of the sea."

"But David and I were together."

"Later, yes." Elina shrugged, as if to suggest it was out of her hands.

"But just being seen…"

"Together with the altercation in the auditorium…"

"*Altercation*?" Petra laughed. "He was goading David. He was insulting us. I was the one who stormed out of the auditorium."

"But David was seen around the time of William Bennett's death."

"By the Chinese woman," Maratse said, picturing Xiá clearly, as she rescued him from more harsh words from the dead man's wife.

"Xiá," Elina said. "Now that you've identified her, I may as well tell you that it was Xiá who reported seeing you. She's quite shaken up, actually. Refuses to come out of her cabin until the investigator arrives."

"And when is that?" Petra asked.

"This time tomorrow, we think." Elina looked at David. "I'm going to have to ask you to stay in your cabin until the investigator gets here."

"For twenty-four hours?" Petra said.

"Yes."

"Okay." Petra stood, tugging Maratse to his feet. "And what about me?"

"You have not been named in connection with William Bennett's death."

"But will you give me twenty-four hours to look into it?"

"What?"

"I'm a sergeant with the Greenlandic police, part of the Danish police. You can contact them if you like, but seeing as a Greenlandic national is being accused of murder, it makes sense that a Greenlandic police officer is accorded some professional courtesy to investigate the crime for which he is accused."

"No one is accusing…"

Petra continued. "Provided that I don't tamper with any evidence, there's very little harm that can be done to the investigation."

"I don't know," Elina said, looking from Maratse to Petra.

"Piitalaat," Maratse whispered.

Petra ignored him.

"Captain?" she said.

"I suppose…"

"Don't suppose," Petra said. "You have to act. You owe it to the travel company."

"What?"

"*Sirius Cruises*. The ship is chartered by them. You captain the ship, but the owners don't pay you, the company does. What will the company say when they discover a passenger has died?"

"We haven't informed them."

"No?" Petra tugged her smartphone from her pocket. She turned the screen towards Elina. "See the Wi-Fi icon? Networks are available. That's the ship's Wi-Fi. Internet is expensive at sea, but if you haven't turned it off, that means everyone has the means to connect. You've got thirty guests, and a similar number of crew. Are you willing to bet that the company knows nothing about William Bennett's death?"

"Why would they…"

"Post about a death on their cruise on social media?" Petra bit back a laugh. "Do you even have to ask?"

"Piitalaat," David said. "We should just wait."

Petra slid her smartphone into her pocket, then turned slowly towards Maratse. She lowered her voice, and said, "You are the most patient man I have ever met. And I know you can sit for twenty-four hours…"

"Because I didn't do anything."

"We both know that. But don't make me sit with you. Let me protect you, just like you protect me. Let me do my job."

"You're not…"

"Ready?" Petra bit her bottom lip and nodded. "I didn't think I was. But now…" Petra took Maratse's hands. "Sometimes you need a shove in the right direction." She dipped her head to nod at the captain. "I just got one."

"Okay," Elina said. "I'll give you the twenty-four hours. I guess it's the least I can do."

Petra nodded. "Thank you."

"But David has to stay in his cabin. He might be a constable…"

"Retired," Maratse said.

"Right, but just Petra. She asks the questions. You stay in your cabin." Elina gestured at the door. "Luukas will be right outside. Those are the investigator's instructions."

Elina stood and walked to the door, an apology formed on her lips as Petra led Maratse out of the captain's quarters, but one look at Petra suggested that the time for apologies was past.

"I'll start in sickbay," Petra said, over her shoulder, as they descended the stairs to the lower decks.

They paused at their cabin, as Maratse entered his enforced period of confinement.

"You'll be okay?" Petra asked.

Maratse picked up a thick paperback from the small desk screwed into the bulkhead opposite the bunks.

"I'll be fine."

"You're not worried?"

"I didn't do anything, Piitalaat."

"I know, but…"

"It's going to be okay."

"You say that, as if you're convinced. How can you know?"

"Because," Maratse said, closing the gap between them, "after all we've been through, we're still alive, still strong, maybe stronger. This is a formality. I was in the wrong place at the right time. Nothing more than that."

Petra took Maratse's hand. "I heard Karl say once that he thought trouble followed you around Greenland."

"He has said that."

Petra wrinkled her nose as she gave Maratse one of her *there-could-be-some-truth-to-that* looks. At least, that was what she said, when Maratse didn't react.

"You can pack all of that into a look?"

Petra pressed her lips to Maratse's ear, and said, "You're not the only one with communication skills."

"What skills?"

"*Hmm,*" Petra said, smiling as she pulled away. "I'll fix this," she said. "It's nothing."

Maratse lifted his book. "I'll be fine."

"I know you will. Besides," Petra said, as she opened the door. "I know where to find you. Stay out of trouble."

The door clicked as it closed, leaving Maratse alone in the tiny cabin. He took a moment to look around him, as a feeling of déjà vu pressed upon him. The distance between the walls, and from floor to ceiling, reminded Maratse of his cell in Vestsyssel Prison. He preferred not to think of it as a cell, choosing instead to collapse on the bunk and open his book. He skipped the introduction, and jumped straight into the first chapter, something about space tearing open around an attack cruiser. But in the darkness of space, shimmering in the light of ancient stars, Maratse couldn't escape the thought that there was a face staring back at him, and that face belonged to the woman called Xiá.

Chapter 24

Qitu felt the vibration of moving furniture in the corridor as soon as he left the elevator, ribbing through the thin soles of his slim shoes as he walked to Kaama and Svea's rented office space. The air was still damp but tinged with the smell of new paint tickling Qitu's nose as he stepped through the open door and into the office. Kaama saw him first, shaking her head as he walked deeper into the room. She pointed at the wall, then called out to Svea to leave the paint for a moment.

"It's all gone," she said, as Qitu walked up to the empty wall. "They even took the pins and post-its."

"Hard drives and computers too," Svea said, stepping into Qitu's line of sight. "We were getting dinner, eating out. When we came back the neighbour said she heard noises in our apartment. She went upstairs and knocked, but she said we didn't answer."

"Because we weren't there."

Svea nodded, adding, "But she said she could hear us, and the music. She wanted us to turn it down."

"Music?" Qitu asked.

"I don't know," Kaama said. "Maybe to hide

the sounds of the robbery."

"Or to send a message," Svea said.

Kaama wagged a slim finger. "Don't start that again, babe."

"Why not? It makes sense. They *wanted* us to know they were taking everything. And they wanted us to come right here and find that everything was gone." Svea turned back to the paint pots, slapping the stirring stick into the open pot. "There's nothing more we can do but paint."

"Everything is gone?" Qitu asked.

"Yep," Kaama said. "That's eight month's work. I mean, we could write the article, but we can't prove anything, can't confirm any sources. And if they can do *this*, then they can make sure the sources don't talk." She cupped her hands under her belly, drawing concerned looks from Svea. "I'm okay," Kaama said. "I just need to sit down."

She continued talking as Qitu moved closer to the wall, away from her lips, tracing the outlines of articles, photographs, and clippings. All gone. He felt the vibration of a new text message on his phone and checked it. Qitu frowned as he turned to look at the office door.

"What is it?" Svea asked.

"A message," he said.

"And?"

Qitu turned the screen towards Svea and waited as she read it aloud.

"*Tell your friends to leave.*" Svea looked at Qitu, waiting for a response.

"I don't know who sent it," he said. "Number

withheld."

"And they want us to leave?"

Qitu turned to Kaama. "It's probably related to this," he said, gesturing at the empty wall behind him.

"But they texted you."

"*Aap.*" Qitu shrugged. "I don't know anymore than you."

"But you would tell us if you did?" Svea held the stirring stick in her hand, paint dripping on the carpet as she pointed the end at Qitu. "Right?"

"Svea," Kaama said. "He's a friend."

"A friend who just got a text telling us to leave…"

"We go," Kaama said, pushing herself to her feet.

"Just like that?"

"Qitu will tell us what it's about. Won't you?"

Qitu nodded. "Of course."

"See?" Kaama took the stick from Svea's hand and slid it back into the pot. "Come on. The sooner we go, the sooner we'll know. Right?"

Svea took a last look at Qitu, staring at him with barely concealed distrust, enough for both her and Kaama. She wiped a dribble of paint from her fingers on a rag, then followed Kaama out of the office.

Qitu sat in Kaama's chair and stared at his phone, wondering if he should text a reply, or just wait. If they knew where he was, he reasoned, then they would also know he was alone. Qitu slipped his phone into his pocket and waited.

Even with perfect hearing, Qitu would have struggled to hear the footsteps in the carpeted corridor. Nor did he feel the vibration of the lift returning, after Kaama and Svea had taken it up to the ground floor. But he did sense the arrival of someone and turned to the door as a young woman walked into the office. She walked slowly but purposefully towards him, waiting until she was close, until she could see he was focused on her face, on her lips, before talking.

"You read lips?" she said.

"*Aap.*"

"My name is Fenna." She stepped to the wall and placed her hand in the space that had been a blank placeholder, just below the one Qitu had filled with a picture of Malik Uutaaq. "This," Fenna said, "was me."

Qitu lifted his head, following her movements as she fetched a chair from the side of the office and returned, placing it in front of him before sitting down.

"You took all their work?"

"Yes."

"You stole their computers and external drives."

"Yes," Fenna said. "Everything."

"Because they were on to something?"

"Closer than they thought." Fenna nodded. "Too close, considering what's going on."

"What *is* going on?"

"Plenty, and nothing at all."

Fenna pointed at Qitu's pocket, holding out her hand until Qitu placed his phone in her palm.

He watched as she removed the back of the phone, the battery and the SIM card. Fenna turned around to place everything on the table behind her.

"Anything else?" she asked, smiling as Qitu shook his head. "Okay then. We can talk."

Qitu waited, wondering who should start, and what he would do with the information once he was given it, if he could trust it, if he could trust her.

"Who are you?" he asked.

"Fenna Brongaard. I work with Canadian intelligence."

"But you're Danish."

Fenna shrugged. "It's a long story."

Qitu glanced at the bare wall, and said, "You were in Nuuk."

"Yes."

"You met him, the Chinese man."

"Yes."

"So, you also know Constable Maratse."

"I do," Fenna said. A sad smile creased her lips, drawing a curious look from Qitu. "He helped me, and then, when he needed me most, I failed him." Fenna brushed an imaginary patch of dirt from the knees of her jeans, silent for a moment, as Qitu watched her. "Do you know him?" she asked, looking up.

"*Aap.*"

"And, is he... well?"

"He's well," Qitu said.

"And he has a happy life – comfortable? No pain?"

Qitu paused for a breath. "Turbulent," he said. "Different kinds of pain. But," he said, as Fenna paled, "he's happy. He has a friend. They are good together."

"A woman?"

"*Aap.*"

"I'm pleased," Fenna said. Her eyes shone in such a way that Qitu believed her. Fenna looked away for a second, back to the empty wall, before continuing. "This isn't about Maratse," she said. "It's about the Chinese man: Hong Wei."

Qitu resisted the urge to reach for his notebook and pen in his satchel. He saw Fenna's gaze switch to his hands, as if she saw the twitch of his fingers, and then, with a quiet understanding – no notes, no record – they looked at each other. Qitu nodded that he was ready.

"What do you know about Malik Uutaaq?" Fenna said. "His picture was on the wall."

"He's a minister."

"Yes. And how would you describe him?"

"Troubled," Qitu said, after a pause. "He gets into a lot of trouble. It's like he's driving a train, fast, the tracks are laid out in front of him, a good distance, but either he doesn't see the direction they are leading him, or he doesn't care."

"He doesn't think?"

"It's not that," Qitu said. "He's too impulsive to think. He's a middle-aged man who hasn't matured enough to understand he's experiencing a mid-life crisis." Qitu shook his head as he laughed. "That's a journalist's purple prose for you."

"No," Fenna said. "It makes sense. I get the feeling he could be very capable, dangerous even, if he applied himself."

"His campaign managers were the dangerous ones – very capable. And dead."

"More than one?"

"*Aap*," Qitu said, counting off on his finger and thumb. "Aarni Aviki and Tipaaqu Jeremiassen. Both murdered. Although, Aarni's death was made to look like suicide, but there was plenty of evidence of torture."

"In Greenland?"

"*Aap*."

Qitu watched Fenna's face, curious at the way her eyes seemed to flicker as she processed the information. He wondered if she was aware of it.

"Malik is under investigation," Fenna said, switching her gaze back to Qitu. "He was in custody before a lawyer arranged for his release."

Fenna let the thought hang in the air between them as she stood, walked to the table with the kettle and mugs to make tea. Qitu watched as she searched among the teabags for a particular flavour. He forced himself to look away, at least for a second, before he got caught up in her precise movements – more processing, perhaps – as he realised *she* was the missing link, that she could be a source. Kaama and Svea's work, even his own work, need not be wasted. She could confirm everything.

Except, she won't, he thought, as Fenna returned with two mugs of tea – green tea, with lemon.

"I need to meet with the officer who is handling Malik's case," Fenna said. "Do you know who it is?"

"*Aap.*"

"And you can arrange a meeting?"

"Yes. Is it about Malik?"

"Yes," Fenna said, as she tugged on the string of her teabag. She said nothing for a long minute, as she focused on the teabag, removing it, squeezing it against the inside of the mug, and then placing it on the table. "I need to put Malik in play," she said. "I need the police officer…"

"Ada Valkyrien," Qitu said, drawing a nod from Fenna.

"I need her to keep tabs on him here, in Copenhagen."

"And when he returns to Greenland?"

Fenna smiled. "Qitu," she said. "You know what I'm going to ask you."

"I'm not a spy."

"No, you're something far worse, far more dangerous."

"A journalist…"

"Who runs a small, independently financed media group, focused on a few interesting cases at a time." Fenna paused for a sip of tea. "How am I doing?"

"That depends," Qitu said. "On what you're willing to give me in return."

Fenna curled her hand around her mug and rested it on her knee. "So," she said. "We're negotiating."

"*Aap.*"

"You don't want money."

Qitu shook his head, and then looked, pointedly, at the empty wall.

"You want a source?" Fenna laughed. "Right. That could be difficult."

"So is keeping tabs on Malik."

Fenna stood and walked the short distance to the wall, pointing at the outlines of the different pictures – hers and Hong Wei's, Qitu noted. Without knowing the extent of her operation, Qitu could only guess at its significance, what it meant for him, for Malik, and for Greenland.

"Bigger than that," Fenna said, as she looked at Qitu. "You're wondering how deep this goes, how wide the reach of it all. Let's just say it goes as far back as your friends…"

"Kaama and Svea."

"Yes," Fenna said. "They were right to think it has something to do with the *Xue Long* back in 1999, but not for the reasons they think, at least not all of them. I'm just a pawn in this game, Qitu. But I'm getting closer to getting out. If you help me get him," she said, tapping the wall where the blank paper reserved for Hong Wei used to be, "then, once I'm out, I'll be your source – anonymous, of course."

"Of course."

Qitu took a sip of tea – cold, as expected.

Who cares about the tea, he thought. *I have a source.*

"I'll contact Sergeant Valkyrien," he said.

"And Malik? What about him?"

"I'll keep an eye on Malik."

Fenna pointed at small pile of phone parts on the table. "I'll text you with another number. Once you have arranged the meeting, contact me."

"And until then?"

Fenna smiled. "Enjoy your tea, Qitu."

Chapter 25

The sickbay of the *Admiral Chichagov* was larger than some clinics in Greenland, and better equipped. Petra waited at the entrance as the doctor wiped the crumbs of his sandwich from his lips and extended his hand to greet her.

"Madhu Rao," he said. "Ship's doctor, for my sins."

"You eat here?" Petra asked, as she studied the short but portly man. His skin was darker than hers, but only slightly, and the hair on his head was thinner than Maratse's wispy beard. Petra caught herself making the comparison, curious that everything had to do with Maratse at the moment, and that she needed to focus if she was going to help him.

"I spend a lot of time here," Madhu said. He lowered his voice to a conspiratorial whisper. "I don't like ice."

"What?"

"Ice," he said. "It bothers me. So much power in it." Madhu pointed at the shelf above his desk. The spines of the books faced outwards, tethered by a length of black bungee holding them in place in the event of bad weather. "These are my favourites." Madhu stuffed the last of his sandwich into the pocket of his examination gown as he skirted around Petra. He lifted the bungee to release a book, pressing it into Petra's hands. "The best of the bunch," he said. "Roland Huntford's biography of Shackleton. His ship, *Endurance*, was crushed by pack ice."

Petra leafed through the pages of the book, noting the various bookmarks – tickets and boarding passes – together with copious notes scrawled in the margins of many of the pages.

"But you're frightened of the ice," she said.

"Yes." Madhu took the book from Petra's hands and placed it back on the shelf.

"But you read about ships getting crushed in the ice."

"It's my passion."

Petra waited for Madhu to make the connection, only to realise he wasn't about to, as if there was no connection to be made. She wondered if his medical skills suffered the same detachment, which brought her back to the investigation.

"I'm a sergeant with the Greenland police," she said.

"I've been briefed."

"So you know I have twenty-four hours to figure out what happened to passenger William Bennett."

"Yes," Madhu said. "He's right through here."

Madhu led Petra through to a second room, the same width but twice the length of the first. William's body was on one of two gurneys bolted to the floor. Again, Petra was impressed by the size of the sickbay and the sophistication, especially considering the age of the icebreaker.

Madhu caught her eye, and said, "You haven't been in a ship's sickbay, have you?"

"Not recently," Petra said.

"We can cope with pretty much anything, and as we have a lot of older passengers, we have plenty of adrenaline and two heart massage machines."

"Adrenaline?"

"To stab in the heart," Madhu said. "In the event of cardiac arrest. I read that in Greenland, in the more remote areas, you only have a couple of doses of adrenaline, enough for two people." Madhu smiled. "Another passion – polar medicine." He paused before adding, "I guess that's *my* profession, too. But, anyway, if the cruise ships that visit Greenland didn't carry adrenaline, then there's no way the small villages and settlements could cope with tourists having heart attacks during a visit."

"No," Petra said. She walked over to William's body. "Are you telling me he died of a heart attack?"

"Respiratory failure," Madhu said. "Caused by paralysis."

"He was paralysed?"

"Yes." Madhu lifted the sheet covering William's head. "See the blue colouring in his lips?"

"Yes."

"Hypoxia, at the tissue level, seen in heart attack victims, but here, he simply stopped

~ 261 ~

breathing."

"Because he was paralysed?" Petra waited for Madhu to confirm, and then asked, "How?"

"That's what I'm looking into. But…"

"You have a theory?"

"A working theory," Madhu said. "Without a proper lab, I can only work with what I can see, together with the patient's history." Madhu covered William's head with the sheet. "Phyllis, the victim's wife, says he had recently been diagnosed with early stages of cancer – lymphatic. This affects his immune system and makes him more susceptible to toxins."

"What kind of toxins?"

"This is where it gets interesting," Madhu said. "If you look into paralytic toxins…"

Madhu stopped talking at a knock on the door leading into the outer room of the sickbay.

"You wanted to talk to me?" Xiá said, stepping into the room.

"Yes," Petra said. "But if it could wait…"

Xiá shook her head. "It can't wait. I'm so sorry. I have to give a lecture. The captain wants things to go as programmed – she ordered me out of my cabin – to give the passengers a diversion, so they don't think of…" Xiá lifted her hand and pointed at William's body.

"We can continue later," Madhu said.

Petra checked the time on her smartphone, nodded once, thanking the doctor before following Xiá through the sickbay and onto the open deck.

The breeze blowing north from the icy

continent startled Petra with thoughts of home, pinching the skin of her cheeks, and bringing a glow to her face. Xiá, she noticed, shivered in the wind, but as the Chinese scholar had chosen to talk on the deck, Petra made no move to go back inside.

"You wanted to talk to me?" Xiá said, hugging her arms to her chest.

"About last night," Petra said. "Actually, it was earlier this morning."

"When I saw your friend."

"Yes."

"He was in the corridor," Xiá said. "Close to Mr. William's cabin."

"And you're sure?"

"I'm sure. Do you think I'm lying?"

The polar light lit Xiá's face, reflecting in her glasses but without disguising the sharp, pointed look in her eyes. Petra bit back a quick reply as Xiá's timid polar scholar image crumbled a little, revealing someone else, someone far more dangerous beneath.

Unless, that's just what I want to see?

Thoughts of Maratse waiting in their cabin, a guard at the door, future unknown, urged Petra on, curious as to how far she could push Xiá, and how far she dared.

"Yes," Petra said, returning Xiá's look. "I do."

"I said I was there. He saw me – Mr. Maratse." Xiá took a step closer to Petra, dropping her hands to her sides as she closed the gap. "Maybe you need to ask what he was doing walking the decks so early in the morning?"

"I don't need to."

"No?" Xiá laughed. "Now who's lying? You're lying to yourself, trying to hide the fact that you both had an argument with the passenger, you both got angry. In fact, you," Xiá said, pressing a small finger into Petra's chest. "You were most upset. Maybe you killed the man, and Mr. Maratse was in the corridor looking for you, or maybe…" Xiá's eyes bulged as if she had suddenly made a breakthrough discovery. "Yes, that's it." Her eyes darted to Petra's face, and she took a step back, then another, shrinking to the wall, further and further from Petra as she reached for the door. "That's what happened. He was covering for you. You did it. Of course you did. He's not the killer. Mr. Maratse didn't kill anyone. You did."

"Xiá," Petra said, with a slow shake of her head. "You have a wonderful imagination."

"This is not imagination." Xiá reached for the door handle. "This is fact. Or it could be. With more evidence. But, when the investigator comes, I'll tell them just what you said, and what I think you did. Then you will both be under investigation, and the ship, the passengers, we will all be so much safer, with you and Mr. Maratse – the murdering Greenlanders. Locked up. Case closed. So much safer."

"You can't possibly think that," Petra said. She reached out for the door as Xiá opened it.

"I don't think," Xiá said, tapping the side of her head. "I know."

And then, with more strength than her body suggested she possessed, Xiá yanked the door fully open and stepped inside the ship. She left Petra holding the door, one foot inside the ship, the other on the deck, and a deep frown on her forehead as she tried to process what had happened. Whereas Xiá's eyes suggested a tough interior to the polar scholar, her actions and words reminded Petra more of a spoilt teenager, than a woman who she guessed was only a few years younger than she was.

"Who the hell are you?" Petra whispered, as she stared in the direction Xiá had walked.

Petra stepped back onto the deck, letting the door close as she turned into the wind and walked to the railing. The ship, like a police helicopter orbiting a football stadium, turned in large but slow circles, within helicopter range of Ushuaia, the southernmost city in the world. Petra walked to the stern as snatches of romantic moments flickered through her mind. *What was it the woman had told them to say?*

Te amo.

Petra smiled at the thought, picturing the sea lions on the rocks by the lighthouse, the picture the tourist took of her and Maratse, falling asleep in his arms as the boat pushed along the tide back to the city.

How did something so perfect turn so ugly so fast?

More time, and more thought might have allowed for a deeper analysis, looking back on recent events, looking for a pattern. Maratse,

Petra knew, would say there was no pattern. *But surely,* she thought. *This kind of thing doesn't happen to everyone.*

Petra stopped when she reached the helicopter pad, suppressing further thoughts as she watched the crew prepare the helicopter for the flight back to the mainland. She thought about how simple it would be to catch a ride back with them. They could pack in seconds, Maratse even quicker than that. Then leave the boat, fly north, and keep going north, where they understood life, and life seemed to understand them.

Not like here, this ship, its rules, and all the crazy people.

Petra remembered the doctor in sickbay. She checked her smartphone, watched the seconds tick away, gone forever, and still no answers. Petra turned and walked, resisting the urge to run, back to the door, then inside the ship and along the corridor to sickbay, to find the doctor – and all *his* examples of crazy, with his fascination and fear for ice. She knocked on the door, pushed it open, and stepped inside, stopping cold when she saw the captain consoling Phyllis, the dead man's wife, with an arm round the older woman's shoulder as Phyllis gulped breaths between bouts of tears and shaking.

"Come back later," the captain mouthed, flicking her eyes to the door, turning Petra around, before she could even get started.

Petra stepped back into the corridor and leaned against the bulkhead. She heard the whine of the helicopter's engines, heard the first heavy swirl of the rotors, and then felt the rumble through the bulkhead as the pilots increased the pitch just before pulling into the air. The shudder of the helicopter cut through the ship, cutting even deeper into Petra as she knew that when it returned time was up for Maratse, that she would have run out of time – for both of them.

"Piitalaat?" Maratse said, as she stumbled into the cabin.

"It's over, and I've got nothing."

"Because there *is* nothing." Maratse pulled her to the bed, curling his arm around her shoulder as she sat down. "There's no case."

"There doesn't need to be," she said. "You don't see it, because you haven't talked to them."

"To whom? Phyllis?" Maratse smiled. "She doesn't like me very much."

"No, and Xiá, the Chinese woman. She must hate us both." Petra turned in Maratse's arms. "You should have heard what she said, what she will tell the investigator." Petra wiped a tear from her cheek. "She really hates us, and I have no idea why. I mean, we met her for the first time yesterday."

"*Eeqqi*," Maratse said. "I don't think that was the first time."

Chapter 26

Xiá leaned into the wind as the downdraught from the helicopter's rotors thumped against her slight frame. She gripped the handrail, squared her feet, dipping her head as the pilot dumped the helicopter onto the pad. The engines whined, straining, as if the metal beast wanted to fly, until the pilot cut the power, stifling the engines and then the rotors as he applied the brake. Xiá let go of the rail and walked up the steps to the ramp, shaking her head and pointing at the helicopter when a crewman tried to tell her to wait.

"She's waiting for me," Hong Wei said, as he stepped out of the helicopter, ignoring the offering of a helping hand as he strode towards Xiá.

"You have to clear the pad," the crewman said. "The helicopter is returning to Ushuaia for a service."

Hong Wei nodded that he understood, and for the crewman to take his bag – a single black holdall. He took Xiá's arm, leading her off the helipad and on to the stern of the ship. "Report," he said, switching to Cantonese.

"Everything is in place."

"And you were discreet?"

"Yes," she said, with a flash of her eyes,

daring him to comment.

"I'm not the enemy, Xiá," Hong Wei said.

"I said nothing."

"No. You didn't have to. But of late, I feel your attitude is changing." Hong Wei gripped Xiá's arm, drawing another bitter look. "Remember, Xiá, what we do and how we do it is for the benefit of the people. It is never about us."

"No?" she said, shrugging her arm free of his grip. "What about this?" Xiá gestured at the ship. "The Greenlander, Maratse. Is this not personal?"

Hong Wei flattened his lips into a thin smile, and then said, "It's *convenient*. There's a difference."

"Convenient and expensive. You bought a ship."

"An asset for China."

Xiá took a step away from the railing, then pointed at the superstructure. "The captain is waiting to see you. I said I would bring you up, just as soon as you landed."

"And yet," Hong Wei said. "There is something more. Isn't there? You have that look."

"I've done what you asked, and I'll play my part."

"I expect nothing less."

"But I want something in return."

"More information." Hong Wei sighed. "About your father."

"Yes."

"Very well." Hong Wei moved away from the railing, drawing Xiá with him. "Take me to the captain and then wait for me in your cabin.

We are approaching the end of this phase of the mission, and you could do with a break. Once we have carried out this *investigation*, then you will take some time – to travel, perhaps."

"I won't leave until you tell me the rest of the story, tell me how my father died."

"I will. Just as soon as I have spoken with the captain." Hong Wei took a cloth package from his pocket. "A pistol," he said, pressing it into her hand. "Diplomatic pouches still have their uses."

Xiá took the pistol and led the way, saying nothing as they climbed the stairs between decks. She took Hong Wei to the bridge, excusing herself as he greeted the captain. Xiá heard their exchange of pleasantries, followed by Hong Wei's subtle charm and even subtler threats as to what he expected and what would happen if the captain or her crew were not sufficiently accommodating.

Xiá had heard it all before. She didn't need to hear it again.

Xiá's cabin was clean, spartan, just as she liked it. It was one of the few concerns that had been raised during training, that she treated the places she stayed as a sterile sanctuary she could leave at a second's notice.

"Admirable, on some levels," her instructors had said, during the penultimate meeting with Hong Wei before she was assigned to him. Xiá remembered standing mute to one side, just as she was ordered.

"But?" Hong Wei had said.

"The problem is she treats these places like a sanctuary…"

"That she can leave in seconds." Hong Wei had frowned, waiting for the instructors to elaborate.

"But if someone were to infiltrate her room, they would know she was a spy the second they walked in." The instructor had, Xiá noted, afforded her a glance together with a pitiful *I-tried-to-warn-you* shrug of the shoulders. "There's no litter, not even *neat* or *tidy* litter. There is nothing. It is sterile. Always."

"I fail to see the problem," Hong Wei said. "She could be obsessive compulsive, or perhaps just extraordinarily tidy – both worthy attributes."

"Of course," the instructor had said, accepting the suggestion. "But Xiá must be all things. Anything she is asked to be. She must be able to deceive. She must expect infiltration and betrayal. She must present a varied disguise, suited to the purpose."

She had tried.

During training, and the first few operations. But Xiá knew that Hong Wei understood, and the reason he had taken her anyway was because he knew the root cause. Over time, Xiá had developed a need to control every aspect of her situation. She had perfected the art of adopting a role, but only so far. When it came to her bolthole, if it was not shared, then it was clean, sterile, ready to be abandoned.

Hong Wei smiled at the familiar sight the second she opened her cabin door, letting him inside after he was finished with the captain.

"You don't change," he said, as he pulled the chair out from under the desk and sat down.

"I don't need to."

Xiá sat on the bunk, eyes fixed on Hong Wei.

"You think your father was lax, don't you?"

Xiá said nothing, just watched.

"He wasn't, Xiá. But from the day you were old enough to think about how he might have died, you have assumed he did something wrong, or that he wasn't quick enough to get away. Not skilled enough."

"They called him incompetent in the reports," she said, closing her fingers into fists.

"They were wrong."

"They said…" Xiá paused, thinking, remembering. "They said he was a fugitive. They called him a traitor. Said he committed treason."

"Covering their tracks," Hong Wei said, resisting the urge to wave the accusations away. He sensed the change in Xiá, that this was perhaps the last time she expected to be told the truth, that she would seek it in other ways if he didn't volunteer it. Hong Wei took a second to examine the room, looking for the wrinkle beneath the covers of Xiá's bed, looking for a knife, or perhaps the pistol.

"Who?"

"What?" he said.

"Who is covering their tracks?" Xiá leaned forward. "The party? The MSS?"

"The Ministry of State Security…"

"Leaked the story they wanted the media to

write." Xiá sneered. "I'm not a fool, Hong Wei."

"I never believed you were. Not for a second."

"But you waited years before telling me the truth."

"You weren't ready."

"And when I was, you spoon fed me – a teaspoonful at a time."

"It was best…"

"For whom? For me?"

Xiá uncurled her fists. Hong Wei swallowed as he noticed. He knew what she could do with the flat of her palm, what he once could do, so many years ago.

"For you?" Xiá said, with a slow bob of her head.

"Xiá…"

Hong Wei's breath caught in his throat as Xiá slid a thin metal tube out of her sleeve.

"You know what this is?" she asked.

"Saxitoxin," Hong Wei said. "It's your current weapon of choice."

"Yes." Xiá snorted. "Have you ever wondered why?"

Hong Wei watched as Xiá assembled the tube, exposing the firing pin at one end of the tube. A jerk of her thumb – not even hard; the lightest of pressure – would fire the compressed gas capsule, forcing the toxin out of the end, the end she pointed at Hong Wei.

"I've been doing my own research," she said, lifting her chin to look at Hong Wei. "Juatan Fortin, the man from Tuktoyaktuk…"

"Yes?"

"He died from paralysis. It took a long time to discover from what – seeing as there was no cause to look into his death, until…"

"The Canadians found your father," Hong Wei said.

Xiá nodded. "When they found him, and traces of him, all the way back to Fortin's house, they became suspicious."

"Yes."

"Together with the surprise visit of a Chinese military ship in the Northwest Passage."

"Xiá…"

"What were you thinking?"

"I was ordered to send a message. Just like you are sending a message."

"Framing a man for murder – in Copenhagen or on this ship – is not the same."

"Isn't it?" Hong Wei crossed his legs, flicking his gaze from the tube in Xiá's hand to her face. "The art of deception is about getting someone to look in one place, while you do something in another. We sailed the *Xue Long* into Canadian waters. We made them look at their own back door, and we sent tremors down the very spine of the Canadian defence and intelligence community, and the world. Think, Xiá… Think what we achieved, arriving on their doorstep, waking them up, causing such alarm."

"Deceiving them."

"Yes."

"Allowing you and my father to sneak into the country."

"One doesn't *sneak* into the Arctic – those long roads, the low, barren ground, the dust trails... We needed a diversion. The *Xue Long* was it; we used it to deceive."

"To conduct espionage."

"Yes," Hong Wei said. "What else?"

"You entered the mine."

"Thomsen Mining." Hong Wei nodded, relaxing as Xiá lowered the tube – slightly, but just enough for him to breathe a little easier.

"And my father was with you."

"In the pickup. He was driving. We stopped a little way outside the mine. I let him off. We rolled Fortin into a tarp."

"Just like that?"

"No," Hong Wei said. "He was sobering up, becoming combative." He pointed at the tube in Xiá's hands. "We used Saxitoxin. Killed him inside of a minute. *Then* we rolled him into the tarp."

"And you left my father..."

"Outside the mine."

"As you gained entry."

Hong Wei allowed himself a thin smile. "Easily. The guards were changing shifts, doing the *handover*. They waved me through the gates." Hong Wei's smile evaporated as he shifted in his seat, uncrossing his legs, leaning forward, closer to Xiá, closer to the tube. "I parked. I walked right inside the main building, avoiding the crew cabins and the bar. The offices were busy, but..."

"You created a diversion."

"A simple one," Hong Wei said.

"A fire alarm?"

"Low tech is best. I've taught you that." Hong Wei smiled, glancing at the tube. Xiá moved it a little, further out of his reach. "The office emptied, I accessed the computers, opened the safe – it was unlocked. And I found what I wanted. The mission was a success."

"Except my father..." Xiá said. "He died."

"Yes."

"Why?"

Hong Wei stood and pushed back his chair, giving him space to pace – not much, but perhaps enough to react should Xiá try to discharge the tube.

"The mine had its own fire crew. Being so far from anywhere, they had to. I knew that. So I wasn't surprised when they discovered it was a false alarm. But I forgot something." He stopped pacing to look at Xiá. "I forgot to prepare for the unexpected."

"My father?"

"Was waiting in the hollow by the road. There should have been no traffic, but a local cop with a huge jurisdiction was in the area. He responded to the fire alarm, driving down the same highway to the mine. He saw your father, Xiá."

"And he saw Fortin?"

"He saw enough to think something was going on. At least, that's what I think. I passed the police officer on my way out of the mine. He was coming in. Pān Tāo described how the patrol car had slowed as it passed him, that he had nowhere to hide. I asked him if the police officer had seen his face. Your father said he had."

Hong Wei paced closer to Xiá, brushing her knees as she looked up with her next question.

"The mission was compromised?"

"Potentially," Hong Wei said. "I couldn't allow it. We had what we needed. All that remained was to get away, to bring back the information, to be one of Sun Tzu's *surviving spies*."

"You created a diversion," Xiá said.

"Yes."

Hong Wei nodded, then reached down, slapping his palm into Xiá's chest with one hand as he ripped the tube from her hands with the other. He pulled back, hand clasped around the tube, drawing Xiá with him as she ignored the shock of the slap and held onto the tube. Hong Wei's eyes widened at the soft click of the firing pin as Xiá pressed her thumb onto it.

"Empty," she said, her face close enough to Hong Wei's to smell his breath.

"You would be dead too," he said, looking down at the tube, not letting go. "Just being in the cabin. You would have caught it."

"A necessary diversion," she said, pulling back as Hong Wei let go of the tube.

"What?"

"If you thought I was willing to die, to kill us both, then…" She shrugged, waiting for Hong Wei to figure it out.

"I would tell you what you wanted to hear."

Xiá nodded. "But there's more, isn't there?"

Hong Wei sighed, his eyes fixed on Xiá's, staring right into them, before he nodded, just once, ever so slight, but so very heavy.

"You would rather die than tell me," Xiá said, holding the tube in her hand.

"Yes," he said.

"And what happens if you do?"

"If I tell you, it will be the end of all things. The end of me and you. The end of your father's legacy."

Xiá pushed away from Hong Wei, her face twisted, eyes narrowed – black, obsidian sharp. "My father has no legacy."

"Xiá," Hong Wei said, as she started for the cabin door. "The mission – we must finish the mission."

Xiá stepped out of her cabin and into the corridor, pausing ever so slightly at Hong Wei's last words.

"Complete the mission, and I'll finish my story. I'll tell you everything," he said.

Xiá looked over her shoulder, fists clenched. She caught Hong Wei's eyes, dipped her head, once, then closed the cabin door.

Chapter 27

Before the helicopter returned, the *Admiral Chichagov* ploughed the waters at the northernmost part of *Drake Passage* in ever increasing circles, bumping the same growlers of ice with its bow as if the captain, fed up of waiting, took out her frustration on the same lump of ice, one circle after another, until it gave up and disintegrated into blocks and brash ice. When the helicopter returned after the last *Drake Passage* circuit, it settled on the pad at the stern with an ominous thud that echoed through the decks.

Petra sat up in the bunk, swinging her feet over the side, cursing the time that she had slept, cursing the doctor for being so elusive – never in sickbay when she visited, always at the other end of the ship when she asked.

"We're out of time," she said, peeling out of bed as Maratse reached for her.

"Piitalaat," he said. "Everything is going to be okay."

"How can you say that? You're *the* suspect in a murder."

"Who says it's murder?"

"They said it was suspicious."

"It's the same thing, until they rule it out. It's

~ 279 ~

what *we* do when we check up on a suspicious death."

"And how many times do we find signs of actual murder?"

Petra paused, halfway through pulling on her jacket. "Okay, it's rare but…"

"But what?" Maratse sat up. "This is a ship. The passengers are older. You said William was fighting cancer."

"Yes."

"Then that's what it is."

"But those women – maybe even the captain – they are trying to put you there, at the time of his death, making more of it…"

"Than they can ever prove." Maratse stood, reaching for his jeans draped over the back of the chair at the desk. "We're going to be okay."

"I don't know."

"You don't have to. This time feels different. Trust me."

"I want to, but so many things are out of our control, David. I don't like it. Right now, I wish we had never met Connor in Kangerlussuaq. I wish we were in Spain, that you were complaining about the heat, that I was laughing at you, that I might even be in a bikini…"

"A bikini?" Maratse pulled a grey t-shirt over his head. "You never said anything about a bikini. I would have gone to Spain."

"Stop teasing," Petra said. "I'm serious, David. *This* is serious."

"I'm serious too, about the bikini."

Maratse caught the smile on Petra's lips. He

took a step closer, brushed the hair from her cheek and tucked it behind her ear, just as he had seen her do so many times. Joking about bikinis was new, strangely exhilarating, as if he was venturing on new ground, discovering new facets of his own taciturn, quiet self.

She did this to me. She made me smile. She made me live.

Not that he had never lived. Maratse knew that he *had* lived, that he had embraced life, but that it had been a solitary life, just him and the elements, him alone on the sea ice, in the mountains, even in the patrol car – alone in the settlements. Although never lonely, once Petra had come into his life, suddenly he realised that there was more to being with people than he had appreciated, more to enjoy, more to share, that being alone didn't always solve problems, but that sharing problems could make the most unbearable things bearable.

And yet some things were almost too much to bear, he thought as the image of Jaqqa Neqi bleeding on the sea ice in Uummannaq fjord flashed through his head. He shook it out of his mind.

"It's going to be okay," Maratse said. "You'll see."

"You promise?" Petra cupped her hand over his, pressing it to her cheek.

"As much as I can," he said.

"Then we'll…"

Petra turned her head at a knock on the door. Her breath caught in her chest and she nodded for

Maratse to open it. Maratse tucked his t-shirt inside his jeans and tightened his belt. He searched for socks on his way to the door, calling out that he was coming when they knocked the second time.

"David," Luukas said, as Maratse opened the door. "The investigator would like to see you."

"Just let me find my boots."

Luukas looked around Maratse, into the cabin. "Ah, he'd like to see both of you."

Maratse glanced at Petra as he picked his boots up by the laces. "Why?"

"He didn't say. Only that you should both come."

"Okay," Maratse said. He grabbed his old police jacket, pulling it on as Petra fastened her laces and took her down jacket from the hook on the bulkhead behind the door.

"It's this way," Luukas said, once he could see they were both ready.

The stairs between decks one and two seemed steeper and longer, as Luukas led them from one deck to the other, and then into the ship's reading room and library. He paused at the door, apologising for everything, before stepping to one side.

"I'm not to come in," he said. "Just to wait, here, for when you come out."

"Okay," Maratse said. He turned to Petra, took her hand and squeezed it. "Everything is okay. Everything will be fine."

Except it wasn't.

It could have been the man's aftershave, a

subtle reminder pricking at Maratse's senses. Or, perhaps, it was the light, the way it cut through thin clouds, clawing at the sun, and pressing on the window, at an angle, just like it did through the buildings in the mining camp at the top of Nuuk fjord. But then, most likely, it was the way the man said Maratse's name, the way he greeted him as if they had once known each other, however briefly, but in such a way that neither man would never ever forget.

"Constable Maratse," Hong Wei said in English, as they stepped into the reading room. "If I had known it was you, well, I would have done everything in my power to come sooner."

"David?" Petra said. "Who is he?"

"Ah, and you must be Sergeant Jensen." Hong Wei walked around the mahogany reading table, hand outstretched, ready to greet Petra, until Maratse stepped between them.

"You don't touch her," Maratse said. "You don't even look at her."

"Constable?" Hong Wei said, feigning surprise. "Surely you don't mean that? I am merely being polite."

"Be polite," Maratse said, nodding at the armchair at the head of the table. "From over there."

"That's so unnecessary, Constable. So rude, in front of your friend."

"Over there," Maratse repeated. He took a small step forwards, and Hong Wei backed away, smiling, eyes locked on Maratse's.

"David," Petra whispered. "You're

trembling."

Maratse took a breath, holding it, trying to *hold* on.

"Of course, regardless of how soon I wanted to get here," Hong Wei said, as he sat down. "This whole situation is quite unfortunate. And yet, curiously fortuitous, don't you think?"

"You're not an investigator," Maratse said.

"No?" Hong Wei opened his palms with an indifferent wave. "I can be many things, Constable. If you remember?"

"I remember."

"And yet," Hong Wei said, continuing after a moment's observation in which he focused on Maratse's legs. "I had heard you were incapacitated."

"I couldn't walk."

"That's what I heard. And now?"

Maratse gritted his teeth, and said, "I recovered."

"No doubt speedily, under the care and perhaps even love of your delectable friend, Sergeant Jensen." Hong Wei leaned to one side to get a better look at Petra. Maratse moved to block him, drawing a thin laugh from the Chinese man. "So protective of Petra," Hong Wei said. "Or is it *Piitalaat*?"

"David," Petra said quietly. "I don't like this."

"No one *likes* this, Petra." Hong Wei stood and moved to the window. "There is nothing to like about this whole unfortunate situation. But at least we are moving again. The captain can stop drilling holes in the sea and resume her course. She, then, among us is happy. As are the passengers, some of whom are, as we speak, getting ready in anticipation of the first whale excursion. Whales have been spotted," Hong Wei said, pointing in a vague direction out to sea. "The boats are being prepared, and all that remains is to fill them. Of course, our mutual friend, the Constable, will not be joining the safari, but you will, Sergeant Jensen. It is expected." Hong Wei raised his hand, cutting off Petra's protests. "As I said, it's *expected*. You are a guide on this ship. And once you are on your way, David and I will have a little chat, right all the wrongs in the world, and clear up any misgivings and misunderstandings there might have been in the last forty-eight hours aboard this *Chinese* ship."

"We're citizens of Greenland," Petra said, stepping around Maratse.

"Aboard a Chinese ship."

"We have Danish passports."

"Irrelevant," Hong Wei said. "You are in international waters. The law of the sea applies, and you are bound to the laws applicable in the country to which the ship is registered. In this case…"

"China," Maratse said.

"Yes, thank you, Constable. That's correct. On this we agree." Hong Wei smiled, and said, "Progress."

Maratse reached for the back of the nearest chair, gripping it as he felt an old but familiar pain pulse through his legs – deep, right down in the nerves. If he closed his eyes, he knew he would be back in the mining camp, he could almost hear the stutter of the generator, the crackle of the metal paddles Hong Wei held in his hand, and the burst of fire on his skin as the electricity bit into his body, spitting fat beneath the paddles, blistering through his nerves. He didn't need to close his eyes to see it, and the fresh varnish on the tabletop wasn't strong enough to erase the sudden smell of charred flesh – his own. Maratse felt the scars on his chest prickle. He thought of Salmonsen in Vestsyssel Prison, and his fascination, albeit short-lived, in Maratse's visible trauma scars.

"David," Petra said. "I'm here."

Maratse felt Petra's hand. The strength of it was enough, just enough, to push back the flow of phantom pain in his legs, to press it down towards the deck. She was there, just like she had been there in the rehabilitation ward in Nuuk when the physiotherapist put Maratse through his training, and again in the ambulance workshop, when Maratse decided he didn't need any more therapy. She was his rock. He knew that now, and regardless of what the Chinese man had done to him, regardless of what Hong Wei intended to do to him…

"Impressive, Constable," Hong Wei said, derailing Maratse's train of thought. "Such fire. I think I understand now how you overcame your injuries, how you overcome so many things." Hong Wei walked to the table. He picked up a slim folder that neither Maratse nor Petra had noticed when they first walked in. Hong Wei opened it, pulling out sheaths of paper, placing them either side of the folder. "This is you, Constable," he said, arranging the papers on the left. "And the good sergeant," he said, adding to the papers on the right. "If I didn't know better... If I was to read these files for the first time, without the slightest knowledge of either of you, then I would be tempted to think I was reading about criminals, not police officers." He tapped different pages in turn. "Organised crime here. Torture porn – forgive me," he said, looking up at Petra. "Here."

"Stop," Maratse said.

Hong Wei waved his hand, ignoring him. "Deaths here..." A tap of a page. "In Greenland. In Berlin." He lifted his head, raising an eyebrow. "Greenland again, and again. Some in Denmark – recently. Another in Greenland, just a month or so ago. So many deaths."

"Stop."

"And one more, here on this ship – this *Chinese* ship." Hong Wei looked up. "It seems that any attempts to curb all this killing, all these deaths, have been unsuccessful." Hong Wei reached for one of the papers, studying it as Maratse watched him. "Curious."

"David," Petra whispered. "We should go."

Maratse dug his fingers into the back of the chair, pressing the tips through the upholstery, drawing a smile from Hong Wei when he noticed.

"Such fire, Constable," he said. "I think,

given the evidence, it's high time someone put out those flames. How fortuitous that that task should fall to me."

Chapter 28

Ada Valkyrien slipped her tiny Chevrolet into a vacant spot at the agreed parking lot. The clandestine meeting made her think of Adam Hansen and his mysterious background, not to mention the needle tracks on his arms, and the life he put on hold each time he entered the underworld.

"But this isn't the underworld," Ada reminded herself, before dropping any further thoughts for fear of discovering just what it was and what she had let herself in for when she agreed to Qitu's cryptic text providing little more than a time and a place.

Ada spun around as someone opened the passenger door and dropped into the seat beside her before she could reach her pistol holstered at her hip.

"I'm Fenna," the woman said, as she reached up to turn off the interior light. "A friend of Qitu's."

"He didn't give me a name," Ada said, unsure as to whether she should keep moving for her pistol or give *Fenna* the benefit of the doubt. Curiosity got the better of her, and she rested her hands on her thighs.

"Thanks," Fenna said. "I appreciate the vote

of confidence." She turned her head, checking all sides, and then taking a quick look over her shoulder at the back seat. "Not that anyone could hide there," she said, with a smile. "Can't be too careful."

Ada tapped her thighs, nodding, waiting for Fenna to speak.

"You're wondering what this is about?"

Ada shrugged. "I got a time and a place. That's all."

"It's about Malik Uutaaq."

"Yes?"

Fenna turned in her seat to face Ada. "I need you to back off."

"He's free," Ada said. "Some fancy lawyer…"

"Bailed him out? Yes, I know that. But still. You need to drop the investigation."

Ada looked at Fenna, then said, slowly, deliberately, "It's a murder investigation. You don't just *back off*."

"And yet, that's what I'm asking you to do."

"On whose authority?"

Fenna took a moment. "Yeah, that's where it gets tricky. I'm not supposed to tell you too much, and it's probably best that you know next to nothing, but let's just say that important people need you to do something important."

"That's not *next to nothing*," Ada said. "That's nothing at all."

"I told you it was tricky."

Ada reached for her car keys, turning them just far enough to make a soft clicking sound, before starting the engine. "You might want to get out," she said. "Or, here's a thought, you could tell me more, and I'll sit here just a little longer, maybe even make up my mind to help you."

"Fine," Fenna said. "Here's *more*." She waited until Ada let go of the keys. "Obviously, I'm Danish."

"Yes?"

"But I work for the Canadians…"

"Canadian intelligence?"

"To a degree," Fenna said. "There are some connections at least, if you looked hard enough. But none of that matters. What I need is to get Malik Uutaaq back to Greenland as soon as possible. But I can't do that if you have him flagged as a person of interest. He won't get past security at the airport."

"He's a member of the Greenland government…"

"Currently associated with an ongoing murder investigation. I know. And no matter what government he's with, that creates friction. It's amazing this hasn't leaked to the press to a greater extent than it has, and I credit Qitu and you with that, plus the sad fact that the suspicious death of a Greenlandic woman simply doesn't draw the same kind of attention as if she was Danish, for example."

"That's a little harsh."

"Sure, but can you deny it?"

Ada thought about it for a second, shook her head.

"But Malik's lawyer, no matter how fancy and expensive, can't give him total freedom. He still has to stay in Denmark until your investigation is concluded. And that means you, Sergeant."

"I'm not strictly working the case."

"That's not what I heard."

Ada wondered just *what* Fenna had heard and from whom, but let it drop as Fenna continued, drawing Ada deeper into her world.

"Qitu might have told you that Malik is being followed. That fits with my investigation and the contact I have had with his followers since being in Copenhagen." Fenna stopped talking as Ada turned in her seat to point at her.

"It was you the other day, outside the metro station. Wasn't it?"

Fenna let the question linger in the space between them, her gaze steady, revealing nothing, not even a denial.

"There was a Chinese woman with a knife," Ada said, continuing. "And two shots were fired." Ada shifted her gaze from Fenna's face to the bulge of a pistol holstered under her arm. "From a gun."

"Pistol," Fenna said, opening her jacket to reveal her shoulder holster. "Old school holster, better for concealing a Browning."

"What?"

"A friend convinced me to carry a Browning." She twisted a length of hair around her ear, looking away from Ada for a moment, giving the impression she was looking far, far away. "It's another long story," Fenna said. "For another time."

"But the shootout in the street?"

"More embarrassing than anything else." Fenna closed her jacket. "She – whoever she was – ran away, and I got Malik into a van, then off the street and into a safe house."

"Where is he now?"

Fenna made a vague gesture at the window. "Out there, loose, figuring things out."

"And if I clear him of involvement in the case?"

"He'll fly back to Greenland. He'll be easier to track, easier to reach."

"If I let him fly?"

"Yes," Fenna said. "That's all I'm really asking you to do."

"And what if it turns out he did kill Tipaaqu Jeremiassen? What then?"

"He didn't."

"But what if he did? Am I supposed to let him walk from a murder?"

"If the evidence suggests it?"

Ada nodded.

"In that case," Fenna said, with the slightest of pauses to make her point. "Get rid of the evidence."

"Jesus," Ada said. "You can't expect me to cover up the tracks of a killer. I don't care who he is…"

"You should." Fenna raised her voice, filling the space between them as she leaned forward, closer to Ada, forcing her to move back to the door. "He's a government minister, and that makes him a person of interest to foreign powers. They have already contacted him, bailed him out, made it clear to him what he can expect when he helps them and, even more so, what they will do if he doesn't. Now, I've tried to convince Malik otherwise, but I have no idea what he is going to do unless you cut him loose and get him the fuck back to Greenland." Fenna jabbed a finger towards Ada. "It's up to you. You're holding things up. There's no telling what the consequences might be. But what do you care? What does it matter if Malik does his Chinese whispers, allowing the building of a new dock here, or the extension of a runway there? No, you don't care, because it's happening so far away, in a country with, what… the population of a small town in Denmark?"

"Bloody Greenlanders," Ada whispered, once Fenna had finished, once she had retreated back to the passenger side of the tiny Chevrolet.

"What's that?"

"Greenlanders," Ada said. "These past few months, I've been plagued by Greenlanders. As if there isn't enough going on in the world? Or even in Denmark."

Fenna laughed. "Actually, I get that."

"Get what?"

"Greenlanders, how they get under your skin."

Ada reached out and gripped the steering wheel as she took a long breath. "There's this one guy," she said, exhaling. "It took me forever to get him to help me out. And even when he did, honestly, I'm not sure who was helping who. He was so damned quiet. I mean not more than a few words at a time, and even then, mostly just a grunt."

"A grunt?"

"Yeah, and his Greenlandic, maybe even East Greenlandic *yes*, like a squeak or something."

"*Iiji*," Fenna said. "Something like that?"

"That's it," Ada said, turning to look at Fenna. "Exactly that."

"Constable Maratse." Fenna sank into the passenger seat. "Of course."

"You know him?"

"Yes." Fenna ran her fingers through her hair, obscuring her face from Ada, as she said, "A while ago. Sometimes it feels like yesterday. Qitu mentioned him." She paused. "I'd like to see him one day."

"It'll have to wait a bit," Ada said. "He's gone south, to Antarctica."

"What?"

"He and his friend – girlfriend, maybe. They were offered a guiding job on a cruise ship. I looked it up. They'll be gone a few weeks."

"But they were in Copenhagen?"

"For a few days. We paid for Maratse to fly down here. He had to appear in court. Then, that first night at the hotel – that was when Malik came into the lobby, right after he found Tipaaqu." Ada mouthed the word *found*, curious that she was already distancing Malik from the actual murder. "Then there's Maratse's ghost.

Someone he thinks he saw, right about the time the hotel lost the data from their computers – all the security camera footage."

"Wait," Fenna said. "Back up a minute. You're saying someone wiped the camera footage?"

"Either that or a freak accident."

"But you said something about a ghost."

"Yeah, Maratse thinks he might have seen someone – a woman – step out of the security room behind reception."

"Hotel security?" Fenna waited for Ada to nod. "And where were they if they weren't in the room?"

"Out front, with me, stopping a riot."

Fenna pulled out her phone, nodding for Ada to continue.

"It was a bunch of Chinese tourists. They arrived late – their driver kept them at the airport, for some reason or another."

"Chinese tourists?"

"Yes."

"Causing a distraction in the lobby?"

"I didn't say that. It looked pretty real." Ada rubbed her arm at the memory of being startled by a stray punch from the driver. "Felt it too."

"And Maratse's ghost?"

"Not much to say. He didn't say much, but I get the feeling he thought it was a woman."

"Chinese tourists fighting in the lobby," Fenna said, as she punched in a number on her phone. "A ghost seen outside the security room, and then I get attacked by a Chinese woman following Malik. Yes," she said, placing the phone to her ear. "It's me. I have more information."

Ada waited as Fenna talked on the phone, lifting her head as Fenna said words like *confirmed* and *strong indicators* followed by *Chinese assets.*

"And Maratse," Fenna said, lowering the phone and pricking Ada's arm with her finger to get her attention. "He was there? He saw the ghost?"

"Yes."

"You didn't?"

"No."

Fenna pressed the phone back to her ear, nodding as she spoke, "Yes. Maratse saw the ghost. No. The police officer didn't." Fenna ended her call with the promise to call again, later.

"Canadians?" Ada said, gesturing at Fenna's phone.

"The worst kind," Fenna said, with a grin. "Thorough, though. You have to give them that. My boss," Fenna said, waving her phone, "suggested Maratse could I.D. the ghost."

"Maybe. He was a bit vague."

"But if it's the same woman I saw in the street outside the metro... *If* I was there at all. Maybe if his description matches mine... Do you have his number?"

"No," Ada said. "But Petra gave me this." She tugged a business card from her pocket and pressed it into Fenna's hands.

"Connor Williams?"

"He's the one who recruited them. He should know how to get in touch with Maratse."

"Thanks." Fenna tucked the card into her pocket. "And the other thing? Malik?"

Ada paused. "You said this was bigger than us?"

"It is."

"Okay, how about this. I waive his flight restrictions, but I have Nuuk police pick him up and remind him that if we find any evidence…" Ada shook her head as Fenna started to protest. "No, I can't let that go. I can't let killers walk free."

"Neither can I." Fenna tapped her phone, and then said, "Fine. It's a deal – *if* you find anything that links him directly to the murder, not just a suspicion, we're talking hard evidence. Right?"

"Hard evidence," Ada said. "Agreed."

"Thank you."

"You're welcome. I'll talk to my boss tomorrow, sort out the paperwork."

Fenna reached for the door handle and opened the door. She had one leg out of the car before Ada stopped her.

"You'll contact me, after you talk to Maratse?"

"Sure, I can do that."

"It's just he seems to have this knack of getting into trouble. I've only known him a short while, but I get the impression he's good at it."

"Getting into trouble?" Fenna nodded. "I have some stories…"

"Long ones?"

"Aren't they all?"

Fenna got out of the car and shut the door, slapping her palm on the glass, a last farewell, before disappearing into the night. Ada looked over her shoulder, watching Fenna until she couldn't see her any longer. All that that remained was a black shadow in a black night. Ada started her car and turned on the headlights, deciding she had had enough of working in the shadows for one night.

Chapter 29

It took Luukas, a second crewman, and much reassuring from Maratse in Danish, to prise Petra from Maratse's side.

"It will be okay," Maratse said.

In any other situation, even those when they were both under the maximum stress and strain, she would have believed him. But in the library of the Ukrainian, now Chinese icebreaker, Maratse had lied to her for the very first time. He did it three more times, in Danish, once in Greenlandic, and then a fifth time – the last time – in a mix of English and scratchy Spanish.

"Piitalaat, it will be okay," he said, and then, "*Te amo.*"

"I'm not leaving," she said, pushing Luukas to one side, fists clenched, teeth bared. After everything Maratse had done for her, everything they had experienced and *survived* together, the thought of leaving him... Petra knew she would die by his side, if that was what it took.

And yet.

"Piitalaat," he whispered, pressing his mouth to her ear, cupping one hand to her cheek, curling the other around one of her fists. "You have to go. I'll be okay."

"You won't," she said, pulling her face back

to look at him. "He's the one," she whispered. "He's the one who hurt you."

"*Iiji*," Maratse said. "But that was then. It's different now."

"How?"

"I won't let him hurt me again. And he can't if you're safe."

"But you can't leave me. I can't let you stay. If anything happened…"

"Nothing will happen."

Petra looked around Maratse's head, and said, "Then why is he here?"

"I don't know. But I should find out."

"I'll stay."

"*Eeqqi*." Maratse shook his head. "I need you to be safe. Away from him."

Maratse looked at the crewman standing beside Luukas. The man was already dressed for the sea, with a bright red jacket and an automatic life vest – the kind that inflated on impact with water. Maratse reached for the radio clipped to the man's vest and pressed it into Petra's hand.

"Keep this," he said, glaring at the crewman, daring him to object. "I'll call you."

"The range…"

"Will be sufficient. I'll make sure of that."

"I don't know," Petra said, turning the radio in her hands.

"I do, Piitalaat. You have to go."

Maratse kissed her cheek, drawing a sigh from Hong Wei as he watched the exchange.

"Touching," he said, as he took a step forward.

"I told you to stay there," Maratse said, turning to face Hong Wei. "Not a step closer."

Hong Wei's face twisted with creases of confusion as he looked at Maratse. "Constable," he said. "Just who do you think is in charge here?"

"You may own the ship," Maratse said. "But you don't own me. You can't hurt me. And I won't let you hurt us." Maratse gripped Petra's hand, pressing the radio into her palm. "Go," he said, nodding once as Luukas gently took her arm, prising her slowly away from Maratse.

They reached the door, and Petra stared back at Maratse, one hand gripping the back of a chair, the other held flat, stiff against his side. She had seen him in difficult situations before, but never so vulnerable. Petra swallowed, fighting the urge to burst back into the room. Maratse shook his head with the smallest, most imperceptible of movements, meant only for her.

And then they were out of the library, and Luukas shut the door.

"Ah, I'm sorry," he said, as Petra stared past him, as if she could see into the library. "The boats are leaving. You need to go on the excursion." He paused. "It's your job."

Petra clutched the radio. She let the crewman guide her down the stairs and all the way to the mudroom, where the passengers were waiting, most of them already dressed, others fiddling with bulky zips and Velcro cuffs.

"Here," Alasdair said, shooing the crewman to one side, and pressing a drysuit into Petra's hands. "Let's get you dressed," he said. "Just kick off your boots and pull this over your clothes."

"He's got David," Petra said, her arms limp at her sides.

"Aye, I heard." Alasdair bent down to untie Petra's laces, tapping each leg as he pulled one boot off her foot and then the other. He guided her feet into the drysuit, then tugged it up her legs, taking the radio from her hand. "Just for a second," he said, as she reached for it. "We'll clip it to your vest once you're dressed."

Petra watched him, staring into his eyes – staring past him, until Alasdair asked her to smooth her hair before pressing her head through the rubber gasket around the neck piece of the drysuit.

"I've a message from the doctor," he whispered, as he feigned a problem with the suit. "He says William Bennett died of poisoning."

"Poison?" Petra said."

"Aye." Alasdair looked at her, curious at the sudden change, as if she had regained both purpose and energy. "Keep your voice down," he whispered.

"What kind of poison?"

"Shellfish. It was his best guess."

"Something Bennett was allergic to?"

"Possibly." Alasdair shrugged. "I'm just a mechanic, remember?"

"Something he ate?"

"No," Alasdair said. "That I do know. There was no shellfish that night. Not even prawns." He helped Petra squeeze her head through the gasket, then spun her around to grip the long rubber tag attached to the zip running from her left shoulder to her right. "This needs to be fully closed," he said, jerking the zip from one shoulder to the other. "No gaps, or the water will just piss right in. Did you hear me?"

"No gaps," Petra said, running on automatic, as her mind swirled with poison and the need to prove it – for Maratse's sake. "I need your help," she said, as Alasdair lifted a life vest over her head, clicking it into place.

"Can't," he said, pointing at the boots he had set aside for her. "I'm coming with you – driving one of the boats."

"After, then – when we get back." She tugged the boots on then straightened, looking Alasdair in the eye.

"Aye. When we get back." Alasdair clipped the radio into Petra's life vest and nodded. "You'll do."

Petra followed him and the last of the passengers out of the mud room and onto the deck. She waited at the railing as the crew guided everyone down the ship's ladder, running at a little less than forty-five degrees, to the floating dock and the rigid inflatable boats waiting below. One of the boats was already filled with passengers. Petra saw the Chinese scholar, Xiá, waiting in the second boat, watching her as she walked down the ladder, all the way until they were sat opposite one another. Alasdair took his place at the stern of the RIB, grasping the long tiller, and starting the large outboard motor. The

150-horsepower motor shuddered into life, exhaling a thin cloud of diesel fumes across the boat, through which Petra and Xiá stared at each other.

She has a radio, too, Petra thought as she looked at Xiá. Her eyes drifted to a bulge just beneath Xiá's jacket, on her shoulder, making Petra wonder if Xiá's drysuit was properly closed. She pointed, and said, "I think you need to fix that."

Xiá shook her head, and said, "Not your concern."

Petra nodded.

It wasn't.

I've got other concerns, she thought, reaching for her radio, willing it to crackle with Maratse's voice, telling her that he was okay, that he was on his way, that he would join her, just as soon as he and the Chinese man were finished.

It was all a big misunderstanding.

Those were the words Petra wanted to hear, to which she would add: *Yes. He died of poisoning. We're just not sure how.*

But, as Alasdair shouted for the crewman on the floating dock to untie them, Petra studied Xiá more closely, curious now, buoyed by the doctor's discovery, ready to suppress her emotions regarding Maratse's situation, and to be more analytical, more useful. There was something about the young Chinese woman, but *what* exactly escaped her as Petra looked away for a second, to shift her grip on the RIB's handgrips, the ones Alasdair instructed everyone to hold onto. When Petra looked back, she saw something else in Xiá's eyes – a fierceness that wasn't there before but flickered with intensity as Xiá glanced back at the ship.

It's not me she's mad at. At least, it's not only me.

Petra caught Xiá's eye one more time, until contact was broken when the first passenger shouted that they could see a whale.

Alasdair brought his boat alongside the other RIB, bumping the side gently as the passengers twisted to better see the whales.

"Petra," Alasdair said, gesturing for her to stand. "Can you tell us a little bit about these whales?"

Petra bit back a curse, and nodded, remembering why Connor had recruited her, with an emphasis on authenticity, not knowledge. She stood in the bow of the boat, looking at the blow from the whales as she desperately tried to recall what she knew of whales in Greenland, and how that could possibly relate to the whales surfacing less than fifty metres in front of the RIBs. She relaxed when she recognised the shape of the flukes the whales presented.

"Humpbacks," she said, tracing the tails with her two index fingers in the air, starting with the dip in the middle all the way to the upturned points at the ends. "They feed on krill, massive amounts," she said, lowering her hands. "I've seen them feed in Greenland, among the icebergs, blowing huge bubbles of air from below." Petra lifted her hands, as if pushing water up from below, towards the surface. She closed her hands like a great mouth, as she raised her arms. "The whale feeds, closing its mouth at the surface – filter feeding, trapping the krill, letting the seawater out." Petra drew strength from the passengers' appreciative comments, and a huge grin from Alasdair. She forgot Xiá for the moment, pointing at the whales, letting the brisk air blow her hair into tiny knots. "They're not feeding now," she said, as the whales continued with shallow dives, encouraging Alasdair and the driver of the first boat to follow, at a discreet distance, towards a large ice floe in the distance.

"If you'll sit down, Petra," Alasdair said, throttling up, the second she was seated. "We'll follow them for a bit, then maybe investigate the floe over there."

"That's a big floe," said one of the passengers. "Are you sure it's not pack ice?"

"Then it's come a long way," Alasdair said. "But we'll have a look."

They followed the whales for half a kilometre before veering towards the large floe, where Alasdair suggested they might be lucky to see seals.

"Maybe even leopard seals," he said. Alasdair grinned at the passengers' reaction, the turning of heads and the fiddling of cameras and long, heavy lenses.

"Can we walk on it?" one of the passengers asked. "On the ice?"

"We'll see." Alasdair waved at the other boat, giving the thumbs up as the driver pointed at the ice. "We'll have a look," he said, speaking into the radio, calling the other boat. "Some of the passengers would like to take a stroll."

The two RIBs sailed close to the floe, their drivers nodding at the thickness of the ice, curious that it should be so big, and have drifted so far, but happy that it was thick enough to moor alongside, and, to the delight of the passengers, considered safe enough to take a short stroll.

"Not too far," Alasdair warned. "And not without your guide."

The crew of the first RIB anchored their boat to the ice, confirming that it was good, and, given the current conditions with hardly any wind or swell, as safe as it could possibly be for the passengers to stretch their legs.

"Don't try to walk," Petra said, as she helped each of the passengers from her boat on to the ice. "You want to slide your feet, slowly, keeping your soles on the ice. If you lift your feet, you'll fall," she said, as Alasdair joined her in the bow. Xiá watched but showed no inclination to join the passengers on the ice.

"You're doing good, Petra," he said.

He left the motor idling out of gear, then took Petra's hand as she helped him out of the boat.

"And you," He said, reaching out for Petra's hand once he had found his feet.

Petra glanced behind her at the *Admiral Chichagov*, far away, but not so far she couldn't see the black windows of the superstructure. She imagined Maratse in the library, curious that she felt stronger now, almost confident that it was all just a misunderstanding, that the doctor would be able to make everything right again.

"Okay," she said, reaching for Alasdair's hand.

She would walk on the ice. And then they would all return for refreshments, sharing experiences over hot chocolate as the voyage south continued. Petra would leave the passengers as soon as it was polite, sooner, most likely, grabbing the doctor and the captain, confronting the Chinese investigator. Solving *everything*.

Everything was going to be fine. Just like Maratse promised.

Except for the fact that she had never seen him so anxious before, never seen him tremble.

It made her stop, made her think, her fingers less than an arm's length from Alasdair's.

"I don't know," she said, quietly, almost a whisper, as the thought of Maratse and his reaction to the Chinese man, leached the energy from her body, and she felt cold – colder than she should be inside her drysuit and the extra layers inside and out.

"I do," Xiá said.

Petra saw the blade of a safety knife, the kind with the blunt tip that all the crew were wearing, as Xiá pulled it from her belt and sawed through the line anchoring the RIB to the ice. Alasdair stumbled towards her, grabbing the line, then slipping on the ice as Xiá yanked it from his hands.

"Back off," she said, pulling a small pistol from her jacket pocket.

"What are you doing?" Petra said, as Xiá cast her end of the rope into the boat.

"Finishing things," Xiá said. She turned the pistol on Petra as the boat drifted away from the ice, too far to leap, either from the ice or from the boat. Alasdair shouted as Xiá slid across the deck to the outboard motor. "Sit down, Petra," she said, as she clicked the motor into gear.

"You can't take the boat," Alasdair said. "You're stranding the passengers."

"Obviously," Xiá said, as she throttled up.

The bow of the RIB lifted out of the water, forcing Petra to grab one of the handrails, holding on as Xiá kept one hand on the tiller and the other gripped around her pistol, pointing it straight at Petra's chest.

But her eyes, Petra thought. *She's not even looking at me.*

Petra watched Xiá as she increased speed. Xiá flicked her attention from the black water in front of the RIB, to the floe on their right, and then back to the ship. The pistol in her hand never wavered.

Chapter 30

Maratse watched Hong Wei as he walked to the window, peering through the sea salt crusting the thick glass as he looked down on the deck below. Hong Wei's reflection, and his haunted eyes in particular, clearer and easier to see as Maratse joined him at the window, gave Maratse at least some hope: the Chinese man was distracted.

Distraction.

Karl had helped Maratse with plenty of distraction, drawing his thoughts away from what had happened in the mining camp in Nuuk fjord, away from Hong Wei, as he forced him to fish, teaching him the best places to set longlines, joking with him about the dogs.

Sledge dogs.

Tinka had been one of the best distractions, bothering Maratse from the first day he set foot in Inussuk, and every day thereafter.

But now that he was here, within a metre of the man who had caused him such pain, cutting short his career with the police, Maratse found it difficult to be distracted. And yet, as he thought about the different twists and turns his life had taken since he discharged himself from the hospital, Maratse discovered that where there had been pain there was comfort, turmoil had been replaced with peace. Maratse had known peace before, but nothing like the peace he found with Petra. The wildest of thoughts flickered in Maratse's mind, as he thought about what he might say to this man, and if he should be the first to speak.

It was a game, after all.

But the rules of the game are defined by those who play them.

"I should thank you," Maratse said, surprising himself and Hong Wei as he broke the silence.

"Really?" Hong Wei pulled away from the window, taking one last look at the small black boats as they motored away from the ship, before giving Maratse his full attention. "I didn't expect that, Constable. Please," he said, gesturing at the table. "Continue."

Hong Wei took the seat at the head of the table, waving Luukas in as he appeared at the door, and taking the radio from the young man's hand as Maratse sat down on the side of the table closest to the window. Hong Wei placed the radio on the table between them, nodded for Luukas to leave, and then waited for Maratse to continue, prompting him when he didn't.

"You wanted to thank me?"

"*Iiji*," Maratse said. "For changing my life."

"I thought I rather ruined it." Hong Wei's chair creaked as he leaned back. "That was part of the plan. Or, rather – *you* were part of the plan."

"To get to Fenna?"

"Yes," Hong Wei said. "It seemed the easiest way to get the information I wanted."

"What about now? What do you want?"

"It's funny that you should ask that. Only, our mutual friend, the Konstabel – *Fenna*, as you call her. She's making problems for me, again." Hong Wei tapped the radio with his finger. "Considering our history, Constable, it seems only fair to speak plainly. I'm here to create a situation that will distract Fenna Brongaard. She feels a certain guilt over what I did to you. She feels responsible." Hong Wei smiled. "I have to admit, her guilt makes this so much easier. You see, if I can play upon that, using you, *framing* you, to the point where she is distracted, then I will have stalled her investigation."

"She's investigating you?"

"Yes."

"What for?"

"Constable," Hong Wei said, with another smile. "Speaking plainly is not the same as speaking openly. I'm not about to tell you everything, but just enough to make you aware of your role – a small but important one – in a greater game." Hong Wei gestured at the radio. "We should get a call, momentarily."

Maratse looked at the radio, frowning as he wondered who might call, and to what purpose.

"It's quite simple, actually," Hong Wei said. "The dead passenger created the opportunity for me to come here in the guise of an investigator, following normal procedure for the investigation of crimes committed at sea on Chinese registered ships."

"What is normal procedure?"

Hong Wei shrugged. "I have no idea. But neither does anyone else on this ship, so I am free to enforce any rules and procedures I see fit. However, a couple of eyewitnesses, placing you close to the scene of a man's death is hardly substantial, and won't hold up to further scrutiny. Even less so when one of the so-called eyewitnesses turns out to be working for me."

"Xiá?"

"The same," Hong Wei said, as Maratse squirmed in his chair. Both men looked at the radio, as if it might crackle into life at any second. "You see my dilemma? With so little to go on, it will be very difficult to prosecute a case without a confession."

"Confession?" Maratse said, as he looked at Hong Wei. Whatever had distracted the Chinese man at the window was gone now, replaced with the next step in his plan.

"*Your* confession, Constable."

Hong Wei continued, but without Maratse's attention, as he focused on the radio, willing someone to use it, but wary of the tightness in his chest at what might be said over the airwaves.

"I've lost you." Hong Wei snapped his fingers in front of Maratse. "There you are. Back again."

Maratse fidgeted in anticipation of sudden, violent action. *Piitalaat,* he thought, now desperate to hear her voice on the radio, regardless of her words, just to hear that she was alive.

"I'm impressed, Constable," Hong Wei said, after a moment's pause. "It's almost as if you can read my mind. Yes," he said, gesturing at the radio, "your sergeant friend is in trouble – imminent trouble. And I'm sure that you will do the right thing, that you will confess, here and now, thus ending this investigation, and allowing the next phase of this operation to…"

"If you hurt her…" Maratse said, his voice low, measured, laced with intent.

"She need not be hurt, Constable. In fact, I would prefer if she wasn't. But I can't always promise one thing or another. Matters will take their course, often out of my hands. In this case," he said, with a nod at the radio, "in Xiá's hands, for better or worse. So, it won't be *me* hurting Petra. It will be Xiá, if…" Hong Wei raised his finger, stalling Maratse as he rose from his chair. "If you cooperate. Then it needn't be quite so dramatic."

"Call her," Maratse said, reaching for the radio.

"That is not the plan."

"Plans change." Maratse slid the radio across the table towards Hong Wei. "Talk to her."

"And tell her what? That you have agreed to confess?"

"*Iiji*," Maratse said, jabbing his finger at the radio.

"You confess to murder?"

"I'll confess to whatever you want. Just call her, now."

Hong Wei reached for the radio, curling it into his palm as he looked at Maratse. "Incredible. Look at you, a retired policeman, unassuming by all accounts, and yet, the heart of a whale. At the merest suggestion of ill treatment towards this woman…"

"Piitalaat," Maratse said, pointing again at the radio.

"Yes, *Piitalaat*," Hong Wei said, testing the name on his tongue. "You don't even know what you're letting yourself in for."

"It doesn't matter. Only she matters. Call Xiá."

"I will, of course, but Constable, please, sit." Hong Wei gestured at the chair, waiting for Maratse to sink into it. "That's better. Now we can talk."

"I've got nothing more to say. Make the call."

"Constable, I insist." Hong Wei used the radio like a pointer, aiming the antenna at Maratse's chest. "You need to know what will happen."

"I don't care."

"No, I can see that. But *I* do, Constable." Hong Wei lowered the radio, pausing for effect, then lifting his hand to count on his fingers. He raised his thumb first. "You confess, and I take you to China, as a convict, to be imprisoned for murder."

Maratse nodded.

"You're not even curious, are you?" Hong Wei waited for Maratse to respond, then extended his index finger. "I reach out to our friend, Fenna, and strike a deal – your release for her information and the termination of her investigation. Of course," he said, with a fake frown, "this could be a drawn-out process, lots of politics, perhaps media attention. In all fairness, you might face six months in a Chinese prison, maybe longer."

"But Petra goes free."

"Yes, that is the deal, once it comes through," Hong Wei said, weighing the radio in his hand. "There are no guarantees…"

Maratse flicked his head towards the radio as it crackled with static.

Hong Wei?

"Go ahead, Xiá," Hong Wei said, pressing the button to talk. "In English."

I have possession. I am ready for the next step.

"Let her go," Maratse said, eyes fixed on Hong Wei.

"In good time, Constable. Calm yourself. Let me handle this…"

Hong Wei's last word stuttered on his lips as Maratse pushed back his chair, grabbing the back as he twisted on his feet and slammed it into Hong Wei's chest. The radio skittered across the floor as Maratse lurched around the table, bending to grab the radio as Luukas burst into library.

"Out of the way," Maratse shouted, as he charged across the deck to the door.

Luukas stepped to one side, twisting his head

from Hong Wei scrabbling to his feet at the end of the table, and then back to Maratse as he ducked through the door and turned right. Hong Wei shouted for Luukas to stop Maratse, as the pounding of Maratse's feet on the stairs thundered into the library.

Maratse leaped the last flight of stairs, slamming into the bulkhead and spinning away from it as he fought to regain his balance. He slammed his shoulder into the door leading to the outside deck, then raced towards the crew pulling a sling under the bow and stern of the last of the rigid inflatable boats, preparing to launch to save the stranded passengers.

"Get it in the water," Maratse shouted.

"We will, but the outboard…"

Maratse tucked the radio into the pocket of his police jacket, then climbed over the side of the RIB. He pulled the cowling off the outboard motor, casting it onto the deck where it clattered past the crew's feet. Maratse examined the motor, pumping his finger in the air, urging the crew to lift the boat up and over the side of the ship.

"It's the cotter pin in the gear case," one of the crew said, as another crewman operated the winch.

"Hmm," Maratse said, as the boat swayed off the deck. He stuffed his hand into his pocket, pulled out a couple of short, flat nails and a length of frayed twine. Maratse bit a thin filament from the twine and wrapped it around the nails, reaching in and stuffing the makeshift pin into the gear case. "Faster," he said, as he looked up at the webbing handle where the strops met beneath the winch hook, twisting over the centre of the boat.

"Stop him," Hong Wei said as he stumbled onto the deck, one hand pressed to a cut on his forehead, the other gripping Luukas' shoulder as he used him as a support.

Maratse caught Hong Wei's eye as the RIB drifted over the side of the ship. He looked at the webbing handle, then back to Hong Wei. The Chinese man stumbled along the deck, drawing closer, shouting at the crewmen to stop what they were doing or suffer the consequences.

The boat spun beneath the hook.

Maratse looked over the side, judging the distance – ten metres to the sea below.

"Constable Maratse," Hong Wei shouted. "I'm ordering you back onto this ship."

Maratse squared his feet on the deck of the RIB, directly beneath the webbing handle, gripping it with one hand as he wrapped the painter from the bow line around his wrist, pulling it taut.

Maratse took one last look at Hong Wei and then released the sling from the hook.

Air whistled around the sides of the rigid inflatable boat as it plummeted towards the sea. Maratse bent his knees in anticipation of the hull slamming into the black water, then toppled onto his side with the crash. He took a moment to pick himself up, ignoring the pain in his knees as he scrambled to the outboard motor, releasing the lock holding it at a safe angle, and dropping the propeller shaft into the sea. The crew on the deck above cheered as Maratse started the motor, throttling it in neutral amid clouds of thick blue smoke, before twisting the throttle to idle and clicking the motor into gear.

Maratse grabbed the radio from his pocket and pressed it to his mouth. He shifted his feet into a firm stance, gunning the boat towards the ice.

"Piitalaat," he said, pressing the button to transmit. "I'm coming."

Chapter 31

The black sea splashed against the hull of the rigid inflatable boat. Petra sat in the bow, her back pressed into the V where the air tubes met, heels wedged against a lip of metal in the deck, hands gripping the loops of rope on either side. She fixed her eyes on Xiá at the stern, and the pistol tucked into the belt of her life vest.

Xiá stared straight ahead, stuffing Petra's radio into her jacket pocket. Spray from the sea flecked her brow, as it burst over Petra's head, missing the Greenlander, plastering Xiá's hair to her forehead. She wiped it away with the back of one hand, keeping the other on the throttle. Petra saw her shiver, more than once, as the sea spray, the breeze, and the chill from the ice combined to bead on Xiá's jacket in tiny globs of ice, in her hair, her eyelashes.

She's cold, Petra thought, wondering when, how, *if* she might act, taking advantage of the environment, and Xiá's obvious discomfort at being in it.

Xiá's glasses were gone. It had taken some time before Petra noticed, and then, when she did, when the rational part of her mind processed the observation, a beat away from the thoughts of abduction, she put it down to being in the boat, being at sea. Further thoughts suggested that Xiá hadn't removed her glasses to stop them misting up in the cold like those of the older passengers. No, Petra realised, it was more likely that Xiá didn't need them, that she wasn't who she was supposed to be.

The floe slipped by on Petra's left, as Xiá continued to sail alongside it, further and further from the passengers, stranded on the ice – too many for one boat, too risky to leave half of them behind. Xiá slowed and stood on her tiptoes, peering forwards in such a way that Petra risked doing the same, turning to look ahead, seeing the lead, the crack in the floe, just as Xiá turned into it.

"Don't," Petra said. "We'll get trapped."

Xiá ignored her, settling onto her heels, throttling up as she made a sharp turn to the right. The boat banked, forcing Petra to hold on with her right hand. Xiá levelled the boat, increasing speed, flushing water from beneath the hull, then cursing as it splashed back over the sides as the lead narrowed. Petra caught a rebounding wave in her face, then another from the other side. She wiped her face, staring at Xiá, the pistol bulging in her pocket, and the bump at her shoulder where Petra believed the zip of Xiá's drysuit was not fully closed.

The boat slowed as Xiá throttled down, reaching for the radio in her pocket as she heard the crackle of static before transmission.

Piitalaat.

Xiá glared at the radio, then again as Maratse

finished his call.

I'm coming.

Petra tried not to react, keeping every part of her body still to avoid provoking Xiá, but her eyes betrayed her, shining at the thought that Maratse was free.

"It doesn't matter," Xiá said, stuffing the radio back into her pocket. "He can't help you."

Petra turned her thoughts to Xiá's motives. It was obvious she was working for the Chinese man, but everything else seemed unscripted, fuelled by the flicker in the young woman's eyes, the way she glanced back at the ship every other minute. Something drove her, and Petra struggled to think that it was her, that she had done anything to provoke Xiá. If anything, the look in Xiá's eyes suggested she was mad at someone, and even at his most dour, Maratse rarely made anyone mad.

Exasperated, yes, she thought, suppressing a smile. *But rarely mad.*

Xiá slowed as the sides of the floe pinched, narrowing again until the first squeal of rubber against the ice forced Xiá to pull to one side, until the ice rubbed against both sides of the boat and the propeller churned the water without any further forward movement.

"Out," Xiá said, cutting the motor.

The sudden stillness caught both of them by surprise, providing a second or so of complete and utter, dense and cold, quiet.

Petra looked at Xiá, brushed her hair behind her ear, pausing as if to say *you still want me to get out of the boat?* A wave of the pistol Xiá pulled out of her pocket confirmed it – *yes, get on the fucking ice.*

"Where are we going?" Petra asked, waving at the expansive floe that stretched for what seemed like a kilometre in all directions.

"Just walk."

"Fine." Petra slid her boots across the ice, curious that the surface layer of snow was powdery, as if it had snowed recently. *Somewhere further south,* she thought, as she struggled to remember much more than a few clouds and plenty of sunshine since arriving in Ushuaia. She paused at the sound of Xiá slipping on the ice, turned to offer her help, only to receive a sneer and a wave of the pistol in thanks.

"Keep moving."

Petra saw the deeper patches of snow, remembered what she knew of ice, how deceptive the drifts were. Strangers to sea ice would gravitate towards the drifts, seeking comfort in the thicker surface, only to be surprised when they discovered softer ice beneath the layer of snow. Petra knew the snow insulated the ice, just a few degrees, but enough to allow the current or waves to bite into that part, weakening the floe. She wondered if Xiá knew the same but decided to keep the thought to herself.

The edge of the ice loomed in the distance, where the shadow of the sea, black against the grey white ice, contrasted sharply. Petra kept walking towards it, until Xiá's voice stopped her. She turned to face Xiá as the young woman pointed her pistol at Petra's head. Xiá pressed the radio to her mouth, holding the transmit button down as she talked.

"In English," Xiá said, looking past Petra. "I want a witness."

"Very well, Xiá."

Petra stiffened at the sound of Hong Wei's voice, then shifted her focus to the pistol wavering slightly in Xiá's hand as she trembled.

"Tell me what happened to my father," Xiá said. "Tell me now, and then we can end this."

Petra saw the tears, saw them glisten as they rolled down Xiá's cheeks, slowing in the bite of the wind, the chill of the ice.

"I passed the police car as I left the mine," Hong Wei said, his voice tinny and distant, constrained by the radio's mono speaker. "I knew he must have seen your father. I knew he would be curious, and would come back, as soon as the fire was reported as a false alarm."

"So you did something," Xiá said, keying the transmit button.

"I acted, Xiá, in the only way I could." Hong Wei paused. "You must understand. The mission had been a success. We had the necessary information. All that remained was to survive, to get back to China."

"So you took my father back to the ship."

"No, Xiá. You know that's not what happened."

"Then you made a plan with my father. So that you could both escape."

"The highway," Hong Wei said. "Is long and

dusty. The Arctic sun does not set in the months of summer. Dust spills from the back of cars on the highway. It can be seen for miles."

"It doesn't matter. You could go back to the village."

"We couldn't go back. They would be waiting for us."

"So you turned around. You picked up my father, and drove south, to a town, or a city, somewhere to hide before getting out of the country."

The static pause cut through the chill of the air on the floe. Petra watched as Xiá paced back and forth, her eyes alternating from looking at Petra, back at the ship, never at the ice. Xiá pressed the radio to her ear, waiting for Hong Wei to continue as she paced, drawing Petra closer, if only to hear the last part of the story.

"The policeman," Hong Wei said, "came back."

Xiá stopped, just a footstep away from a drift. Petra saw it, glanced at it, then shifted her gaze back to Xiá's face.

"Xiá?" Hong Wei said. "Are you still there?"

Xiá clicked the button twice in response.

"We would have to attack the policeman to get away, we would have to shoot him."

"So, you shot him," Xiá said.

"Your father shot him, Xiá."

"He had to," she said. "You said so."

"Yes, but the policeman was faster than Pān Tāo expected. Your father was shot. He was bleeding. The policeman died but they would come looking for him when he didn't report in. They would close the road. If we were going to get away, we had to leave right there and then."

"You had time."

"We had no time."

"My father was wounded."

"Badly."

"You could save him."

"No, Xiá. I couldn't."

Petra watched as Xiá whirled on the floe, turning her back on Petra, glaring at the ship, as Hong Wei's words crackled through the speaker. She took a step forward, sliding across the ice, wary of the pistol, now lowered, hanging loose in Xiá's grip.

"Tell me," Xiá said, her voice crackling like Hong Wei's. "Tell me you didn't leave my father to die."

"No, Xiá. I couldn't."

Petra stopped, just two metres from Xiá, close enough to lunge, and to miss, if Xiá pulled back, just a fraction of a step.

"Xiá," Hong Wei said. "You know I had to do it. For the good of the mission. It was necessary. It was the only…"

Xiá cut Hong Wei's voice in half as she pressed the transmit button and screamed into the radio, firing the pistol at the distant ship, blasting it with useless bullets, spiralling short and fast on the ice, spent of energy, just as Xiá was spent, or so Petra hoped as she closed the distance between them.

Petra couldn't remember the last time she had

been in a fight, but her body could. Sparring in the gym during training had prepared her for Friday nights arresting drunks in the city. The drunks had taught her to react, fast, confident, ending a fight before it could begin. But there was little in her training that prepared her for fighting a trained assassin.

Xiá ducked and whirled as Petra lunged at her, making the most of her slight size as she ducked under Petra's arms, then rising, faster than Petra anticipated, faster than a drunk or a sparring partner, to crack the radio into the back of Petra's head.

Petra crashed onto the ice; fingers splayed in the spindrift snow coating the surface. She rolled onto her side, grabbed a handful of snow and threw it into Xiá's face as she attacked. Xiá snarled, bursting through the soft snow cloud to slap at Petra's hands, grabbing her hair, pulling Petra to her feet, pulling her as she stepped backwards.

"Xiá," Petra said, dipping as Xiá pulled her head down to her knees. "You don't have to do this."

"He killed my father," Xiá said, tugging at Petra's hair. "Shot him in cold blood, so that he could run, so that he could live."

Petra reached for Xiá's hand, clawing at her fingers, trying to break free, only to feel the thud of cold metal to her temple as Xiá pressed the pistol to her head.

"He killed my father and ruined the life I could have had. Now," Xiá said, pulling Petra as she walked backwards. "When I take your life, when I spoil his plans, I will ruin *his* life. It's his turn to be ruined, to know how it feels, to feel the wrath of a rotten legacy, to know what that…"

Xiá stumbled into the deep snow of a drift and crashed through the ice, plunging into the water, and dragging Petra with her.

Chapter 32

Hong Wei pulled the radio away from his ear as Xiá's scream cut through the speakers, electrifying the warm library air until Hong Wei pressed the mute button. He stared at the radio for another minute, turning the various outcomes of the current mission over and over until he knew what to do, the *only* thing he could do.

Hong Wei climbed the last flight of stairs to the bridge, entering without knocking, striding past the bridge crew until he reached the window.

"Captain Mäkelä," he said, pointing at the large floe in the distance. "I want you to take us to the ice."

"To the ice?" Elina held up her hand, as a question formed on the helmsman's lips. "You realise that Xiá – whoever she is – was broadcasting on an open channel?"

"Very aware," Hong Wei said, tapping the window. "We need to get to the ice."

"I have sixteen passengers and four crew – six, including Xiá and Petra – stranded on the ice because Xiá took one of the boats."

"Yes?" Hong Wei turned, flashing a look at the helmsman, urging him to increase speed with a wave of his hand. "And you should have charted a course for the ice as soon as Xiá took the boat."

"Should have?" Elina snorted. "With respect... No, to hell with respect. I don't care who owns this ship, I am the captain, I give the orders."

"You're treading a very thin line, Captain..."

"Yes, all the way to the ice, to rescue stranded passengers..."

"You will proceed to the ice, Captain," Hong Wei said, closing the distance between him and Elina. "And then on, further, following the path that Xiá took with the boat. The passengers will be fine."

"You're confident of that?"

"Quite confident."

"And how confident are you of holding your position as investigator, or whatever rank you hold in whatever service you are attached to?"

"I don't have time for games, Captain. Have your helm increase speed, or..."

"Or how about I decide on our course, and speed?" Elina nodded for the helm to adjust course. "And then you can explain to the owners what happened when a Chinese spy – correction – *two* Chinese spies commandeered a vessel in international waters."

"This vessel," Hong Wei said, his voice rising. "*Is* Chinese. It is an asset, owned by the People's Republic of China."

"Fine," Elina said. "And she's yours to command, just as soon as I have picked up my passengers. People, not assets."

"Captain," said one of the crew, holding one

hand over the mouthpiece of a handset. "There's a call."

"Put it on speaker."

"It's for him," the man said, turning to Hong Wei.

"Speaker," Elina said, settling into the captain's chair, as Hong Wei strode to the crewman's station and picked up the microphone.

"This is Hong Wei," he said, in English.

"I think you know who I am."

Elina looked at the speaker as the voice of a young woman filtered into the bridge.

"Konstabel Brongaard," Hong Wei said. "It's been a while."

"I missed you in Copenhagen," Fenna said. "Although I'm pretty sure I met a friend of yours."

"And you discovered I was here?"

"Yes."

"How?"

"It seemed like the most logical place."

"I'm sure I don't quite follow you, Konstabel."

The speakers crackled with soft surges of static as the helmsman steered the *Admiral Chichagov* closer to the ice.

"Konstabel Brongaard?" Hong Wei said.

"I'm still here."

Another pause, more static.

"I'd like to speak to David," Fenna said. "Constable Maratse."

"Yes," Hong Wei said, turning to the window. He held his thumb against the transmit button, pressing lightly, as he watched a black speck charging across the sea, leaving white arrows of surf on the surface of the water. "He's unavailable just now, Konstabel. Perhaps you could try him later?"

"I know what you're trying to do," Fenna said.

"And what's that?"

"You used your assassin to draw me out in Copenhagen, and now you want to use David to…"

Elina opened the armrest of her chair and keyed the microphone hidden there. "David is fine," she said, adding, "This is the captain speaking."

"Captain?"

"It's an open line, Fenna," Hong Wei said, before tossing the microphone at the crewman. He pressed his hand to the cut on his forehead, examined the blood on his fingertips, and then walked towards the door. "You," he said, pointing at Luukas. "Come with me."

Hong Wei ignored Fenna's questions, and the captain's answers. He took the stairs quickly, snapping his fingers for Luukas to hurry up.

"Do you have a rifle on board?"

"Yes," Luukas said. "But…"

"That's all I need to know. Get it for me and meet me in the bow."

Regardless of what the captain told Fenna, Hong Wei understood that everything he had worked for was unravelling. He could still hear Xiá's scream in his ears, and for the first time in a very long time, he understood that some things – just one, in fact – were more important than others.

Forgiveness.

Nothing else mattered. The machinations of Chinese intelligence, the power struggle for the Arctic, even the very future of his beloved country – nothing mattered.

Only Xiá.

Only her forgiveness.

Hong Wei strode across the deck, shivering as the wind cut through his thin jacket. He reached the bow and climbed the short ladder onto the raised deck – an observation platform, littered with signs warning passengers to be careful.

The time for being careful, Hong Wei mused, was past.

He heard Luukas jogging along the deck and turned to watch him climb onto the observation platform. Hong Wei took the rifle from his hands, then clicked his fingers and pointed at Luukas' jacket.

"I'll take that too," he said.

Luukas shivered as he handed Hong Wei his jacket, then, as soon as Hong Wei turned his back on him, he retreated to the ladder, slipping down onto the deck, and running back to the warmth inside the ship. Hong Wei let him go, zipping the jacket with but an idle thought at how effective it was against the wind, before picking up the rifle and searching for Maratse through the scope.

The black dot of the rigid inflatable was too

small and too far away to shoot, but the scope afforded at least a better view of where Maratse was going as the ship followed in the wake of the tiny boat. Hong Wei lowered the rifle, then sighted again, picking out the brightly coloured jackets clumped on the ice, and nodding as he realised where Maratse was headed. He turned his head to look up at the bridge, willing the captain to order the helm to increase thrust, pushing the ship faster to reach the passengers as quickly as possible.

On that point, at least, they agreed.

Hong Wei slung the rifle over his shoulder, pulled the hood of the jacket over his head and stuffed his hands into his pockets.

If Xiá hadn't screamed, ending their call, he would have told her more, how Pān Tāo could not be saved, that his wounds were fatal. The closest medical centre was at the mine. Even Xiá would have understood how that was not an option, especially not with the blood of a Canadian police officer on their hands, and the body of a Thomsen Mining employee rolled in a tarp by the side of the road.

Xiá would have understood that. I taught her as much.

There had been but one option.

Hong Wei steeled himself as the memory of that day on the Inuvik-Tuktoyaktuk Highway blistered into his mind, as gnarly as ever, just as jagged as it was when the night horrors wore Pān Tāo's face.

"Go," Pān Tāo had said. "Leave me."

"I can't leave you."

"You have to. The police…"

Hong Wei remembered the grimace stitched across Pān Tāo's face as the bullet in his gut twisted another bout of pain through his body.

"I'll stay with you," Hong Wei said, crouching beside Pān Tāo as he took his hand.

"Don't be stupid." Blood spilled over Pān Tāo's lip as he looked at Hong Wei. "Go. Leave now. I'm dying, but not fast enough. They'll catch you if you stay."

In the bow of the *Admiral Chichagov*, the wind played tricks on him, whispering in his ear, blowing phantoms into his pockets, curling the hair on the back of Hong Wei's hand, until he imagined he still grasped the hand of his friend, Xiá's father. The phantom grip took him back to the dusty Arctic road.

"You'll look after her," Pān Tāo said. "Promise me."

"I will."

"She never met her mother. She'll need a father."

"She *has* a father," Hong Wei said.

"Only for a short while. She will need another for the rest of her life. I want it to be you."

Hong Wei nodded – on the side of the road in his memory, and in the bow of the *Admiral Chichagov*, bearing down on the ice, the stranded passengers, Constable Maratse in his tiny boat, and Xiá, the daughter of his long dead friend, in another.

"I will look after her."

Hong Wei's memory synched with his present, as he walked through his past, through the dust, to the policeman's body. The policeman's aftershave mixed with the smell of blood, prickling Hong Wei's nostrils, details he would remember later, forever. Hong Wei fought the urge to bend in the bow as he bent down in his memory, picking up the policeman's pistol, lifting it, levelling it at Pān Tāo's head, swallowing as he increased pressure on the trigger.

"Look after her," Pān Tāo had said.

His last words.

"I will."

Hong Wei pulled the trigger.

He jerked on the bow as the memory hit home, harder than before. He tried to swallow with a desiccated tongue clinging to the roof of his mouth. He felt the tears roll down his cheeks and stuck his tongue out to catch them, to put them to use, only to curse the irony as they slowed, freezing, just out of reach.

The weight of the phantom pistol was heavy in his grasp. The thought crossed his mind, that, if it was real, he might have taken his own life.

"I will look after her," he said, forcing the words out of his mouth.

Hong Wei stared into the wind, searching the ice for signs of Xiá.

He saw the black lead cutting into the floe, like a crack in white paving. He saw Maratse's boat bump into the side of the ice, saw him throw a line to one of the crew on the floe, watched as he crawled over the side of the boat and onto the ice.

If Hong Wei had been on the bridge, he would have ordered the captain to plough into the ice, scattering the passengers and crew, chasing Maratse, splintering the ice at his feet, hurling ice spears and crystal shards at his back. There would be blood before the end, before the adamant bow of the icebreaker rose up to crash down on the floe, burying the Greenlander beneath metal and ice, submerging him before pushing on in search of Xiá.

"I will look after her, Pān Tāo, I promise."

Hong Wei spoke the words aloud in the bow of the *Admiral Chichagov*, just as he had spoken them aloud on the dusty Arctic highway, taking one last look at his friend, before slipping the pistol into the policeman's hand, and walking back to the pickup.

Xiá.

Pān Tāo's daughter – *his* daughter. Out there. On the ice.

"I will look after her."

Hong Wei took one last look at the passengers, saw Maratse point at the ship, and then watched as the retired Constable started to run, across the floe, towards the very tip of the lead, towards Xiá.

"And this is how it ends," Hong Wei said, securing the radio in his pocket and tightening the sling of the rifle over his shoulder. He climbed down the ladder and strode along the deck to where the crew made the ship's ladder ready to deploy. He felt the engines shudder as the ship slowed, heard the crew talk about lowering the floating dock.

"The captain won't want to get near the ice," one of the crew said.

Hong Wei turned his head, curious as he wondered why, and how ironic that a captain of an icebreaker was frightened of ice.

Why?

Hong Wei stared at the retreating figure of Maratse, taking long, slow breaths, calming himself for the inevitable chase to come.

Chapter 33

Alasdair caught the painter as Maratse threw it to him, holding it tight and securing the boat against the ice. Maratse clicked the motor into neutral and let it idle. He grabbed a boat hook from the deck before climbing onto the floe.

"The ship's coming," Alasdair said, with a nod to the *Admiral Chichagov* in the distance.

"*Iiji*," Maratse said. He scanned the passengers, looking past the bewildered faces as he studied the floe. "Where did she go?"

"She took the boat that way." Alasdair pointed to his right. "Then curled around that point. It looked like she was going up the ways, through the ice, but I guess there's a lead."

Maratse followed Alasdair's finger, then stepped around him, staring towards the middle of the floe, squinting at two bright spots hunkered low on the ice.

"Wind's picking up," he said. "Take the boats. Get everyone back to the ship."

"What about you?"

Maratse tapped the metal end of the boat hook into the ice at his feet. "I'm going on foot," he said.

The first few metres of ice were thick, resisting the metal hook as Maratse tested his route. The ice ahead of him was white, glassy in places where the wind had scoured the surface snow away to reveal the darker ice beneath. The patches stretched, joining to create a path and Maratse ran along it, barely lifting his feet. From a distance a casual observer might have thought he was ice skating, but closer inspection revealed the skill of the hunter, avoiding the deep drifts of snow, keeping his weight balanced on the whole foot, not the toes, especially on the thinner sections of ice. Maratse used the boat hook when the ice thinned, tapping with the metal end to test the thickness. When the ice thinned even more, he used the soft and rounded end of the wood shaft, tapping lightly, slowing as he did so. The ice in the middle of the floe was older, with the undersides chewed by currents and warmer stretches of sea as the floe moved northwards across *Drake Passage*. An idle thought flickered through Maratse's mind, that the floe was extraordinary to have remained whole for so long. But a shout in the distance, closer now, drove him on, and he resumed his course, picking his way across the ice to Petra.

"She's gone through the ice," Petra shouted, as Maratse ran to her side. "Her drysuit isn't sealed. It's filling up with water."

Maratse slowed, approaching slowly, pressing his hand on Petra's shoulder, squeezing it once to say *I'm here, we're safe* before kneeling beside her and thrusting his hands into the water, grabbing Xiá's arm.

"I think her feet are caught," Petra said, her voice hoarse, as if she had been shouting or crying, perhaps both. "She wouldn't let go of the gun," she said, nodding at the pistol on the ice. "Kept pointing it at my head, until I could take it." Petra shifted position as Maratse nodded that he was ready to lift. "It's empty," she added, with another glance at the gun.

"Now," Maratse said, as they pulled at Xiá's arms, inching her out of the ice, but no further than her stomach. "She's caught. Hold her."

Maratse reached for the boat hook, then chipped at the ice around Xiá's body. She stared at him with black eyes, turning grey as her face paled to a dirty white, like the ice.

"Hurry, David," Petra said. "She's slipping."

Not slipping, Maratse thought. *Dying.*

The collars of Maratse's jacket flapped in the wind, creasing his wet sleeves with salt-stained ice. Maratse rose to his feet, working his way around Xiá until the hole was bigger and there was a ring of cold black water around her body. He worked steadily, head down, his breath clouding with the exertion. He didn't see the bow of the *Admiral Chichagov* bite into the floe.

Neither of them did.

"Again," Maratse said, dropping the boat hook and pulling Xiá's arm. Petra did the same, crying out as they lifted Xiá's body out of the sea, slowly, an inch at a time, until she was on the ice. "Into the boat, out of the wind."

They carried Xiá between them, dragging her feet along the ice, heaving her body up and over the side of the inflatable.

"Start the motor," Maratse said, as he climbed back onto the ice. He pushed at the bow wedged into the floe, then dropped onto his backside, kicking at the rubber, fighting to release it from the icy gums of the floe gripping it. Maratse scrabbled to his feet as Petra started the motor.

The cough of the motor disguised the first gunshot as Maratse ran to the hole in the ice, bending down to pick up the boat hook. A second shot cracked through the wind, snapping past Maratse's shoulder as he looked back towards the *Admiral Chichagov*, and the figure in the bright red jacket walking across the ice towards them.

The third shot clipped Maratse's arm, spinning him onto the ice.

"David!"

The outboard motor coughed once and died as Petra scrambled over the side, running to Maratse. She swerved, slipped, and fell as a fourth shot slapped into the ice to her right. She picked herself up, then ran, slid, and stopped at Maratse's side, turning him over, oblivious of the danger the shooter presented, caring about one thing only.

"You're alive," she said, dropping onto Maratse's chest, cupping his cheeks in cold hands, covering his face with ice-beaded hair as she kissed his forehead.

"*Iiji*," he said, curling one arm around Petra.

"Okay," she said. "We're okay."

"Piitalaat…"

"Yes?" She lifted her head.

"He's coming."

Petra rolled onto her side, staring back across the ice as Hong Wei approached, working the bolt of the hunting rifle, then stopping to tug it into his shoulder.

"Go for the boat," Maratse said.

"I won't leave you."

"You have to," Maratse said, pushing her with one hand, urging her to move.

"I won't…"

The sixth crack of the rifle sent a bullet into the ice beside Petra, cutting her cheek with shards of ice. Maratse pushed her away, but she clawed at his arm.

"No," she cried. "Not like this."

"The boat, Piitalaat. Please."

Petra turned her head, searching the ice for Hong Wei. She let go of Maratse, frowning as she stood.

"Piitalaat?"

"He's gone," she said.

Maratse propped himself up on one elbow, scanning the ice.

"He was right there," Petra said. "And then… Wait." She pointed. "There."

Maratse and Petra watched as Hong Wei clawed his way onto the ice, jerking his arms forward, stabbing leaden fingers into the surface snow, slipping, then gripping, heaving himself out of the water.

"Hmm," Maratse said, thinking of the path he had taken, the patches of thin ice he had crossed.

"Help me up," he said, taking Petra's hand. She pulled him to his feet, and Maratse took a step forward.

"What are you doing?"

"He needs help," Maratse said. "He fell through the ice."

"No," Petra said.

She moved in front of him.

"Piitalaat?"

Maratse moved to the side, stepping around Petra. She took another step, blocking him.

"He'll freeze to death."

The ice in Petra's hair rattled across her cheeks in the wind. She pressed her lips closed, staring straight into Maratse's face. When he moved, she moved, blocking him a third time, then a fourth. Maratse took her arm, gently pulling her out of the way.

"No," she said, slapping at his arm, then slapping his chest, pushing him back.

Maratse walked to one side, Petra ran ahead of him. She pushed, both hands, flat into his chest, pushing him back towards the boat. When he stumbled, heels slipping, she stood there, staring down at him, daring him to get up.

Maratse crawled onto his knees, cradling his useless arm as he regained his feet.

"Piitalaat?"

Petra stood in front of Maratse, eyes fixed on his, her hands at her sides, fingers clenched.

"*Constable.*"

Hong Wei's voice drifted across the ice, licking at their feet, no higher, no stronger. His cries sifted into the windblown snow scratching the surface of the ice.

"He needs our help."

"No," Petra said. "He doesn't."

Maratse saw it then, saw his own reflection in Petra's soft brown eyes. They were on the sea ice, but another time, another place.

"You understand?" she asked.

Maratse dipped his head. "*Iiji*," he said, his voice barely a whisper.

"When this is over," Petra said. "We move forwards."

"Piitalaat…"

"No, David. No more words. Go back to the boat. Go now."

"I can't just…"

"Yes, you can. You did this for me. It's my turn. I won't have him come between us. He fell through the ice. We couldn't help him."

Maratse opened his mouth to speak. Petra stopped him, tears streaming down her face as she walked towards him.

"I want a life," she said, voice crackling as she pushed at Maratse, beating him back towards the boat, slapping at his chest, hard slaps, growing softer with each step. "Understand that – *please* understand, that this can't go on. These people will destroy us if we let them. I won't let him take you away."

Petra sniffed as Maratse stopped.

"I won't let him."

She stepped closer, pressing her head into Maratse's neck, curling her arms around his waist.

"He can't hurt us. I won't let him hurt us."

Maratse stared through the filter of Petra's hair. Hong Wei stared back at him, stared *through* him, as the cold leached the life out of his body.

"*Iiji*," Maratse said. "I understand."

They left Hong Wei on the ice, turning their backs to him as they worked to free the boat. Xiá's pulse was weak when Petra checked it. She lay beside her, protecting the young woman from the wind, pressing her warm hands against Xiá's frigid cheeks. Petra smoothed her fingers through Xiá's hair, whispering that she was going to be all right, as Maratse reversed the boat out of the lead, turning it as soon as the channel was wide enough.

Maratse steered the boat to the floating dock on the starboard side of the *Admiral Chichagov*. Alasdair received them, calling for crew to take Xiá to sickbay, before helping Petra out of the boat.

"She'll be all right," he said, as Petra watched the crewmen carry Xiá up the ship's ladder. "We'll get her warmed up."

Petra nodded, then turned to Maratse, taking his hand as he stepped onto the deck.

"Bullet?" Alasdair asked, reaching for the tear in Maratse's jacket.

"*Iiji.*"

"And the Chinese man?"

"Fell through the ice," Petra said, before Maratse could answer. She took Maratse's arm, pulling him away from Alasdair. "I'll take him to sickbay."

The captain met them on the deck, lowering the binoculars in her hand as Petra led Maratse off the ladder.

"These are treacherous waters," she said.

"Yes," Petra said.

"Accidents happen. And..." she paused, handing the binoculars to Luukas as he joined them. "It's been my experience, that successful icebreaking is as much about avoiding the ice than crashing through it. I don't know how this floe got so far north, but I'm going to take it as a bad omen. We've had enough bad luck on this cruise. I don't think we should encourage any more, do you?"

"No," Petra said.

"Then we agree. Good." Elina looked at Luukas and held out her hand. "We found this in Xiá's cabin," she said, taking the clear plastic bag with the metal tube from Luukas' hand. "It looks innocuous, but Doctor Rao assures me it is a delivery system for something quite deadly. We'll be passing it on to the authorities the minute we arrive in Ushuaia."

"We're going back?" Petra said.

"Yes, I'm afraid so. I'm sorry but Antarctica will just have to wait."

"I'm not sorry," Petra said. "I'm ready to go home."

"What about you, David?" Elina said.

"Hmm?"

"You're not curious?"

Maratse turned to look south, only to find his gaze drifting across the ice floe until he found the lead, then following the crack of black water to the spot where he last saw Hong Wei. Sea ice was temporary, its existence threatened by warm waters, strong currents, and winds. Hong Wei's last resting place was already degrading, and soon it would disappear. Maratse turned his back on the ice. He took Petra's hand.

"*Eeqqi*," he said, with a shake of his head.

"That means *no*," Petra said, tugging him away from the captain, off the deck.

The captain's last orders to retrieve the dock, the boats, and the ladder followed them to the door.

"What about the body?" one of the crew asked. "Should we go and get it?"

"No," Elina said. "The ice is too dangerous."

Petra caught Maratse's eye, gripped his hand and pulled him inside.

Epilogue

Malik pushed the earbuds into his ears and pressed play on his phone. Tipaaqu appeared on the screen, pressing her face to the camera, as if she was holding it, drawing it to her face. The sweat on her brow trickled down the sides of her cheeks, and Malik imagined the run she had just finished, one of her quick *jogs around the block* – the kind that usually finished him.

"You listening?" she said, pulling the camera back.

"*Aap*," Malik mouthed, ignoring the passengers fidgeting beside him as the flight assistant made the last rounds before landing in Nuuk.

"Good, because, it's not about the money. Remember that." Tipaaqu walked as she talked, giving Malik a tour of the gym as she picked up her towel on the way to the showers. "Money will only get you so far. But a voice, Malik – *your* voice, pitched at the right level, will take you all the way. You let me worry about the money, while you concentrate on your voice. And," she said, pausing at the door to the women's changing rooms. "If you're a good boy…" Tipaaqu opened the door just a crack, as if she was taking him inside.

The video ended with Tipaaqu's thumb covering the lens, seconds before she turned the camera off.

My voice, Malik thought, as he tugged the earbuds from his ears and wrapped the wire around his phone. *I used to have a voice, used to have words.*

The De Havilland Dash 8 bumped onto the runway in Nuuk, turning at the far end and taxiing back to the airport building. Malik stared straight ahead, oblivious of the snow on Sermitsiaq, Greenland's most famous mountain, or the cars on the airport road filtering more snow through their headlights.

Malik followed the passengers out of the aircraft, across the short stretch of ice-covered apron, and into the tiny baggage area.

This past year, my voice has been silenced.

He bumped elbows with his fellow passengers, stepping out of the way until all the luggage had been taken, apart from one black case turning round and around on the carousel.

Either they won't let me talk, or they don't like what I say.

"Is this yours?"

Malik looked up and took his case from the police officer.

"*Aap.*"

"Malik Uutaaq?"

"Yes," he said, focusing on the police officer's face.

"I have a message," he said. "You're to call in at the police station, first thing tomorrow.

~ 351 ~

Okay?"

"That's okay," Malik said. He shifted his grip on the handle of his case, extended it and pulled the case behind him, wheels bumping past the passengers waiting for the return flight to Kangerlussuaq.

I know what I want to say, Malik thought, ignoring the few passengers who greeted him, as he walked to the door. *But I need time to organise my thoughts, my words, my voice.*

He stopped at the door, bracing at a cold blast of air.

Malik zipped his jacket, tugging gloves from his pockets, pulling them on as he wondered where he was going.

"Home?" said a voice. "Malik? Do you want to share a taxi?"

"Qitu?" Malik said, looking up, suddenly aware someone was talking to him.

"*Aap*," Qitu said. "Tertu and I were on the same flight from Copenhagen. Do you want a lift?"

Malik shook his head. "I'm not going to my apartment."

"Okay, somewhere else then?"

"*Naamik*. I'll make my own way."

Malik waited for Qitu to leave, ignoring the curious look on the journalist's face.

I'll make my own way.

It was what Tipaaqu wanted, what she teased him about. But each time he had tried he had been foiled – murder and death, responsibility twisted into humiliation. Each time he had trusted someone he had been abused. Abandoned each time he had relied on someone.

Not anymore. I'll make my own way.

Malik turned his collar up, grabbed his case and stepped out into the thick-flaked snow so familiar in Greenland's capital. He took the next taxi in line, gave the driver the address, nodded that he was Malik Uutaaq, and *yes* he was *that* minister in the government. But, thankfully, there was nothing more to confirm, no salacious gossip, only the driver's concerns about fishing quotas, a topic that took them all the way from the airport to Malik's old house.

The drive was covered in deep snow, and the snow continued to fall long after the taxi pulled away. Malik paused, wondering if it was the right thing to do, if he would be welcomed, if he would be forgiven.

"*Ataata?*"

"Princess," Malik said, as Pipaluk opened the door. He waved at her, curious to see how much she had grown in such a short time. He had been away for less than two weeks, but already his teenage daughter was rapidly becoming a young woman. "Is anyone else home?"

"Sipu and *anaana*," Pipaluk said. "Everyone."

"Malik?" Naala stepped into the light, her hand curling around her daughter's shoulders as she peered out into the dark winter evening. "What are you doing?"

"I wondered if I could come in?"

"Now?"

~ 353 ~

"*Aap.*"

"Sure," Naala said, stepping back as Malik walked across the snow to the front door. She watched as he bent down to kiss Pipaluk's cheek, then took his hand in one of those awkward greetings reserved for estranged couples.

"*Qujanaq,*" Malik said, kicking the snow from his shoes before stepping into the house.

"What's going on?" Naala waited for Malik to speak, pulling Pipaluk close, then Sipu as he bounded down the stairs, stopping short at the sight of his father.

"I've done some things," Malik said. "I haven't always been nice." He looked at Naala. "Sometimes I've been nasty. But I need to come home, and I need you – all of you – if you'll take me back."

"I don't know. It's too soon," Naala said, her voice falling into a whisper.

Malik pressed his hand to his mouth, nodding once, before turning to the door. Pipaluk stopped him as he reached for his case.

"He needs our help," she said, dragging it from the door and further into the hall.

"Pipaluk?" Naala said.

"We're going to help him," she said, looking at her mother. "And he's going to be a father again, he's going to be your husband." She took her parents' hands, pulling them together. "We'll start again. We'll be a family."

Malik looked into his wife's eyes. "Naala?"

She took a breath, then looked at Sipu. "Daddy's going to sleep in your room. Okay?"

"Okay," Sipu said, followed by a wild look in his eyes, as he realised having a parent in his room might affect his late-night gaming.

"You'll have to share," Naala said, calling after Sipu as he ran up the stairs.

"*Qujanaq*," Malik said, squeezing Naala's hand.

"Do you want to eat?"

"*Naamik*," he said. "I need to write."

"You mean work?" Pipaluk said.

"Yes. But more than that." Malik let go of Naala's hand to pull his daughter close. "It's important."

"What are you writing?" she asked, plucking at her father's fingers.

"My manifesto," he said. "For Greenland."

The End

Acknowledgments

I would like to thank Isabel Dennis-Muir for her invaluable editing skills and feedback on the manuscript.

Chris

October 2020
Denmark

About the Author

Christoffer Petersen is the author's pen name. He lives in Denmark. Chris started writing stories about Greenland while teaching in Qaanaaq, the largest village in the very north of Greenland – the population peaked at 600 during the two years he lived there. Chris spent a total of seven years in Greenland, teaching in remote communities and at the Police Academy in the capital of Nuuk.

Chris continues to be inspired by the vast icy wilderness of the Arctic and his books have a common setting in the region, with a Scandinavian influence. He has also watched enough Bourne movies to no longer be surprised by the plot, but not enough to get bored.

You can find Chris in Denmark or online here:

www.christoffer-petersen.com

By the same Author

THE GREENLAND CRIME SERIES
featuring Constable David Maratse

SEVEN GRAVES, ONE WINTER
BLOOD FLOE
WE SHALL BE MONSTERS
INSIDE THE BEAR'S CAGE
WHALE HEART

Novellas from the same series

KATABATIC #1
CONTAINER #2
TUPILAQ #3
THE LAST FLIGHT #4
THE HEART THAT WAS A WILD GARDEN
#5
QIVITTOQ #6
THE THUNDER SPIRITS #7
ILULIAQ #8
SCRIMSHAW #9
ASIAQ #10
CAMP CENTURY #11
INUK #12
DARK CHRISTMAS #13
POISON BERRY #14

MADE IN DENMARK
DANISH DESIGN Story 1

THE WHEELMAN SHORTS
PULP DRIVER Story 1

THE DARK ADVENT SERIES
THE CALENDAR MAN
THE TWELFTH NIGHT
INVISIBLE TOUCH
NORTH STAR BAY

UNDERCOVER GREENLAND
NARKOTIKA

THE BOLIVIAN GIRL
THE BOLIVIAN GIRL

GUERRILLA GREENLAND
ARCTIC STATE
ARCTIC REBEL

GREENLAND MISSING PERSONS
THE BOY WITH THE NARWHAL TOOTH #1
THE GIRL WITH THE RAVEN TONGUE #2
THE SHIVER IN THE ARCTIC #3
THE FEVER IN THE WATER #4

Made in United States
North Haven, CT
16 July 2022

21449942R00217